The Place You're Supposed to Laugh

a novel

by Jenn Stroud Rossmann

7.13 Books

Brooklyn, NY

Printed and distributed by 7.13 Books. First paperback edition, first printing: November 2018

Cover design: Gigi Little
Author photo: Leda & Cleo Rossmann

ISBN-10: 0-9913687-2-X
ISBN-13: 978-0-9913687-2-3

Library of Congress Control Number: 2018950754

For information about permission to reproduce selections from this book, contact the publisher at https://713books.com/

No matter where you go, you are what you are, player
And you can try to change but that's just the top layer
Man, you was who you was 'fore you got here

Jay-Z

Holy Calamity

On the quiet drive to collect his dad from jail, Chad Loudermilk stared out at a surreally warped Palo Alto. Downtown boutiques and restaurants distorted and refracted. The Caltrain's whistle modulated into a different key. Chad peered down Palm Drive at Stanford, the rows of palm trees a mellow West Coast version of stately columns on older, stodgier campuses. He was nauseous with disorientation.

In the last year the effervescence had gone out of the dot-com fizzy lifting drink. The number of FOR SALE signs was way up. *It's a buyer's market these days*, his mother said, though his parents were the only renters on their street. Traffic on the once-sclerotic freeways had thinned, and it was easier now to find a seat on the train. Silver linings. People were walking their own dogs again, instead of subcontracting to the recently defunct RoverComeOver.com.

But the queasy delirium Chad felt now wasn't just the malaise of a Valley that hadn't figured out what would come next; it was the acute, specific vertigo of his unprecedented mission. Beyond the car, his hometown was unfamiliar and newly forbidding.

"Thanks again for the ride," Chad told his neighbor Mrs. MacAvoy.

Her response was a grim nod, a tightened grip around the steering wheel.

Chad had spent the night at his friend Walter Chen's, and had barely entered his own house when the phone rang that morning. Groggy but revved by the box of dry Froot Loops he and Walter had called breakfast, Chad wasn't sure whether to believe the voice telling him his dad was in need of a ride, and perhaps a family member into whose care he could be released.

"Is he all right?" Chad asked the voice. "Do I need to bring, like, bail?" But the call had ended, and he was left alone with his questions. *What is happening? Are you sure you called the right number? That you have the right Raymond Loudermilk? Am I still asleep on Walter's living room floor?*

His new dog had padded toward him when he walked in, gazing mournfully with head cocked while Chad took the call.

With his mom out of town, the only adult Chad could see asking for a lift was his next-door neighbor, Scot MacAvoy. Scot's MacAvoy.com with its flagship, Latte, was one of the Valley's invincible titans. Scot's bulletproof prosperity was ambiguously correlated with the time he spent at home on his game console, besting Chad at alien annihilation or simulated street racing.

Something looked different as he walked toward the MacAvoy house, though Chad couldn't have said what it was. He swung open the unlocked front door. Unusually, the TV wasn't on. "Scot?" Chad called. "He's not here." Mrs. MacAvoy appeared from her kitchen. "Seattle. Or Portland. Or somewhere." She flung her wrist and gave a vague, magisterial smile. "I'm sure he'll be ready to play with you when he gets back."

"Um, sorry for barging in."

"That's quite all right." She half-turned, dismissing him. Her sleek, multi-paneled exercise clothes looked expensive; Chad felt self-conscious about his sleep-rumpled plaid flannel pants and t-shirt, even though they were essentially both wearing pajamas.

"My dad needs a ride? But I don't drive yet?" Chad swallowed hard to stop his voice from cracking. Fourteen was a calamitous age. "I was hoping maybe Scot could take me to get him."

Mrs. MacAvoy stared at him, hard. "My husband's car is in the shop," she said carefully, placing each word like an interlocking tile. "It needed an oil change."

Chad nodded. That's what had been different: the SUV was absent from the MacAvoy curb. "But, um, is there any chance that you could take me?"

Now, the car was quiet. Already-grounded-on-the-way-home-from-a-party quiet. *I don't care that your friends were all there too.* Leaving-your-grandma's-funeral quiet. Car-commercial-quiet. It was that kind of car, with leather seats and plush floor mats. Going-to-pick-up-your-dad-from-jail quiet.

Chad had begun to consider the possibility that his

dad was playing a practical joke. Most of Chad's child-hood birthdays had been surprises, with his dad going to insane lengths to divert him from the real party plan. Gleeful at the revelatory moment, jazzed at having pulled it off.

One of these ruses had involved a feigned injury, a panicked dash to the backyard when his dad claimed to have been bloodied by his old-fashioned push lawnmower—a rotating cylinder of blades whose resemblance to a torture device had been remarked upon by Chad's mom. "It finally happened," she was muttering as they rushed outside with armfuls of gauze, to discover not a bloodied Ray but a scrum of eight-year-olds eager to deploy the bucket of water balloons his dad had been filling when they'd thought he was mowing the lawn.

So it was not implausible that Chad's current unease was simply part of another Ray Loudermilk setup that would end in cupcakes. This would be kind of messed up, but consistent. In the meantime, Chad hoped he would not vomit on the buttery leather of Irene MacAvoy's car.

She reached to turn up the air conditioning, and a vent blew icy air. Even the vent was quiet; somewhere a fan turned silently. For a long moment the only sound was Mrs. MacAvoy's nails tapping the steering wheel to the beat of an unheard song.

He supposed the lack of forced conversation—*and how is school going this fall?*—was a relief, except that the silence trapped him in his own head.

Over the summer, Chad's Grandma had died, and ever since, his mom had been strangely absent—there, but not really. Some nights she'd just throw dinner together, emerging from her room with red-wild eyes to commence scrambling eggs with a vengeance.

Chad and his mom spent great chunks of the summer watching Grandma die. At the hospital, Grandma Marchese was shackled to an IV pole dripping chemo into her arm. This had surprised Chad: a humdrum, un-terrifying way to deliver poison that killed all the cells, good and bad alike, a poison so powerful it erased his grandmother's thick, dark eyebrows. Somehow he'd expected something different, maybe with gas masks.

These were his choices: get stuck at home, while his dad went to work and Walter was at math camp; or sit at Grandma's bedside and watch her shrivel into her own ghost, clacking her useless rosary beads.

But if he hadn't gone, his mom would've been alone. His mom's sister, Chad's aunt Diana, had declined the invitation to Grandma's hospital room. And Grandma Marchese wasn't married to his grandpa anymore, hadn't been since before Chad came into the picture. Not that Grandma herself had ever appeared lonely or in need of anything that any other human might provide.

Chad sat at Grandma's bedside so his mother would have someone's hand to hold. His mom, of course, felt compelled to make small talk. Tried to coax Grandma into caring about each new roommate she got in the ward. "Ma," she'd say, "She says her favorite film is *On the Waterfront*."

"Sweet Jesus," Grandma said, rolling her eyes at Chad. He loved her for the very "obstinacy" his mother scolded her about. Still, he wasn't sure why his mom thought people would be clamoring to socialize with the withered, hairless person his Grandma had become. Frankly you'd prefer to avert your eyes: bruised arms with hardened veins that shut out IV needles and forced them to install a weird sci-fi port in her shoulder; and a bag flopping from under her sheet, slowly filling with urine as his mom chatted and Chad sat there getting skeeved out.

At the beginning of a cycle, after she'd had two weeks to recover from the last chemo dose, when she was almost herself again, Grandma had the energy to tell Chad's mom to knock it off. "I don't want to make friends in here," she said.

"Okay," his mom said.

"Stop *managing* me, Allison," said his grandma. "It's like the way you straighten out other people's children."

"They're at-risk," said his mom.

Grandma waved this away. "Who isn't?"

Allison grimaced.

"You always try to take care of people who aren't your responsibility," Chad's grandmother went on. "Me, your sister, Chad—."

"Chad is my son." Her voice was hard. She looked straight at him. With her eyes she was telling him: we are a team. No matter that people couldn't tell by looking. *We picked you*, she had always said. It was too intense for him, her insistence on this; he looked down at his sneakers. One of the IV pumps began beeping, and his mom reached over to unkink the tubing. "The way I see it," she said, "we're all each others' responsibility."

"It takes a mother-loving village," pronounced Grandma.

The Place You're Supposed to Laugh

This weekend his mom was visiting Chad's grandpa and his wife, her first such trip since Grandma Marchese died. Chad had used his plans with Walter to deflect her Come-Visit-Your-Grandfather-Who-Loves-You-And-Who-Knows-How-Many-More-Chances-He'll-Get-To-See-You? offensive.

This argument, admittedly, had gained traction. But Chad had plenty of chances to see his grandma eking out the last months of her life, and part of him would've been willing to miss some of those chances in order to remember her the way she was before. So his mom made the trip solo.

Almost at once, Chad and his dad Ray fell into a bachelor torpor that resisted meal planning and cleanup and favored takeout and disposability. With his mom out of town, "screen time" was no longer rationed. After school he could spend a couple hours playing video games with Scot MacAvoy next door, then come home with new cartridges in hand, and his dad would wave him over to the TV. "Ballgame's on," his dad said: the cartridges were a fistful of foreign currency that was worthless on this side of the border. The Oakland A's were coming off a three-week winning streak, but now they were losing to Anaheim.

"Anaheim," Ray muttered, shaking his head. He dropped a spring roll onto his plate, made un-hungry by the sour taste of his team's suffering, by the way the A's roster, nurtured from seedlings by the management, had been dismantled by wealthier teams when they'd sprouted. "This is what happens to underdogs who start to make good. They get their star players bought out by the Yankees and Red Sox."

"We just won twenty straight, Dad," Chad said. "That's a heck of a rebuilding year."

"It's the principle," his dad said.

Chad wasn't quite sure he followed, but his dad gave a decisive nod, confident he'd made his point.

Most of his dad's dot-com clients had had the wind knocked out of them, and there was much less need to advertise companies that no longer existed. So maybe he felt a little underdog-ish himself, especially renting the house next door to the Valley equivalent of the Yankees, Scot MacAvoy.

During the seventh-inning stretch they called his mom. She sounded tired, a little bored with the grand-parental routine. Probably she wasn't sleeping well, on that pullout couch. Then again, she had been tired for months now. Chad spoke with one eye on the game, trying to distract himself from the guilty pinch in his gut. After supplying the requisite small talk, he passed the phone to his dad.

The handoff was a relief; he could hear his mother's laughter through the phone as his dad told a work story. It was almost like he'd storyboarded it: he sketched a few of his coworkers for Allison, and then described a startup that was hoping to go public. The startup would not be a new client, as his agency had erred on the light side: "The company is called Jumpy-Monkey.com," his dad said. "And they want gravitas."

Chad's mom's laugh was an amazing sound, after the long mirthless summer of Grandma's decline. She only ever laughed like that with his dad. Next to him, Ray spun another quick tale before they said their goodbyes.

"I'd be there myself except for this pitch on Friday,"

his dad told Chad. "Southwest Airlines," he added by way of explanation.

Work was like that, sometimes; his dad had missed Chad's confirmation service last weekend, too. His absence was surprising since Chad had been under the impression he was going through the whole Confirmation experience for his parents' sake more than his own.

Also, the Loudermilks were pretty much the last single-car family in California. (One of his parents' most obnoxious traits was their way of describing their single-car household, and his dad's easy walk from the train station, as if they were moral victories and not economic constraints.) So on Sunday, Chad and his mom carpooled to the church for the confirmation rehearsal, and were counting on his dad for a ride home after the service. When they couldn't find him, Chad's mom asked for a ride first from the family who had brought them, who'd had to decline, as they were already late for their brunch reservation; and then from a series of other families, until she found a couple in the parking lot who had room for two more, once they slid a splayed umbrella and a stack of papers onto the floor in the backseat.

A few days later, Ray came home with a dog. "Happy confirmation, son," he grinned. "Should we take him for a walk?"

Watching baseball with his dad, his apology dog at his feet, Chad was willing to grant that Southwest Airlines, much like a sleepover at your best friend's, was a valid reason not to accompany a woman, your wife maybe, who'd just lost her mother, on her first trip since to see her father. Because sure, they might've helped her out with small talk and errands and moral support, but you know: Southwest Airlines.

Maybe his dad would get her a dog, too. Chad swallowed hard and burped up plum sauce from the mu shu.

Well, maybe the phone call was part of a prank, or maybe his dad had tied one on after yesterday's Southwest Airlines meeting, had gotten rowdy on the train. Ray was a chronic jaywalker: was that an arrestable offense? They turned onto California Avenue, and Chad realized that he hadn't told Mrs. MacAvoy where they were going to pick up his dad; she had simply programmed her GPS and begun driving. This seemed to support the notion of cahoots, and of surprises.

Corinthian Leather

Ray's mouth was sour and fuzzy, the unmistakable stale regret of a hangover. Outside the car it was cartoonishly bright, as if the sun's rays were targeting him. He shielded his eyes with his hand. "I don't suppose you have any sunglasses," he said.

Irene MacAvoy gave him a look: unpreparedness for sunshine, after fifteen years in California. *Really.* She flicked a hand toward the glove compartment.

Squashed between receipts and a collapsed cigarette pack, he found a pair of large white plastic sunglasses. "Thanks," he said, slipping them on.

Irene gave a light shrug, but did not smile.

Ray struggled with the seat belt, unable to coordinate the two halves of the buckle. He studied his hand with scientific curiosity as his rubbery fingers failed to actuate. Tried not to feel Irene watching him. His fingertips were stained black with ink.

She reached for his seat belt and clicked it into place, in the automatic way she might've done for an infant. It was the closest his neighbor's wife had ever been to him, and he was sure this was the worst he had ever smelled.

"Thanks," he said, "I didn't get much sleep last night."

In answer, she turned on the radio. An ad for garlic pills made improbable claims. Ray winced.

"Just a misunderstanding, Chad," he said. He glanced at his son in the backseat. Chad looked hurt and hollowed out. Ray's throat closed in. "Son, of all the people—"

Chad blinked hard. "I went over to ask Scot—"

"Scot?" Ray turned too quickly; his head continued to vibrate after the motion stopped.

"Seattle," Irene said, brisk.

"I'm sorry to have put you out." He said. When she did not respond he felt unsure whether he had spoken aloud or only thought this. "I'm sorry," he said again, or perhaps for the first time.

In response she emitted an almost imperceptible "mmm."

Outside was weekend traffic, the road's shoulders full of bikers in neon lycra. Everything too bright, too fast. He turned back toward his son, but Chad was staring out his own window.

Ray tried to sound upbeat. "I bet you're as wiped as I am, huh?" Saying this, he mentally prescribed for them both a wanton day of naps and junk TV.

He turned back to the window and grinned at his reflection. Irene's white sunglasses were perfectly absurd. Ray Loudermilk, disturber of peace: he almost laughed out loud.

When Scot and Irene MacAvoy had first arrived on their cul-de-sac, they had seemed like ideal neighbors. Irene brought a pie to Allison's Independence Day barbecue, and Scot helped Ray with the fireworks display. Scot held the ladder while Ray wrapped trees with sparkling holiday lights; Irene was a discerning judge for the pumpkin carving contest. Ray allowed himself to believe that he had achieved a form of what his own parents had back in Nutley. Community. A couple you could trust with an extra key.

For the sake of being neighborly, Ray had struggled to abide the hypersensitive alarm on Scot's SUV, the MacAvoy lawn's confounding greenness even during times of water rationing. Even his name was irritating: what was with that missing t? Ray mistrusted unusual spellings, having spent fifteen years in the ad business and knowing full well that a product called "Kwik Kleen" was likely to be neither as quick nor as clean as promised. And then there was the renovation, months of noisy chaos as a second floor was added to the MacAvoy home, resulting in an unbalanced house that looked like a sketch by a child who had not yet learned the rules of perspective. Ray could hardly change a light bulb without the notarized permission of their landlord. The flood had come, the Valley had been judged; and Scot MacAvoy had built himself an ark, shellacked the hull and measured cubits, instead of rounding up species to save.

Ray shifted in the leather seat of Irene MacAvoy's car. The ache in his back was how it felt to be closing the distance between the type of man he'd meant to be and the type he was.

Irene adjusted the air-conditioning vent, and they continued to ride in silence. Ray slouched behind the sunglasses, trying to look like talking, not talking, it was all the same to him.

Why did he keep letting Chad down? A week ago he'd been late to Chad's confirmation.

He'd only meant to prep for the Southwest Airlines pitch meeting, and had lost track of time. In truth Ray did not enjoy flying on Southwest, with their free-for-all unassigned seating and jokey-casual announcements. This was *human flight*, he wanted to remind the attendants making sarcastic references to oxygen masks and flotation devices: take this all more seriously.

But self-aware irony was his agency's wheelhouse, as they built campaigns for companies disguising their ambitions and ruthlessness in cute corporate names and schlubby hoodies. Magazines praised their "startlingly unforced whimsy." Somewhere along the way, it had become suspect to show up for a meeting in a tie, as if *this* were inauthentic.

Forcing himself to focus, Ray made notes on several of his team's pitch ideas, and when he surfaced he saw he was about to be late for church.

He arrived as the minister was offering a prayer of welcome. Standing at the back, Ray spotted his wife and son sitting at the end of a pew.

He had met Allison in college, when a group of them had roadtripped down the shore from Rutgers. She was a lifeguard, two years younger than Ray, watchful eyes on the horizon. But oh, how she could laugh—how they could make each other laugh. He loved her joy, her strength, and her certainty about everything from the meaning of the swim flags to her plans to go to graduate school; he loved not least that she'd found Ray more charming than his friends. Once she had placed her faith in him, Ray felt he could do anything.

Anything, that was, except walk up the aisle of the church on the day of Chad's confirmation to meet her.

The pen set in his breast pocket—a solid gift, engraved Chad H. Loudermilk, suitable for their boy destined for Stanford or Berkeley or, maybe, Princeton—was a gold-wrapped box of reassurance: he was a good father.

Ray let one hand rest on the edge of the back pew. His fingers traced the smooth, curved wood until they encountered something sharp and angular. It made a clean incision, like a papercut. Ray pulled his hand away and saw the plaque:

THE SCOT MACAVOY FAMILY

Goddamnit. Wincing, Ray felt for the pen set in his breast pocket but found its heft unsatisfying.

It came to him how foolish this was: for his fourteen-year-old son he had bought a retiree's parting gift. He might be the chairman of Union Pacific bestowing an engraved pocket watch on a railman he had never met. He hated the gift, and he hated himself for having thought his son Chad wouldn't notice its falseness.

He couldn't sit through the ceremony, finger leaking MacAvoy-drawn blood, and offer this folly to his son. He had to leave now, before Allison noticed him and shot him that where-have-you-been-we-were-counting-on-you look. His wife possessed a range of finely calibrated expressions indicating the degree to which Ray had most recently let her down, and it worried him that his son had picked up several of them. His lateness, his pathetic gift, would surely earn him another. He wanted to apologize to his son for his failings, beginning with the well-meaning part that he'd had shaved into five-year-old Chad's hair, going through the baseball team he'd continued to coach long after Chad had lost interest, and ending (for now) with the pen set.

Out of the sanctuary, back through the narthex, and out to his car, he heaved himself into the driver's seat, short of breath. His finger appeared to have stopped bleeding, though a pale lip of skin hung over the cut, a vivid illustration of his frailty.

Pulling out of the church parking lot, Ray made the tires squeal, and an inner voice that sounded like his father reminded him not to take it out on the car.

The thing was, he wasn't entirely sure what Chad would prefer to the pen set.

He had expected to know his son better than he did.

Ray drove by the new juice bar, where young people in workout wear sucked pureed fruit through straws. Dogs tied to the parking meters outside. He passed the similarly crowded bagel shop. He saw the old men drinking coffee outside the Greek café, standing together in their wordless brotherhood. Wordless brotherhood sounded just about right to him. He pulled into the parking lot and took a deep, long breath.

He should've stuck with wordless brotherhood,

instead of going out with the guys to commiserate over the failed Southwest Airlines pitch. Was that only last night? At several moments last evening he could've, should've said, "Guys, I ought to be getting home." He felt certain that he *had* said it aloud, at least once; he remembered someone saying back, "C'mon, your wife is out of town, what's to go home *to*?" He remembered laughing in response, accepting the role he would play. His co-workers *expected* mischief of him, having escaped a weekend with his in-laws; he ought not to let them down. To them, his time in the drunk tank would be a badge of honor. At least they'd have *something* to show for the futile Southwest Airlines meeting.

Disappointing now that he could barely recall his time with the guys; he had a dim memory of having missed the last train, and being driven home by someone with a coconut-scented air freshener. Just the memory of this scent caused his stomach to flip. Thank God Irene MacAvoy's car smelled like nothing at all.

For the sake of wordless brotherhood, he'd missed Chad's confirmation, stranded his family at the church. It was a few days later, on his walk home from the train after work, that he'd spotted a dog in the animal shelter. The woman inside said he was part Viszla.

Ray thought the dog looked wise. A soulful companion for his son to take on long walks. And so much better than a pen set.

"You can learn a lot from a dog," the woman said, the beads on her blond dreadlocks rattling. "Like how to shake things off, you know?"

He shouldered a bag of kibble and scratched the back of the dog's head.

When he got home, Chad was in the living room, his eyes on the digitized form of a sword-wielding kung fu expert. With his thumbs, Chad was causing the fighter to spin, kick, and leap menacingly at another digitized figure. He did not turn when Ray entered.

"Hello," he said heartily, anyway.

His son's on-screen alter ego kicked ever faster, accumulating points in the upper left-hand corner of the screen, as Chad pounded a button on his handset.

Perhaps it was unfair to compare this glaze-eyed, inscrutable teenager with the boy who had leapt into his arms, who had clung to his neck when Ray lifted him onto his shoulders. Unfair or not, he couldn't help it.

Ray brought the dog inside, and the two of them went unnoticed until the dog gave a short, cough-like bark, and Chad turned with a face that said, *Great, my dad is actually barking now.*

"Happy confirmation, son," Ray said. At once he wanted to take back the sentence: he'd meant to say "I love you," or "I'm proud of you," or "I'm sorry I missed the ceremony," and he'd meant to say "Chad." He released the dog's leash, imagining that it would pad across the room into Chad's outstretched arms. But Chad was still on the couch, watching bemused as the dog took two steps away from Ray and then lifted his leg on the corner of the rug.

It was the wrong gift, again. The right one had been the game cartridge, the artful contrivance of bits and bytes into digital entertainment. His asshole neighbor had known this, but Ray had not.

So Ray took the goddamn dog for a walk. Scot greeted him at the end of the driveway with false bonhomie.

Ray pulled up on Red's leash, in front of Scot's amplified house.

"Say," Scot said, "I've been thinking. You know I hardly ever drive this thing." He rapped the bumper of his SUV.

"Uh-huh," said Ray.

"Why don't we let Chad use it, now that he's ready to learn how to drive? That thing is crazy safe. It's got like seventeen airbags. Head-on collision, the CD player won't even skip."

"Chad's only fourteen," said Ray.

Scot shrugged this off. "An empty parking lot some weekend, he'd love it."

The dog chose that moment to circle a tree in MacAvoy's yard, then loop back to Ray and shit on the edge of Ray's front lawn.

Startlingly unforced whimsy.

Now, in Irene MacAvoy's quilted front seat, Ray had a vague memory of shouting, "Why don't we let Chad use it now," late last night as he attacked the SUV with a baseball bat, but the memory dissipated as he reached for it, like a half-remembered dream.

As he'd stepped out of his coworker's coconut-scented car, Ray had stumbled. It was late, his empty house was dark. His rented house. His wife visiting her father; his son at Walter's for the night, no doubt playing MacAvoy's games. Emptiness was all that awaited him.

His co-worker drove off with a curt little wave, and Ray struggled to stand. His briefcase flew out of his hand and whacked a hubcap on Scot's SUV.

At once the shrieking alarm. Jesus, it was loud. He scrabbled to retrieve his bag, but the alarm continued. Was it actually getting louder?

Angrily he flung his briefcase at the vehicle. It made a wet smacking sound and slid to the ground.

Why did this cursed alarm not rouse his neighbors? Couldn't they have drowsily found some button to disarm it? Was their brand new second floor suite so well-insulated that they could not hear it?

He should have gone with Allison to visit her father. It had only been a month since they'd buried her mother. Ray ought to be wrapping his arm around Allison on the couch, as she sat with her dad and stepmother. This must have been awkward and sad and lonely, and instead of offering her comfort he had chosen the Southwest Airlines pitch.

Goddamnit.

He did not remember going into his house, opening the trapdoor in the garage ceiling, reaching up for Chad's old aluminum bat. But surely he had done this, because it was Chad's bat he swung at the windshield, the headlights, the shiny black doors of Scot MacAvoy's monstrosity.

Smashing, shattering, crunching. His shoulders were sore now, but he'd been powerful with that bat. The metal and glass no match for his rage. His satisfying, glorious rage. A whack for all the sleepless nights this cursed vehicle had caused. A whack for its owner's improbably lush lawn, his unjustly charmed life. A whack for Scot's having stolen his son's affection and attention. Each whack a new exhilaration. It felt incredible, not like something he'd regret by morning, his mouth filled with the taste of metal, as if he'd consumed the car itself.

It was the car itself that had called them, the cops said when they arrived. Some on-board computer had sensed that the car was in danger.

He realized now that he shouldn't have laughed when he saw the extent of the damage, the behemoth listing to one side like a doomed ocean liner. Oh, but he had laughed: he'd laughed like a man who'd never laughed before. This was not the contrition the cops might've hoped that he'd display.

No, he wasn't drunk, this wasn't a disturbance, did anyone look disturbed?

"Just me," the cop had said, snapping cuffs onto Ray's wrists.

Irene MacAvoy's passenger door swung open to release him. Sleep-deprived and sun-blind, Ray staggered up his driveway. His son guided him inside, where Ray collapsed onto the couch. Chad put the manila envelope of Ray's belongings on the side table.

"So, um, if you're okay here, I'm going to walk the dog."

Ray couldn't bear to make eye contact, so he didn't know where Chad's own eyes were fixed, or how full of shame or pity. He needed time to find a way to explain himself. He needed sleep. Ray nodded permission that Chad hadn't asked for, and slid deeper into the couch.

Disaster Preparedness

Alone, Chad walked from the lab building to the gym, trailed by the sound of girls' laughter. *Not at you*, he told himself, trying hard to believe it. He stared at his feet and kept moving. A few more steps of September sunlight before the cavernous gym.

Because the Palo Alto High School campus was composed of many small buildings, the walk between classes gave you a moment outdoors. The sun shone in its mellow Northern Californian way. For a moment you could soak up that easygoing sunshine, breathe the mentholated eucalyptus in the air, and consider yielding to the palm trees beckoning toward pools and fields. But you had only seven minutes between classes, so you had to grit your teeth and ignore those sweet lazy rays. Tune out the whistle of the train that could whisk you north into the city. You had to hump that backpack over to Brit Lit without complaint. Or in this case, trudge into the gym for the memorial assembly.

Inside, the bleachers were almost full. If this were an awards program or a rally for the football team, everyone would be talking and laughing. It would be easy for Chad to slip up the bleacher stairs, into a row near the top, without attracting attention. Even Chad himself would hardly notice his singularity, his lack of a clan to join. But today the mood was quieter, a wound-nursing shell-shocked hush. Chad felt himself being inspected as he tried to find a seat.

"Excuse me," said one of the giggling girls behind him, and she and her friends pushed past. Cheerleaders: pleated skirts and ponytailed indifference.

Chad took a seat in the second row. The girl next to him moved away almost imperceptibly, putting an extra millimeter between their thighs.

Some committee of upperclassmen had painted signs: WE REMEMBER, and FDNY. Chad muttered, "FD-freaking-NY," as if his friend Walter Chen were beside him to agree on the ridiculousness of California high school students expressing their allegiance to these valiant but distant heroes.

In Walter's absence the only response to Chad's remark was the choreographed look he got from the seniors sitting in front of him, practically medieval in its disdain: a feeble-minded member of some lower caste prone to talking to himself. Chad wanted to evaporate.

The girl next to Chad said then, "I'm actually saving this." Her voice rose at the end, but it was not a question.

He looked at her for a long moment, then inched further down the row.

The assembly marked the one-year anniversary. Chad had watched the endless loop of airplanes, smoke, and pancaking towers on television, with the rest of his eighth-grade class; it was too cinematic to be real. It came at them from screens mounted on hospital brackets in the corners of their classroom, where their teacher had told them they would be watching Current Events and Civics videos. It was the second week of classes; they had not yet firmly distinguished Alexis J. from Alexis F. and Alexa C. But after that day in September, the TV in Chad's classroom sat dark for the rest of the year.

Now, the cheerleaders held candles that fire regulations did not permit them to light; the chorus sang anthems; several teachers spoke. The naked emotion crackling their voices embarrassed Chad. It was a strange thing to commemorate; already, it seemed so long ago.

After all, he was in high school now. He went to Paly.

You didn't want to let the innocuous-sounding nickname, the mission-style campus and palm trees, fool you. Palo Alto High School was high-stakes poker. Every interaction was a rope bridge across a ravine, with half the slats missing and a madman holding a knife to the cord. Chad took pains to be as inconspicuous as the one black kid in a school of 1,500 could possibly be.

He could imagine an alternate existence that was less excruciating. Maybe if he'd been at the pool all summer, instead of at his dying Grandma's bedside;

maybe if his best friend hadn't just transferred to another school; maybe if he looked more like everybody else; maybe if he cared less about computers and more about free weights or skiing. Maybe if his dad's weekend escapade hadn't left Chad destabilized and confused. Then again, it would still be high school.

Danger was everywhere at Paly, as immediate as the guy at the next urinal staring you down into pee-shyness, or matter-of-factly elbowing you into the wall. Your backpack getting flipped inside out with a nylon *fwoomp*, dropping your notebooks onto the hallway floor. The muttered comments pitched too low for a teacher to hear. That internal X-ray that identified weakness, and his classmates' deadeye aim. The rigidly stratified social classes: the Model UN didn't dare talk to the water polo team, except to buy uppers or coke; the Asian kids allowed just one extracurricular by their college-minded parents, who had some explaining to do if it wasn't orchestra; and you had to be cautious about acknowledging people you ran into off-campus, out of context, because your assigned caste stayed with you.

But you couldn't hold an assembly for each hallway snubbing, or light a candle for every sophomore heartbreak. Instead, you memorialized the fallen towers; and you prepared for the unthinkable with monthly Shooter Drills.

Only a day or two after the memorial assembly, the Drill alarm rang; Mr. Farris said, "Okay, you guys, here we go," and each student in Chad's World History class climbed under his or her desk. Each student except Kara Stevens.

Kara had been designated to post a color-coded

sign in the window—a signal to the emergency personnel who would be arriving if this were not a drill. Green meant everyone inside the room was fine; yellow meant three or more in need of non-urgent medical assistance; and red meant that at least one person's injuries required immediate attention, or that the shooter was inside or near their classroom. For the purposes of the drill, Kara had been asked to post a yellow sign.

According to Kara, this was very much like what they did in Texas for tornados. She'd moved from Dallas in the middle of last year and offered herself up to Paly: a willing lamb. She was just too forthcoming, sharing unsolicited comparisons between Dallas and Palo Alto; that these comparisons generally favored Dallas did not ease Kara's way. She also gave feedback to teachers, even when they hadn't explicitly asked, and long before the teachers got to the point of desperate pleading—*C'mon, you guys, I know someone here has an opinion about Tess's relationship with Alec d'Urberville.* Kara's sheer willingness to speak deprived her classmates of the spectacle of educators groveling, and she would not be forgiven.

If there were a key to surviving high school, it was appearing unconcerned about your chances. Pretending the unwritten rules that could make or break someone didn't bother you one way or the other. The Poker Face. The proper shrug was paramount.

Here was the real Sherlock Holmes part: the goal, Chad believed, was not to seem like you cared what other people thought. Yet Kara, who patently Did Not Care, was ostracized. So what the fuck did Chad know?

From under his desk, he could see only a few of

his classmates. It was hot for September, especially without air conditioning in school, and as the girls crouched under their desks their legs and arms made a jumble of confounding uncovered skin. Next to him, a tank top hung loose on a girl already hunched into a cleavage-enhancing position. Chad struggled to focus on the lower half of a map of the Ottoman Empire. To ensure the stability of various peninsulas.

Based on what Mr. F. had told them, the Empire had been a good deal for the sultan, what with the harem and the fist-sized emeralds and the jewel-encrusted everything. This was likely why a sultan's job security was for shit; the guy couldn't even trust his concubines not to slit his throat as they rinsed the shampoo from his hair. Probably ran his own version of a Shooter Drill several times a day.

Shooter Drills were the final straw for the Chens. They had weathered the assemblies and cultural performances that ate up valuable instructional time. But they would not accept the Shooter Drills. As of a week ago, they had removed Walter from Palo Alto High School and enrolled him at the posh private school, five miles south. "That's what I get for talking to my parents," he told Chad grimly.

At first Walter had joined Chad in sneering at his Academy uniform, and had changed into a t-shirt and shorts before coming over to Chad's after school. But one day he'd been running late and had only removed his jacket, then loosened his tie when he saw Chad's shorts. They looked like First Class and Steerage, which had seemed as if they'd be funny nicknames but, as it turned out, were not.

Chad missed Walter now. He wanted to roll his eyes

during the Shooter Drill at someone who would understand. He could only assume that Walter, surrounded by guys in cheap sport coats, had to stop himself from saying things like "Back when I went to public school," or "That's not how we did it at Paly."

After school he went to the music store downtown where he and Walter used to hang out. Every place he could think of going was a place he and Walter used to go together. All of downtown Palo Alto was haunted, from the Apple Store to the bagel/smoothie boutique, the Posh Nosh.

The record store was papered with posters for bands like Death Cab for Cutie and The Mountain Goats, and the place smelled of teriyaki sauce from the restaurant next door. A few customers browsed the new releases. Chad slapped through a tray of used CDs, rolling his shoulder to get rid of the ache he'd developed in his Shooter Drill crouch. He half-listened to two guys ribbing each other.

"I *like* imports, Marcus," said one of the guys. "So sue me."

There was no way these two went to Paly; if they did, they would've been featured along with Chad in the "Diversity" section of the school website. (Paly was mostly white and Asian, so "Diversity" was kind of overstating things. *Bi*versity, maybe.) Also, their baggy jeans and earrings weren't exactly Paly standard. Even if Chad's mom had remembered about back-to-school clothes, she would've bought him polos and jeans that fit properly: no gangster sag on her watch. This wasn't so much about her being white as it was about her being Grandma Marchese's daughter. Since polos were more or less the Paly uniform this suited Chad fine; it was readymade camouflage.

A question occurred to Chad, as he watched these two black boys with their loose-jointed swaggering ease: If a black kid had white parents, was he still black? It sounded like a bad joke, and it had worried him a thousand times before, but at the moment it was piercingly urgent.

"Tell you what," the first boy, Marcus, said to his friend: "For ten bucks I'll make you a set of little yellow stickers that say IMPORT, and you can make everything in your collection bona fide, just like that."

The other guy suggested that Marcus shut the fuck up.

Chad snickered. Both guys glared at him.

"Seriously," Marcus said. "You want to pay extra for the Japanese version of your Eurotrash music, God bless."

Chad smiled at this: *God bless* had been a cherished passive-aggressive phrase of Grandma Marchese's. Sample usage: *Your grandfather and his ladyfriend decided to move out west, I say God bless.* He ducked his head so the boys wouldn't misinterpret his smile.

The boy who liked Imports stiffened. "What you calling Eurotrash?"

"Andre, look," Marcus began. Then, startlingly, he waved the CD case at Chad. Even more startling: he spoke to him. "Settle this for us, man," he said. "These guys in their skinny ties, here, what do you think of them?"

Chad's throat locked tight with panic.

Marcus flipped over the CD. "Christ, Andre, there's

a song on here called 'Pain au chocolat.'" He made a face at Chad: *Can you believe this?*

Chad assessed the risks of alienating Andre, who was already pissed; Marcus, who he pegged as the charismatic leader of the twosome; or both of them at once. The perils were both physical and social. Then again, having never seen these two guys before, he might ensure his short-term safety by declining to comment. Then again *again*, these two guys might be his only shot at avoiding another quiet afternoon of solo Playstation and rubbing one out.

"Help us out," Andre said, thrusting the CD into Chad's hands.

He pretended to evaluate the disk. He knew the band well; they were a favorite of his next-door neighbor Scot.

"Eurotrash, right?" Marcus persisted.

His mouth felt dry on some absolute scale beyond any previous human experience of dryness. "Actually," he said in a strangled, scratchy voice, "three out of these five guys are American."

Andre grinned.

Marcus shook his head at Chad. "Whose side are you on, dude?" But he didn't look pissed.

Chad felt himself regaining strength. "I guess it depends," he said, "on whether you think of Eurotrash as a geographic or a *cultural* distinction."

"Oh, it's most def a state of fucking mind," Marcus laughed. He stuck out his hand and introduced himself.

In short order Chad learned that Marcus and Andre were also freshmen, but at East Palo Alto, where they filed through metal detectors each morning on the way to homeroom. He suspected they would not be particularly impressed by the details of a Paly Shooter Drill. Being unshockable, he sensed, was important to Marcus and Andre: it was one of the top three things they wanted the world to know about them.

In his head he could fast-forward to see the three of them leaving the store together, maybe heading over to the Posh Nosh, but he couldn't see how to get there.

Chad's dad said this was the problem with the whole Valley: people wanted to get to the IPO and be millionaires before they'd put in the hours. Like all it takes is a cute name and a slide deck that charms a VC, he scoffed. Nobody's good with his hands anymore.

The store door jingled as a black-haired boy pushed it open. He struggled with a heavy messenger bag and headed straight for the rack of used CDs.

When the boy looked up, Chad saw that it was Walter, still wearing his blue academy blazer. "Hey," Chad called.

Walter looked at him, and at Marcus and Andre. Chad watched him noting the Rocawear, the saggy jeans, the earring. Counting Chad, Marcus, Andre: one, two, three black boys in a record store. "Hi," Walter said softly.

Chad said, "How's it going?"

"Ummm...okay." Walter was frozen. "I think I forgot my, um, book back there. Later, maybe."

Chad watched him back out of the shop. A small bell rang as the door swung shut behind him. Chad's throat got all squeezy again. "That was my best friend," he said.

"Yeah, obviously you're tight," said Marcus.

Shoeless

For days Chad had been waiting for another shoe to drop. Cops at the door, badges flashed, or a sudden vacation that required half-assed packing and an eye on the rearview mirror.

Part of him was disappointed that the outlaw road trip had not come to pass, but he realized that even as fugitives, his parents would've still stopped at organic farm stands instead of bingeing on Quick Mart snacks, would've still painstakingly tabulated all their receipts, and would've still sung along to Joni Mitchell tapes rather than let Chad make the selections.

Anyway, they weren't on the run. As far as Chad could tell, his mom was unaware of the "misunderstanding," as his dad and Mrs. MacAvoy had both called Ray's night in jail. This didn't mean it was a secret, necessarily; maybe it had truly been nothing, so that there was nothing to tell. Regardless, Chad was disinclined to tell his mother what little he knew. The various scenarios he could envision all involved her getting upset—whether it be at Ray, at Chad, or most likely of all, at herself for having been out of town and unable to help—and after the year she'd had, he didn't want to pile on.

Early in the summer, Grandma Marchese had still seemed like herself. She slept a lot, and her body was withered and small, but she had sharp words for the food—*Chad, call Moon Palace and get a large MSG. This hospital has misdiagnosed me as allergic to flavor*—and the night nurses—*Am I supposed to give her an A for effort when it takes her an hour to find a vein?*

"Mother," Chad's mom would still say then, as if she were shocked. "You're too much."

But Grandma wasn't too much. She was just right. Until there was not enough of her. Now she would've been great fugitive company. Chad would've hit the road with Grandma M. in a heartbeat. Her man Sinatra on the stereo, salty jokes and shit-talk about everyone whose path they crossed. The rhythmic clack of rosary beads as Frank crooned.

By mid-July, things had changed. Grandma barely touched any food, even with smuggled-in spices, and when Chad brought in the chicken cheesesteaks that used to be her favorite, she got sick just from the smell.

Chad and his mom were used to it by then, the vomit and the other stuff—it was terrible, what you could get used to. His mom tending to her own mom, feeding her and wiping her butt: this was the circle of glorious life.

She still cried sometimes. Mostly in her room, so he only noticed when she emerged with puffy eyes, but sometimes standing at the stove with a spatula, or folding laundry in front of the TV. Tears just pouring onto the stacked t-shirts and shorts. Sometimes Chad almost thought she was crying because she felt bad about crying so much.

So why pile on? To tell a story he couldn't finish?

All he had done was get his dad a ride home. He reminded himself of this.

On Friday morning, his mother made him fried eggs for breakfast. No weeping involved. She was even humming one of her old folk songs.

"Thanks," Chad said, surprised. He typically poured his own cereal or grabbed a granola bar before he walked to school.

"I have a client this afternoon," she said. "I thought we could meet here?"

This meant one of her at-risk girls at the kitchen table, possibly sitting where Chad sat now, trying not to talk about whatever had gotten her referred to Chad's mom. Teachers and vice-principals had Allison on speed dial. The minister had sent her several clients; one from the rabbi; none at all from the Catholics. But the Protestants outsourced. The eggs were a bribe, to buy her an uninterrupted hour.

"We have any Tabasco?" Grandma Marchese had taught Chad to eat eggs this way.

The mention of hot sauce rattled his mom, like a skip in a record. She stopped humming and blinked hard as she set the bottle down.

"I should've gone with you to Grandpa's," he said.

"We did miss you," she said. "But I'm sure you and your father enjoyed your freedom."

Chad choked down the things he wasn't saying. Drank fast to help the swallowing.

During the Shooter drill he'd thought about how it might go down, if an actual shooter arrived. He could picture the door swinging open, a figure entering armed like he'd raided that gun stockroom in *The Matrix*.

Wondering: would he be brave, a hero lunging to protect his classmates? A diplomat attempting reason? Or would he cower under his desk, piss pooling on the linoleum beneath him? Would Chad be shot while he was still deciding: frozen, like the guys in Pompeii, in this pathetic crouch? Wondering, too, whether Mr. Farris had considered these odds himself, intentionally placing an earnest boy from the track team in the desk closest to his own, counting on the hurdler's sense of Boy Scout duty. Afterward, Mr. F.'s suspicions confirmed as he surveyed the damage—*Ah, Loudermilk. I always figured him for a coward.*

Chad finished his eggs and carried his dishes to the sink. He glanced out the window at the place Scot's SUV usually sat. He had forgotten that the neighbors across the street had a persimmon tree. In a month it would be laden with fruit, its branches propped with two-by-fours to keep them from snapping under the weight. A lot could happen in a month.

The car that was gone was the car Scot had promised him driving lessons in, the one Mrs. MacAvoy had said was in the shop for an oil change when he'd gone to tell her about his dad needing a ride—a week ago. When he walked past on the way to school, he saw that the pavement glittered with fragments of broken glass. Tiny, too small to sweep up.

Since kindergarten, Chad's best friend had been Walter Chen. He missed the easy way they had together, their inside jokes, how they disguised their mischief to evade Walter's strict mother and her constraints—the back patio always off limits to them, and blanket forts forbidden because they invited ghosts into the house. So they'd gone to the park, hiked up to the giant satellite dish on the edge of Stanford's campus, to freedom.

He would've liked to hang out with Walter now.

But every time he started to think about calling Walter, he remembered that moment in the record store, that moment when Walter could've walked over like a normal person and said, "Hi," maybe even introduced himself to Marcus and Andre. But instead, he'd bolted.

"I hate to tell you this, man," Marcus said, "but your best friend is kinda racist."

"He can't be racist—*his best friend is black*," Andre laughed.

"Maybe he didn't know how black you were, 'til he saw you with Negroes such as ourselves," Marcus said.

"Nah, fool, dude looks white next to us, like how girls look skinnier when they stand next to a fat chick." Andre's skin was three shades lighter than Chad's, so this wasn't about what you could see on the color wheel.

They were sitting outside the Posh Nosh, at a table made of perforated metal. Marcus tore into a sesame bagel. The 3:40 train whistled, four horn blasts, as it rumbled past.

A bird hopped over to investigate a dropped chunk of bagel, and Andre stomped his foot, causing the startled bird to fly off.

Chad remembered an afternoon when he and Walter had made an increasingly hysterical series of prank phone calls, busting themselves up with such hilarity it became difficult for them to be understood by the prank-ees. Chad demanding a pizza with extra "Pianoforte" and "Frappuccino." Walter asking a travel agent for information about visiting East Africa, specifically Djibouti, because he was very much hoping to get all up in Djibouti.

Afterward, Chad's mom escorting them to each business to apologize for wasting the employees' time and being disrespectful.

"Hey, where'd you go, man?" Andre laughed. "Daydream much?"

"Sorry," Chad said, feeling his face get hot. He was going to screw this up, he could feel it. These guys would pull away from him, just like Walter.

"So, what about it?" Marcus asked, re-asking the question he'd posed while Chad was watching birds and stewing about Walter Chen.

Be bold, Chad told himself. "Yes," he said. "Definitely."

Marcus's eyebrows rose, and Chad panicked: maybe it hadn't been a yes-or-no question.

"Well all right," Marcus said. "What're we waiting for?"

And that was how Chad invited his new friends over: accidentally, and pretty much in spite of himself. While they walked back to Chad's house, Marcus unspooled a theory relating the new *Fellowship of the Rings* movie to *Star Wars*. "The Orcs are basically Storm Troopers. Faceless and fully controlled by the top evil dude."

"And top evil dude equals top evil dude," Andre said. "Saruman, Count Dooku."

"Too easy," Marcus said. "Next you're going to tell me Gandalf is Obi-Wan, and Aragorn is Han Solo. Up your game, man." He riffed to demonstrate: "Hobbits are Ewoks, furry comic relief but capable of acts of cuddly violence when under duress."

Chad tried: "The Nazgul are the Siths, right?"

"That works," Marcus allowed, stepping over a broken place in the sidewalk.

Andre harrumphed. The only thing worse than not getting Marcus's approval was watching someone else bask in it.

Chad's Playstation occupied the rest of the afternoon; the three of them digitally eviscerated each other as they wore soft craters into the Loudermilk couch.

"This is a nice house, man," Andre said, and Chad was surprised that this didn't feel like a compliment. It felt like a stiff arm to the chest: you are different from us. Your plush beige couch is entirely too plush and too beige.

Also, it felt like being a third wheel in his own living room. Andre was a nonstop source of references to East Palo Alto kids Chad didn't know, slang he only half understood in context. Although Andre was speaking to Marcus, Chad expected this was not the way he spoke when he and Marcus were alone. Marcus was Andre's Walter Chen, Chad saw, and Chad was a blue blazer.

"Real nice, even though your folks are obviously *bargain shoppers.*" Andre gestured at one of the framed family photos: Chad, flanked by his white parents.

He tried to see his house through Marcus's and Andre's eyes: the overwhelming plush beigeness of it. The picture window view of the driveway, and of Scot MacAvoy's SUV next door (which had rematerialized). He wondered whether there was a subtle way to reveal that the Loudermilks were only renting, to reveal the stained undersides of the couch cushions, or to make them attentive to the picture window: Scot's expanded house making Chad's look smaller and, he hoped, more modest.

"New Jay-Z drops next month," Marcus reminded Andre. "You best call your pals in Scandifuckinavia and get them to hook you up."

Andre shot him the finger.

"Dude," Marcus said, waving a hand in front of Chad's eyes, "you look like you're taking an algebra test."

Chad took a deep breath. "I was thinking: Jay-Z is always sort of proclaiming himself, right?"

"Always saying where he came from," Marcus agreed.

"And how his skills rate," Chad said. "'Yeah I rhyme sick, I be what you're trying to do.'"

"Still, Nas was asking for it once he shaded him in Ether," Marcus said.

"Shade, hell, that was a solar eclipse." Andre said.

"That's one way to announce yourself," Chad said. "Light the other guy on fire. Like how many raps are about saying, Here I am. Recognize me, respect me."

"'My name is, *what*? Slim Shady,'" Andre offered.

"Exactly," Chad nodded.

"Eminem sucks," Marcus said, disappointing them both.

On Friday afternoon, he was playing Izzo for some hand-me-down confidence, and had the volume up so loud he didn't hear the phone. His mom knocked to tell him it was Walter.

"Hey," he said. "What's up?"

"Nothing," Walter said. "Definitely not writing my Religion paper."

Walter had a whole class on Religion, now that he went to a Jesuit school. Probably a step up from the photocopied handouts they received at Confirmation class. "Still finding God in all things?" Chad quoted the Academy motto.

"Yeah, that dude is pretty much everywhere."

Chad snickered.

"You doing anything tonight?"

He'd agreed to meet Marcus and Andre in East Palo Alto, then go to a party at their friend Kevin Hernandez's. He wouldn't have minded bailing, hanging out with Walter instead. But he could imagine how Andre would spin his failure to show. Then again, he could invite Walter to join them at the party, except for the way he'd weirded everyone out at the record store.

"Chad?" Walter prodded.

"Yeah, I have plans, sorry. Catch you later?"

Kevin Hernandez lived in a narrow townhouse down the street from Marcus. There were bars on most of the ground-floor windows, and some of the second-floor ones too. An older man sat in a folding lawn chair on a tiny patch of concrete in front of his house, a cylinder wrapped in a brown paper bag at his feet. Chad felt the man's watchful eyes on him as they passed.

Inside, music was blasting and people were wall to wall. As they entered, Marcus was greeted with enthusiasm. "Yo, Johnson!" Chad was jostled by each new high five, back slap, embrace. He accepted a plastic cup of beer from Andre, and they clacked them together, said "Cheers."

The crowd was black and Latino, throbbing to the beat of the music as if organically connected to it. The thrum of conversation a low murmur, punctuated with trills of laughter and the occasional bellowed "HELL no." Chad sipped from his solo cup.

Within minutes, Marcus had cornered, or been cornered by, a gorgeous girl in short denim shorts and a tank top that glowed against her dark skin. The girl laughed like bells as Marcus leaned in. He gave the impression of having focused his entire being on her, locked into firing position like a fighter jet.

Chad's clothes were wrong. He'd chosen a black polo shirt and jeans: recipe for invisibility at Paly, but here they were too generic, too nondescript. He yearned for a t-shirt with someone else's name on it; he ached for a baseball cap.

But even the hats were different here at Kevin Hernandez's house. They were unlike the caps his Paly peers molded lovingly, rubber-banding them under the mattress like baseball gloves, curving the brims into soft arcs. Muted colors and frayed stitching, worked over to look aged and old school. Instead, the caps at Kevin Hernandez's party looked crisply new, their bills still flat, their logos flashy and primary-colored.

Andre, after delivering Chad's beer, had joined a group circling the keg. Chad caught his eye, and resolved to go over. But Andre shifted his weight to turn away from Chad.

"Look out, dude," said a guy pushing past as his drink sloshed onto Chad's arm.

The loneliness of a crowd was well known to Chad, and he sank into it. In his mind he composed the riff he'd offer Walter, if he were here—or to anyone who happened to stand next to Chad long enough to listen. Chad had been thinking about the book in Mr. Farris's classroom, with ash castings from Pompeii: negative space left by people who never saw it coming—forever Woman Seated, or Guy Picking His Nose or Kid Rubbing One Out. If disaster struck now, Chad's ashen hollow would be gripping the ghost of a red solo cup, watching the feet of the partygoers passing him by on their way to the keg.

Don't Call It A Comeback

Diana caught a taxi to the conference hotel and checked in, her tongue dulled to numbness by the long silent travel time. "Diana Marchese," she tried to say, "I'm checking in?"

Her voice sounded muffled, strangely accented— even though she'd practiced this phrase in Catalan in her head.

The desk clerk pursed his lips and squinted at her.

"I am Diana Marchese," she said again, more firmly. "Stanford University?" She felt she was auditioning for the role of herself, and she was not impressing the director. At best, she would be the understudy.

Here in Barcelona three hundred of her fellow physicists were assembled. To present and discuss their work, yes, but of more immediate concern was that they would be welcoming Diana back to their wise and rumpled fellowship for the first time since she'd given birth to Molly, nineteen long months ago.

The clerk sniffed intensely before deciding to trust her, sliding over a room keycard, and pointing out the conference registration table. There, Diana accepted a laminated nametag and a canvas tote bag filled with papers and brochures for the conference sponsors and industrial exhibitors. In the elevator she was surrounded by men all carrying the same tote bag.

Not yet hungry and unable to nap, Diana put on her Speedo and made her way to the hotel pool. In the water, she did not allow herself to think about Molly, or the talk she was presenting, or the classes she was missing at home and whether the TA lecturing in her course would cover as much ground as she'd hoped. (She had provided a detailed syllabus and her own precise notes.) If she thought at all, it was to count her strokes and focus on controlling her kicks and preventing her torso from twisting too much when she breathed.

After a shower, she called home. Molly was her usual blur of anxious energy. She said Tommy had painted her nails blue, and they were going to watch *Nemo* that night.

"Are you going to have popcorn?" Diana asked.

"No," Molly said. "Daddy made spaghetti."

Diana was guiltily relieved. Not *osso buco*, not Welsh rarebit, just spaghetti.

Intellectually, she knew she was not in a competition with Arthur. They had decided to share Molly. They had explained—to their parents, to her sister— how deeply they believed in Molly having parents who were equal partners. But some days she couldn't help weighing what Arthur offered—a stable, loving relationship; a spacious, well-furnished house; nutritious home-cooked meals—against what she herself managed to provide.

Diana remembered—as a teenager—telling her mother that she intended to have children who liked to read, and at least one who would play the cello, because she would enjoy listening to someone practice the cello. Her mother gave a thorny chuckle and said, "Good luck with that." At the time she had heard in the laugh only her mother's disenchantment with the sort of daughter Diana had been, but now she understood that that was only part of it.

"I think you'd like it here, Mols," she said. "They have a park with cool mosaics and curving walls, and it's all so colorful." She was describing pictures in her guidebook; she herself would hardly leave the conference hotel grounds.

Molly chirped back, her voice on the phone sounding somehow even younger, more vulnerable than it seemed in person. Her eagerness to talk, and this small voice, were a reproach.

Her daughter saw clean through her, rated her correctly as barely competent, her methods as *ad hoc*. Often, Diana felt sure she was taking mental notes for a bestselling tell-all that would reveal Diana's maternal inadequacies to a scandalized but unsurprised readership.

What an exceedingly good idea it had seemed, three years ago, to have a baby. Diana had just been told by her chairman that the department had recommended tenure. And although Diana knew said chairman was only giving her time to catch her breath before he added the expectations she'd need to meet to make full professor, she took that breath-taking moment to heart. I'm in a pie-eating contest, she thought, and the grand prize is more pie.

Not that her six years pre-tenure had been entirely joyless: her best friend Arthur dragged her to movies and, at least once a week, towed her to some Palo Alto restaurant. And, soon after her discussion with the chair, she said to Arthur over their second round of margaritas, "What would you think about the two of us having a baby?"

This had been their backup plan, a contingency arrangement between a straight woman and her gay best friend: when one of us is ready; if there's no one else around; when we turn thirty. But their milestones had come and gone, and Diana—tenured, alone, thirty-three and a half years old—was ready for something besides the pie-eating contest, and Arthur, after discussing it with Tommy, said yes.

She was aware of the risks. Her own department chair had praised her: "You know, Diana, you're not like the rest of them. Not so emotional." Showing up in one of those maternity blouses with a bow just under the bustline, lumbering through the hallways, would do some damage to this perception.

It had taken her years to wrest control of her identity away from parents and classmates who wished to define her, often in contrast to her older sister Allison; only in college and grad school had she felt that she was truly forging her own identity, becoming an independent woman who unashamedly understood physics and who swam laps at lunchtime. But she had not realized how much being Professor Marchese mattered to her until, for seven months, she was only Mom.

The Place You're Supposed to Laugh

Getting back to teaching and research had been reasonably smooth. There was the occasional hiccup when baby Molly had a fever, and Arthur wasn't available. The daycare's policies meant Diana sometimes dosed Molly with infant Tylenol in their parking lot, hoping to buy herself four hours on campus before the drug wore off and her daughter's teacher called her office to alert her that the fever was "back." Still, but for the baby pictures on her desk, she was a nigh unchanged Professor Marchese.

International travel, though, was trickier. Five days was a long time to be away. She'd considered bringing Molly along, and finding childcare at the conference hotel, but Arthur and Tommy assured her they'd be fine.

This was both reassuring and not.

And, a transatlantic flight with Molly would've been a nightmare. She'd taken Molly on short trips, and seen the way her fellow travelers rolled their eyes and tapped their feet, broad cartoons of impatience, as Diana struggled to collapse the stroller, take off her shoes, and coerce Molly through the metal detector. She boarded early, with a bag full of diapers, wipes, toys, snacks, and Benadryl to be strategically deployed. The first time she'd flown with Molly she'd packed a paperback for herself, that's how naive she'd been. If Molly cried—and who could blame her for crying, with the pressurized, stale air recirculating and the whine of the 737 engines—passengers glared openly at Diana. She made theatrical efforts to soothe Molly, believing that her fellow travelers would be more patient with her if she made an effort, the way the French softened up if you seemed like you were trying, if you managed a

Bonjour or a *Je voudrais café au lait* that sounded half-convincing.

She knew that it was different for Arthur. When he had Molly, people gushed; they beamed warmly, as if they were proud of him. And if it were Arthur and Tommy, well, that was even better. The flight attendants would have brought them extra packs of pretzels and made a fuss over Molly's *trés chic* outfit.

When she'd been pregnant she'd appreciated the aptness of the word *expectant*. Because she was, more than anything, waiting—for her and Arthur's baby to be born, and to see what life was going to be like. She was anxious, full of hopes and vows (she would demonstrate a graceful balancing act admired by her colleagues and students alike). She looked up *expecting*, in fact, and traced this back through *expectations* to *expect*. What it said was "to look forward to; anticipate the occurrence or the coming of: *to expect guests, to expect a hurricane.*" That's exactly right, she'd thought, I'm expecting a guest-slash-hurricane.

The last time she'd flown Before Molly had been a trip east, just before her mother got sick. Her mom's Cherry Hill condo felt smaller than Diana remembered it—and so did her mother.

She wondered now if her mother had known she was dying, had known that the cancer was back. Had instead pretended to be comfortable and calm. More lies meant to protect her mother rather than Diana.

Diana kept a list of her mother's lies:

    (1) In college, boys will appreciate the smart girls, and you'll be the popular one.

(2) Patience is a virtue.

(3) They call you names because they're jealous. And why not?

(4) Picking up the phone on the first ring makes you seem desperate.

(5) If you can read, you can cook. Even that marble-mouthed giant Julia Child says so.

(6) You'll regret giving up the oboe.

(7) When you're older, you'll understand.

For some time Diana had lived, and been soothed by, these lies. But ultimately, she'd admitted that each of these refrains, no matter how frequently repeated, had been untrue. It was Lie Number Four that had finally broken her: Diana was a busy person, too busy to wait for her mother's prescribed two-and-a-half rings. Now she answered briskly, announcing her name to preclude the whole "May I please speak with Professor Marchese" rigamarole, since most callers assumed Diana's contralto must've belonged to the professor's secretary.

Lie Number Five had presented its own share of problems, until Diana had accepted that she happened to be that rare Italian woman with no gift for food preparation. She'd forgiven herself for the countless crunchy risottos, bland meatballs, and unsticky potstickers she'd presented to friends and relatives. "I followed the recipe," she would say, arms raised in helpless surrender to the kitchen gods; she suspected cookbook authors of practical jokery, of snickering to themselves in their gleaming test kitchens: *let's see them try this at home*. Arthur was her most frequent victim, chewing bravely at odd textures until Diana finally said she'd order pizza.

Xander Klein—another part of her pre-mother-hood life—had found both her culinary failures and her obstinate refusal to abandon her cookbooks part of her charm. Then again, since Xander worked 3,000 miles away, at Columbia, they didn't dine together often, and he wasn't the one trying to choke down her gelatinous gnocchi. It was he who had suggested she explore the prepared foods section, friend to the small kitchens of Manhattan; he had liberated her at last from the lie.

When Xander was in town, AWOL from his own campus and his wife, he brought her bagels and smoked trout, and on one occasion a bottle of Veuve Cliquot. He said she seemed like the sort of woman who ought to have a bottle of champagne in her refrigerator, and to Diana it hadn't sounded like a line, like a sly way to get a bottle in there for later.

It was almost excessive that he was brilliant too; brilliance in Diana's world so often excused poor social skills or peculiarities of hygiene that it appeared to be their cause. Xander contradicted all of her assumptions.

A lover who occupied only a few hours each month was in some ways an ideal arrangement. But a lover who caused her to doodle idly on papers she'd been asked to review, who leapt into her thoughts with abandon—whose mere touch made her feel voluptuous, ripe with sensuality; this kind of lover only worked in the movies, when audiences would've been waiting for the icy physics professor to fling off her glasses and let down her hair, unleash her inner bombshell. And when this lover was someone else's husband, well, he didn't work at all.

It was not even reassuring to fantasize a Mrs. Klein who was foolish, or overweight, or unadventurous. Such a wife would have diminished Xander.

Diana understood the conservation of energy and so she knew whatever mental resources she spent on Xander were unavailable for research, or teaching, or even for Arthur. She was too good at time management—even then, before Molly—not to recognize that he was a bad investment.

She did not issue ultimatums or demand more of him. There had been no smashing of dishes or hurling of wine bottles. Voices were not raised. Xander left seeming almost resigned, as if Diana had been a failed experiment. Diana had smiled, to show she knew you couldn't force the data to fit your own conclusions. Her empathy wounded him still further.

Four months prior, he'd proudly called her "rational" and "calm," as if she were a marvelous creature, the first-ever joining of these traits with a righteous set of tits. But maybe after all he'd wanted her to wail, to require him for her own stability, to make unreasonable demands, to come undone at the merest glimpse of life without him.

Serene, instead, she bought a new swim cap for her lunchtime laps, and fine-tuned her stroke. Within a few weeks after she'd called things off, she'd been approved for tenure; and soon afterward, she and Arthur had resolved to have a baby. She gave Arthur and Tommy the Veuve Cliquot.

If Diana had followed her mother's advice she might well now be a happily married woman with a large, well-kept house. She might, in fact, have become her sister Allison. When Diana visited her sister, she would study the knick-knacks carefully, hoping to find a whorl of dust trapped in a curlicue; dust would mean that Allison had found something better to do with her time.

Allison had been the Good Daughter. Through it all, and right up to the end.

Diana had shirked her dying Mom duty, letting Allison be the one to perform the summerlong vigil at the Marchese bedside. But surely Allison had a more soothing bedside manner and was far more useful than Diana would've been, and on top of this Diana had still been nursing Molly last summer. Not exclusively but at bedtime, and sometimes during the night. Obviously she couldn't be sitting in the hospital when Molly still needed her. And Allison loved being the Good Daughter, was born to it.

Now the grief was her sister Allison's reward for putting in the work. She nurtured her grief, caressed it as if it had value, as if it transferred that value to her. Basked in the glow of it. Well, Diana thought, she could have it.

Academic conferences had once felt to Diana like opportunities to mingle with the field's great minds, to hear peers speak about their research and about the state of the field. More recently, she'd realized how many of the greatest minds avoided the planned sessions to congregate in the hallways or at the nearest pub.

Diana's own plenary talk, perhaps because it preceded the opening of the hotel lobby bar, was surprisingly well attended. The ballroom was well lit but windowless, with the usual garishly patterned carpet; Arthur had explained that these patterns hid stains well, which to Diana was insufficient compensation for their hideousness. Around the world, these conferences had the same carpet, the same nylon tote bags, the same nametag badges, the same outrageously priced room service hamburgers. Only the fact that smoking was allowed inside the hotel made her feel sure she'd left California.

She nodded to familiar faces who arrived early enough for her to pick them out, but the room was soon filled to a capacity that made it difficult to distinguish individuals. This was a conference that strictly enforced its self-made hierarchy, with five classes of presentation from the hour-long plenary down to ten-minute talks and down still further to the poster sessions during which you were supposed to stand next to your poster like a model at a car show, beaming in an appealing and non-threatening way, until someone read enough of the poster to ask you a question about it. If the poster was being presented by a graduate student, the conference organizers attached a red balloon on a string to the top right-hand corner, which had the unfortunate consequence of suggesting that the presenters should be patted on the head before being offered lollipops. "Welcome to our profession," the balloons said, "you sit at the kids' table."

After a hyperbolic introduction and applause, Diana said, "It's just physics," with a shrug whose modesty could be read as honest or pretentiously false, depending on your impression of Professor Diana Marchese.

For an hour she played herself on the small stage

of international physics, and no one found her miscast or unconvincing. This thought warmed her with pleasure.

After her talk, Diana accepted kind words from a handful of men before begging off. She had agreed to chair the next session in place of someone who'd had visa trouble.

When she arrived at the Dali ballroom, a tentative grad student approached her with a remote control for the computer and a lavalier pack.

She welcomed the small crowd and introduced herself, offering a preview of the session by reading the paper titles and authors. "Fourth up is—" *it couldn't be; she rattled the page to shake the letters into proper alignment; God, it was, Shit God Shit*—"Xander Klein, who's at Columbia." She offered a wan smile to the group. "And our final talk will, um, follow Dr. Klein." The first speaker thanked her and began his presentation.

She heard nothing. She thanked the speakers after their talks, called on the questioners, and kept her gaze focused on the projected slides. But Diana's head pulsated with a panicky flutter that whispered, insistently, *It's him. Why here, why now, why him?*

Then, as she called on a white-haired man behind him, she met Xander's eyes.

Suddenly what amazed her was that she had gone three and a half years without seeing him. It was goddamn unbelievable. The first year, when she'd been preparing her tenure packet and then trying like hell to get pregnant and then steeping in pregnancy, she understood. But Molly was nineteen months old. And here was Xander.

She turned slightly to steal another glance. He

appeared unchanged, wearing a checked shirt with a tie she'd always disliked, and though she could not see them she felt sure he had on his well-worn brown suede shoes. His beard was clipped close and appeared to contain precisely the proportions of salt and pepper she remembered.

Xander was old school; he used transparencies that he'd written by hand on the plane. The session technician was visibly perplexed by this, but he lifted an overhead projector onto the table near the laptop, and spent several moments adjusting the focusing knob while Diana smiled blankly at Xander and willed herself not to check her watch.

Now Xander was talking, in his vigorous way; his voice was higher and faster than usual, as if he could not quite contain himself, so eager was he to share the secrets of the universe with them.

He did put on a good show. Still had that glint in his eye that promised there was more to him than tweed and chalk.

Diana was conscious of her hips. Xander had made much of them. Could he tell now, just by looking, that she had given birth to Molly? Would he, who'd known each inch of her, detect the new looseness in her joints, the softness of her middle? When—*if*—they made love, would he notice?

If.

When.

If.

She stared at Xander, daring him to look back.

Abruptly she remembered their touring a museum, during a break from one of their conferences. She had marveled at some Degas pastels, which were somehow more brilliant and more vivid than any she had seen before. Xander pointed out the special fluorescent light, a particular wavelength that brightened the artwork. Diana found this revelatory. Understanding *how* and *why* always, always, enhanced the *what*.

The man next to her began clapping politely, startling Diana into clapping too. Xander's eyes were on her, and she clambered to her feet. "Right. Any questions for Dr. Klein?"

She looked out at the sparse audience—most of them just passing time until a lunch appointment or their taxi to the airport. Several men had even brought rolling suitcases with them to the conference room, and a line of identical black bags stood at attention in the back, their handles already raised for faster getaways. "Questions?"

One woman, silver-haired—the only other woman in the room—fanned herself with the conference schedule. So much for sisterhood.

Goddamned session chair etiquette: it would be up to her to ask Xander questions. Why couldn't this reunion have occurred during her own plenary session, with Xander rising from the still-dazzled crowd to ask *her* a question? Why did he appear only *now*, at this session for which she wasn't prepared, in which she hadn't invested?

"So, Jupiter," she said lamely.

Xander nodded.

"I wonder if you could tell us more about your modeling assumptions."

He blinked at her.

"The continuum assumption, in particular; does it hold?"

Lame, lame, lame. She sounded like an undergraduate. If her audience were not so bored they would be snickering at her, whispering among themselves. Diana Marchese, they would tell their colleagues when they returned home: she used to be pretty amazing but wow, what an airhead. Well, the colleagues would say, you know *she had a baby*. Ahhh, would come the answer. Of course.

Xander had stopped talking. She noticed that he had placed a transparency titled, "Appropriateness of the continuum model," on the projector. She had a hazy memory of having seen this slide during his talk. *Shit*.

"Thank you for expanding on that," she told him. She turned again to the audience. "Any other questions for our speaker?"

Near the back, a man stood and exited the room. Diana glared at his retreating tweed.

"I find it remarkable," Diana said, "that in one session we've gone from the flow of human lymphatic fluid to the red spot of Jupiter."

"The universe in a grain of sand," Xander said.

"How unfortunate for Dr. Hofmann that he was unable to attend."

Xander considered this. "How fortunate for us that you stepped in, Dr. Marchese."

She looked at him. His eyes were bright, his smile boldly sexual. She smiled back. *Perhaps.*

"Well, it's been quite a trip," she said. What the mind tries to forget, the body remembers.

"So far," said Xander Klein. Yes, perhaps.

The grad student rang the bell signaling the start of the next talk.

Afterward, when they faced each other, he said, "So…Long time."

Diana made a face that said, *has it been so long?* but aloud she said, "Good to see you, Xander."

"I've missed you."

"I've been busy."

"Me, too."

"Right, Jupiter."

"Not *just* Jupiter." A familiar wolfish gleam in his eyes.

I'm not her anymore, she ought to tell him. I'm someone's mother now. But Xander's expression made her feel at once three years younger, the woman she'd been before Molly. She remembered his kisses, the feel of his hands at her waist. If that waist had softened a bit, so what? They would remember how to be with each other.

She felt the outline of her room key in her front trouser pocket.

"I saw your talk this morning," Xander said.

"Did you?"

"Good turnout."

This frustrated her; it was as if he had recognized the newness of her outfit without saying that he liked it. Perhaps he meant to spare her feelings. Or perhaps he was just Xander, she reminded herself: attentive to all the wrong details.

He invited her to lunch, and she thought that she might get more out of him—some feedback on the plenary, some sense of whether her performance had rung as true as it had felt. She felt herself listing, less sure of her center of gravity now.

"We could share a pitcher of sangria," he said, invoking memories of languid afternoons past.

Perhaps, indeed.

Skate or Die

"I'm beta-testing Tony Hawk," Scot called from the couch. "You want in?"

On screen, a virtual skateboarder sped across an empty plaza. The simulated sound of hard plastic wheels on concrete reverberated in Scot's living room. His digital avatar ollied to stalefish against the side of a building, then smoothly skitched a ride on the bumper of a passing station wagon.

"These graphics are pretty sweet." Scot nodded toward the second controller for Chad. "I should find out who does their render coding."

"You're going to poach them?"

Scot tossed a pretzel into his mouth. "*Poach* is such an ugly word, Chad," he said, crunching. "I wouldn't want your mother to hear you using that sort of language. What I might do, is briefly outline our benefits package. They might then decide that Development at MacAvoy was something worth exploring."

Chad shook his head, and pressed two buttons to launch his own animated skater into action.

"Truth is, Development used to be me and Mike, a Unix box, and a case of Dr. Pepper, right?"

"Guess you're not half-assing it, these days," Chad said.

Scot tilted his head to consider this. "I never got that. Is giving a *full* ass's worth, like, doing a good job? Or, would *no* ass be preferable? How much ass should I be aspiring to?"

Chad and Scot exchanged a look. Finally Chad said, "Is the ass half full or half empty?"

"And there it is." Scot got up to get another drink.

Hanging out with Scot was pretty chill. It was almost like hanging with Walter, or Marcus and Andre, except Scot's TV was bigger. Also: there were no parents at Scot's house to tell them to keep their feet off the furniture, or to say that those pretzels would ruin their appetites. There was only Scot's wife Irene, who sometimes stood with her hands on her hips, shaking her head at the two of them and saying she hoped Chad would be a good influence on Scot, although she more often ignored them.

Once, when Chad had been walking his dog, Mrs. MacAvoy asked him what breed Red was. "I don't know," Chad admitted. "He's from the shelter?"

She'd smirked. "Every dog in this town is a so-called rescue. Even if you researched the breeder, drove out of state to pick up your pedigreed puppy, and you're feeding him nothing but quinoa, you still say, 'we think he's part-spaniel, maybe,' as if you're only guessing."

Chad shrugged, confused by how much this

sounded like something his dad would say in one of his rants about Authenticity and the Hollow Bounty of the Microchip.

If Mrs. MacAvoy remembered driving Chad to the County Jail, she showed no indication that their friendship had been deepened by the hour together. And, lately, she wasn't around much at all. Today, for example, Scot said she was shopping, which was lucky since they were running low on pretzels.

From the kitchen Scot called, "You want a soda?"

Soon, he would have to pry himself out of the comfort of the couch, of Scot's game-playing den; his mom would expect him for dinner. If his dad had called to say he'd be stuck at work late, again, then his mom would be especially tense. This had happened almost every night this week. The two of them sat at the table with Ray's untouched plate, trying not to react to every set of footsteps outside.

But for now, Chad was at ease on the MacAvoy couch.

Scot returned with their drinks and unpaused his frozen skateboarder, though not before noticing that Chad had created a new avatar, a ponytailed blonde. Scot let out a whistle.

"Who's she?"

"She's a cartoon, dude," Chad said.

Scot's skater ollied over a conveniently placed milk crate. "She's real enough," he said. "Who is she?"

"She's no one." Chad took a drink, and when he looked back up saw that Scot was still staring at him, waiting. "She's new, from Texas."

"Ah. The New Girl. Now we're getting somewhere."

"We're getting nowhere," Chad said.

Soberly, Scot sipped soda from his bendy straw. In an attempt to change the subject, Chad brought up the Big Game TV logistics.

"Sure. Whatever. Seriously, C-man, what's her name?"

His stomach was a miserable whirlpool of carbonated acid and pretzels. "Kara."

Scot grinned. "Now that's nice." He tapped Chad's game controller, nodding toward the screen. "Blonde, huh?"

"It's, um, kind of reddish blonde?"

"Oh, my boy, I'll bet it is."

"Could you, like, not enjoy this quite so much?"

Scot paused the game. "This is the only reason to grow up," he said, "so you can stop being a freaking symphony of awkward about every girl you see. At your age, I was a nonstop series of inconvenient hard-ons."

"That's not a bad band name," Chad said. "I'll tell Walter, for our list." Was Walter still keeping the list? Chad realized he didn't know. The whirlpool in his stomach churned anew.

Scot was not put off by the dodge. You could see how he'd gotten where he was in the Valley; he was relentless in pursuit of a product. "Kara from Texas," he said, musing.

"Don't," Chad pleaded.

Mrs. MacAvoy failed to materialize with or without pretzels, and as it inched closer to dinner, Chad had a fleeting thought of inviting Scot home with him. He knew his dad wasn't Scot's biggest fan, but then again his dad wasn't likely to make it home for dinner, either. He could picture the table: him, Scot, and his mom, staring into space.

Scot's cell phone buzzed, and he said, "Sorry, man, I've got to take this." But instead of excusing himself, he paused the game and started talking. Chad slid off the couch and wandered into the hallway, where a row of framed articles served as a MacAvoy Hall of Fame. One of these included three black-and-white photos of Scot talking to his interviewer. He held a mechanical pencil in one hand, and in the middle photograph he was pointing it toward the camera. The photographs flattered him; he was as handsome as he was in person, but in black-and-white the shadows on his face made him seem more serious than he looked in color, further down the hall, with his bare feet in the grass outside his first office building. The headline of that fawning article was "The Valley's Merry Prankster."

For those who've been hibernating, Scot MacAvoy runs a digital empire. At twenty-two, he and his college roommate wrote a program that became Latte, the now-indispensible Macromedia tool. He has fought off takeover bids from Microsoft and AOL and even an internal coup. He wants you to know he's a regular guy. He wears t-shirts stamped Google or eTrade, and makes sure to tell you that he got them free, at tradeshows and conferences. He lives with his wife on a cul-de-sac that he calls "Main Street, USA." And he—always—makes his own coffee. It's strong and black and his cup (also a conference giveaway) has a chip near the handle. When pressed by an interviewer, he will describe the moment of Latte's inception in a Berkeley dorm lounge at 3 am.

Q. And the rest was history?

A. Not quite, man. It takes more than a good idea. You have to have the idea at exactly the right moment. A buddy of mine worked at this company, it was a startup before they called them that, and back in the mid-eighties they were trying to sell a portable computer. "Fits in a legal envelope," they said. "Do your work on the plane." Nobody thought they needed to work on the plane. They were watching the movie and eating their chicken with peas and carrots. So the company, and my buddy, were SOL.

Q. How important is being in the Valley? There is a burgeoning techworld in Manhattan, and other hotspots are beginning to perk.

A. For now, it's still the place to be. The VCs, the angels, the money guys, are here. The real estate's expensive and parking is a bitch, but I wouldn't want to be anywhere else. Not that I think all good ideas have to happen here, but it's like, if you're a great band you can be from Sandusky, Ohio, but sooner or later you are going to make it to New York because that's where CBGB is.

Q. Pac-Man or Space Invaders?

A. I had the sweetest game when I was ten, man. It was text-based and it ran on my Apple IIe box, and it was Star Wars. You were Luke Skywalker and you could swing with Leia across the chasm. You could blow up the Death Star. I played that shit over and over again. Also I liked One on One. You played Dr. J. against Larry Bird in these ASCII graphics. Unbelievable. I mean if a computer could let you be Dr. J., or Luke fucking Skywalker, that was just it for me.

"Chad," Scot called from the living room. "You still playing?"

"I'll be right there," Chad called, glancing at

another framed piece of MacAvoy folklore, an article highlighting the "uncorporate culture" at MacAvoy-dot-com: foosball, and nap pods, and "not your father's company cafeteria."

Scot MacAvoy gave his employees a free lunch everyday—and not pizza, either, but gourmet free-range chicken with polenta and kale. Or salmon with mango salsa. This was helpful, he'd explained to Chad, in retaining top talent. Lunch, and all the Skittles and Mountain Dew they could eat.

He knew what his dad would say about that.

He did the math, again, about his dad's night in jail coinciding with the vanishing of Scot's giant SUV, a pretty potent symbol of excess. The dust of broken glass on the street.

"I should go," Chad said.

"We didn't even finish this level."

"Next time, man."

"Okay, Big C. Best to your folks."

Chad promised to relay this, but when he got home, Allison was on the couch, alone, again. She hugged him, held it a little too long, and said she hadn't got around to cooking anything.

This was what he had: a dad with a chip on his shoulder, absent; a mom present but sleepwalking through life.

Chad pulled out a bag of frozen burritos. "Chicken or bean," he asked, but she didn't answer.

His mom had put on an old album, and for a long time the only sounds in the house were the whirring microwave, the thump of Red's tail on the dining room floor, and Michael Stipe urging them not to go back to Rockville.

The Best Place on Earth

The last segment on the nightly news was sports, highlighting the latest indignities inflicted on Ray's teams. Back when Chad was about six, the two of them used to go over the box scores together. What Ray had liked most about this, apart from the closeness of Chad as he sat in Ray's lap sliding his finger under each line, the sweet smell of him so near and warm, was that they were establishing something that would stay with them forever. That Ray would be able to ask Chad about at-bats and ribbies and games back and be truly saying, *How are you, I love you, Take care of yourself.* He would say these things too, but he knew from experience that even in commercials such lines could come off cheesy. So he was glad to have crafted a backup. Even though Chad now preferred computer games to box scores.

An infomercial promised to simplify everyday life

with an exciting new pair of products. One was a device that assisted in the opening of milk cartons, and the second was a plastic contraption that aided the making of French braids: you could get one of each, if you acted quickly, for $19.99. It was not clear what united these two products besides remarkably maladroit consumers. Actors fumbled with milk cartons, causing the milk to gush onto the counter or onto themselves, looking to the camera with a desperate, *There's-got-to-be -a-better-way* grimace. Actresses began to braid their own hair only to wind up with a tangled mess that they—emitting a theatrical frustrated sigh—then began to comb out.

Ray thought of Chad, who (judging from the sporadic keyboard clicks emanating from his room) was on the computer, headphones on, blocking out Ray and everything else. This was what would keep Ray up all night: if milk cartons and ponytails were too complicated to be resolved without mass-manu- factured intervention, how could a father and son ever figure out how to connect?

He lacked Allison's ability to reach out, her keen sense of the right way forward. The deft manner with which she could persuade clients, Chad, or Ray himself that they'd made the decision themselves. Ray thought of her sometimes as a third-base coach who could urge bravery or caution based on her reading of the field, saving Ray from an embarrassing out at the plate, permitting him a moment of glory. If he sometimes tired of needing permission, well, that was only natural.

After Sports, the TV anchors made empty chatter, like people who'd found themselves on a long elevator ride and felt obliged to keep things breezy and familiar. They concluded the broadcast, as always, with a segment in which average viewers celebrated the Bay Area. A graphic spun onto the screen: "Best Place on Earth."

Generally, it wasn't the bridges or the beach that people mentioned, but the guy who made their coffee in the morning, or the bookstore where the manager, Nick, could always recommend something perfect, or the farmers market offering six kinds of heirloom tomatoes. We are all pretending we live in a small town, Ray thought, as if becoming regulars at a pizza place (*I don't even need to tell them my order anymore*, testified a guy from Oakland, *I just say my phone number and they say, We'll have that right out for you, Ted*) or having a hookup for your kimchi was the same thing. We are striving for Nutley, New Jersey, in 1975.

Yes, our tech stocks might've tanked, but here in the best place on earth we diversify, and our real estate does nothing but appreciate. No need to mention the poor bastards who had to bolt when the bubble imploded, whose houses now stood empty with sun-faded Coldwell Banker signs out front. Their portfolios shriveled and whitened, like limes abandoned in the fruit drawer after the gin had run out. Instead, let's rejoice in the less-crowded freeways without them, and congratulate ourselves on our smoother commutes.

Ray shifted on the couch. The cheery self-aggrandizement sickened him, the American missionary zeal with which the anchors and Ray's friends and neighbors slapped each other on the back and proclaimed their own genius for having taken the job or chosen the college or missed the train or married the girl that had brought them here. This magical place where you could get rich on a larky idea some college dropout had for a business. Yes, you might lose it all, but another larky idea would surely come along.

Just before it had all hit the fan, it seemed like everybody you met was a millionaire. Even Ray's grocery checker was daytrading between shifts, bragging about stocks he'd shorted, rattling off "major wins" while Ray bagged the food. He might've been a blissed-out Roman in the last days of the Empire, accustomed to indulgence and oblivious to any possible way things could go south.

The MacAvoy virus had infected almost everyone. Ray felt, now, like a survivor after a plague. Yet somehow patient zero was still standing, too.

Sometimes, although she'd chosen not to press charges, and refused his offer to pay for the repairs, Irene MacAvoy called Ray "Criminal." His crime was their secret; Irene told Scot she'd had a fender bender at the grocery store. She lied easily, like water, like silk. Ray might've wanted Scot to know about it, to see the damage he'd inflicted, but this became less urgent when Irene bade: "Come here, Criminal." Irene was the kind of jailer who would make you want to stay behind bars, yearning for her anger.

That first afternoon, she'd called him next door after his post-jail nap, saying she'd made the coffee it looked like he might need. His fingertips were gray-black with police-issue ink, and he'd wanted to wash them before touching her, but she told him, quietly, no.

Now, on his couch, the cushion conformed to himself, Ray took stock: he had a good family, a wife who found him exasperating but loved him nevertheless, in the way of a sitcom wife far more capable than the nominal man of the house; even though she'd been kind of out of it since her mother died. And ever since his night in jail, about three times a week, sometimes four, he got to have lung-searing sex with Irene MacAvoy. This was something wonderful, something that didn't have to hurt anyone—except, maybe, Scot, who more than deserved it. Irene made Ray feel so powerfully good that even at midnight, sunk into a worn valley on his couch, he smiled at the memory. Some accident of serendipitous geography had planted her right next door. Best Place on Earth, indeed.

The next morning, Ray sat in a meeting with three executives from the makers of Sammy's Salmon. He tasted Sammy's Salmon on toast, Triscuit crackers, and cucumber slices; and in a salad made with red onion, tomatoes, and capers. He nodded, took notes. By lunchtime, he could still taste the salty capers, yet he couldn't think of anything memorable to say about Sammy's Salmon.

Perhaps it went without saying that there was no Sammy behind Sammy's Salmon. Sammy's Salmon was fished, cooked, canned, and distributed by a multifarious conglomerate that was also responsible for a line of boxed pasta dinners, the nation's top-selling peanut butter, several breads and bread products, and the glass-cleaning spray Allison used on the bathroom mirrors. However, the label on the canned salmon featured a plausibly handcrafted logo and little evidence of the conglomerate's involvement.

The obvious choice, Ray knew, was to hire an actor to play Sammy, to put him in waders and a nice fishing hole, and zoom in for a close-up of a silvery-pink, still-wriggling salmon on the end of the actor's line. Come up with a tagline about freshness and clean taste; maybe find some subtle way to suggest that canned salmon was a canned fish product homemakers could feel good about, as salmon fishermen (e.g. Sammy) were unlikely to be bringing up any playful, innocent dolphins with their catches. Quick cut to a mother, face unlined by environmental guilt, serving Sammy's Salmon to the kids. Nothing so heavy-handed as to negatively impact sales of the conglomerate's canned tuna and albacore products.

But really it was bullshit that his agency was even talking to the guys from Sammy's Salmon, because their specialty had been the quirky dotcom guys. They had mastered a kind of meta-ad steeped in irony for an industry that no longer needed them, and now they were taking any meeting they could.

Maybe, if he hadn't blown the Southwest Airlines chance, Ray wouldn't be sitting at his desk with a dry but briny mouth. And maybe, if he could figure out how to sell canned fish to the organic-everything Valley, he could keep paying the rent on his house. He pictured one of the infomercial actors struggling to operate a can opener, bashing the can of Sammy's Salmon against their kitchen counter in despair. He let out a desperate chuckle himself, and smiled weakly at his coworkers.

The partners in Ray's firm had decided that having all their creative types in one large space, without offices or cubicles, would be conducive to a highly charged creative environment where ideas were freely and energetically exchanged. This was how Goldsmith & Wong marketed its culture on the company website, calling the firm's "studio atmosphere" a "vibrant intellectual community." What it mostly felt like to Ray was an institutionalized lack of privacy. At a neighboring desk, his colleague used a battery-powered shredder to erase all evidence of his ideas, rather than freely and energetically exchanging them.

Ray worried about Sammy's Salmon for a couple of hours, and then caught an early train back to Palo Alto. His seat was on the sunny side of the cabin, and the window glass was warm on his dozy forehead. He felt half-asleep as he walked home.

The car was not in the driveway; Allison must have been meeting with a client, or doing errands. Chad was still in school. Ray let the dog out, and got a bottle of beer from the fridge. It felt illicit, having a beer in the afternoon, like being in public with no pants on. Now that he considered it, his pants did feel hot and itchy —he had walked home faster than he'd meant to, and it was warm outside. He walked to the bedroom to remove and hang them, then returned to the kitchen. He drank his first beer standing at the counter. In his boxer shorts and loosened tie, he felt terrific.

He felt ten years younger: invigorated by the walk, the beer, his lack of pants. He was twenty-five again. Everything was potential, opportunity. He would change the world; advertising was a conduit for reaching people, for connecting. He could allow himself to be earnest without seeing everything through a cynical cloud. He believed in himself and that he was owed the spoils of the Best Place on Earth.

Irene had done this for him.

"I was wondering," he'd said yesterday, in the Stanford Court Hotel.

"Yes, Criminal?" Huskily.

"I wonder what your husband was like, fifteen years ago."

"You want to talk about my husband?" She wasn't even thinking about him. Advantage: Loudermilk.

He kissed her. "Please," he said.

"Okay," she said. "Fifteen years, I couldn't say. But ten years ago, when I met Scot, he was so goddamn golden that he practically glowed."

Ray nodded, as if glowing golden boys had pretty much grown on trees back in Nutley, New Jersey.

"I was his TA," she said. "And everybody thinks they can bullshit through art history. It's slide shows in a dark room, right? Scot could've blown it off, he could've bullshitted like the rest of them. But he wrote beautifully, and when he spoke in class even the back-row stoners listened." Irene paused, one hand on the strap of her slip. "He was always the smartest, most interesting person in the room," she said, "but he made you feel like you were."

Her eyes were glittering and narrowed, like a predator's.

"You're amazing," Ray said, as sincerely as he had ever said anything.

They went at each other hungrily, hoping to leave a mark.

Standing in his own kitchen in his shorts, Ray could see that she had left bruises on his thighs. Yet he was feeling no pain. He shook away a fleeting notion that what Irene liked about *him* was how much he disliked her husband. He let the dog back in and watched him curl into a contented twist. The dog had been a good decision.

The Place You're Supposed to Laugh

He had just gone to the fridge for a second beer when he heard a key in the door, soon followed by the voices of Chad and his friends Marcus and—Ray tried to remember—Andre. They were laughing, and one of them was saying, "No *way*," over and over.

Ray felt his knees lock up. Should he go out and say hello, even in his boxers? He felt sure that this would embarrass Chad and put further distance between them.

He heard the television come on, too loud. The *thunk* of feet in heavy sneakers landing on the coffee table.

"See?" said Marcus's voice. "This is what I'm talking about."

Ray heard someone, maybe Chad, say something he couldn't make out. He moved closer to the swinging door.

He was an anthropologist, granted a rare opportunity to observe his tribe of interest. A chance to watch a focus group and learn through one-way glass. He knew he was failing Chad: perhaps a little market data was what he needed. He held his breath and leaned his head against the door to listen.

"Oh my God," said one of the other boys. "It's like all they show is ads."

"You know they have these old songs on commercials, and you wonder, how come they sold out, for sneakers or some car or website or whatever?" This was Chad's voice.

"Yeah," said another boy's baritone.

"That's my dad's *job*. He gets the bands to sell out."

Shit. This sort of thing happened with focus groups: Ray always wanted to discuss the group's opinions with them, to negotiate. *When you described Sammy's Salmon as salty, is it possible that the fish tasted so fresh that your mind just made an association with the sea?* He might've gone out to the living room, to begin an impassioned discourse with Chad on the subject of *selling out*, provide a little perspective, but there was the problem of his lack of pants.

Beer: a welcome distraction. The bottle was cold, damp with condensate. He used his thumbnail to peel away at a corner of the label.

Ray heard footsteps approaching the kitchen door and panicked. He fell to a crouch behind the kitchen island.

False alarm, though—the footsteps must've been headed to the bathroom, or to Chad's room. The kitchen door remained closed. He stood up again and looked out the window toward the supersized MacAvoy house.

Their lawn was gorgeous and immaculate, a rich green blanket. Irene's rosebushes, deadheaded now for winter; a box from Amazon on the front steps. He wondered what Irene was reading. She had mentioned something about a book group, but he'd only been half listening.

He had drunk too fast and needed to piss. The bathroom was just through the living room, the first door in the hallway that made the long side of the "L" of his house. He could see himself taking long strides to reach it, feeling the metal doorknob in his grip. But he had waited too long to enter the living room; if he had gone in right away, said a quick hello to the boys, even his pantslessness might have been accepted. If he walked out now, it would be clear that he'd been hiding in the kitchen, and his best hope was that Chad would be embarrassed. Worse and far more likely was that he'd think Ray had been spying on him. Either way, Ray's wardrobe was a complicating factor.

His best option, as he saw it, was to relieve himself into the kitchen sink, staring out at Irene's roses. Afterward, he poured a good half-cup of dishwashing soap into the sink. Pumped Purell into his hands for good measure.

Outside he saw an unmarked white truck pull up to the MacAvoy driveway, a shallow trailer behind it loaded with mowers and weed whackers. A crew of four disembarked, discussing something in animated Spanish. Gardeners.

He should have known Scot MacAvoy didn't spread his own fertilizer.

Back in New Jersey, a lawn service was an extravagance. In his hometown, no one hired out. Ray's dad did a quick circuit with an engineless push mower every Sunday, until he passed the torch to Ray. But in Allison and Ray's neighborhood, things were different. When they'd driven the local streets with the rental agent and seen all the brown-skinned men busy with yard work, Allison had said pleasantly, "I suppose this is a Hispanic area," and the agent had regarded her blankly until Allison said, "Oh."

The agent explained that, in many cases, gardeners "came with the house," that they showed up a week or so after new people moved in, and explained the range of their services, and the reasonableness of their wage. Indeed, Ray had been visited by a man named Jorge who made a very strong case for himself, but whose services Ray declined on Nutley principle.

Scot MacAvoy's crew had split into pairs, one team gassing up the mower and then pushing it to the backyard, and the other team unfurling a thick green hose. A man dragged one end of it toward the raised beds behind Irene's roses, and his partner went to attach the hose to the faucet.

The faucet he used, the one nearest the raised beds, was on the side of Ray and Allison's house. He heard the pipes rattle as water began to flow.

"What the *fuck*," he muttered.

The gardener whistled brightly, and generally failed to look furtive as he crossed the driveway to water the MacAvoy roses with Loudermilk water. This, Ray understood, was standard operating procedure.

"You have *got* to be shitting me," said Ray.

He stalked through the kitchen to the door that led out to the driveway. He took a deep breath and then shoved the door open. The breeze fluttered his boxer shorts.

The men turned toward him and offered neighborly nods before returning to their work. Their affability did not soothe Ray's soul.

"Mi agua," Ray called.

The gardeners looked up, surprised.

Ray pointed emphatically at the faucet. "*Mi* agua," he repeated. "No su agua." He felt he was being quite reasonable.

"Agua?" the man watering the raised beds asked.

"You're working for Mr. MacAvoy. You should use Mr. MacAvoy's water." He walked over to the faucet and twisted the handle closed, then looked up at the men with an expression that said, *I believe I've made my point*. He said, "I believe I've made my point. My water.

Mi agua. Not Mr. MacAvoy's water."

The man holding the hose asked the other something in Spanish; the answer was a flurry of words of which only one was "agua." He thought one of them might have been "loco."

"Si," Ray said, "I am a crazy man wearing my underwear and a little drunk at three in the afternoon. Fair enough. But you," he said, "should not take things that do not belong to you. And this is *mi agua.*"

He waved at Mrs. Abdelnour across the street who was tending her azaleas.

"Hello, dear," she called. "Is everything all right?"

"Just fine," he said. "Just clearing something up with these fellows."

Ray shook hands with both men, and said again, "Mi agua," before heading back into the kitchen. From the window, he saw the men searching for a faucet on Scot's exterior wall, pushing aside bushes to check.

It was a good day. He had at last found evidence of the theft of his water — if not by Scot himself then indirectly, by his proxy. He was neither crazy nor paranoid. He looked forward to explaining this to Allison when she returned. They could toast his vindication, and the calm yet decisive way he had handled things with MacAvoy's men.

As he opened the fridge for one more beer, he heard the door behind him. Turning, he saw Chad and Marcus.

"Good afternoon," Ray said, a little grandly.

"Dad?"

"I got home early." He hit this just right: not defensive, not making excuses for his standing in his underwear, just the plain fact of the thing.

"You need some help with those dudes outside?" Marcus asked. "Dre has three years of Spanish."

His warm feeling curdled as he imagined how he must've looked to the boys through the living room window. The sellout having a freakout.

"Or was it another misunderstanding?" Chad said.

They stared at each other in silence across the small but unbridgeable kitchen.

Soup Night

"My mom has, like, no idea." Allison leaned closer to her client, Gretchen. She looked into the girl's large blue eyes, rimmed with black eyeliner.

"She just doesn't get it," Gretchen said. "She doesn't get *me*."

Gretchen was sixteen. Being misunderstood was important to her; she believed this marked her as distinct from other girls, as if each of them didn't also have a mother who was forever *not getting it*, who spent her days wishing for some other daughter than the one she had.

Allison herself had had such a mother. It would've been easy for her to tell Gretchen her own stories, to laugh about the universal cluelessness of mothers. They would *never* get it, would they? Even on their deathbeds, while you were tending to them, they would

still second-guess your choices and disrespect your son. They would still baldly prefer your selfish prodigal sibling. But she asked Gretchen, "What could you do to help your mother understand you better?"

Gretchen rolled her eyes. The knees of her jeans were meticulously shredded. From the location and décor of Gretchen's home, Allison knew they were the *right jeans*.

As a teenager back in Cherry Hill, Allison had not worn the right jeans. Once, she had believed this deprivation was the worst damage her mother had inflicted.

"My mother," Allison said, "died this summer."

"I'm sorry," Gretchen said automatically. She gazed into the boy-band poster over her bed.

Allison held up her hand. "I miss her," she said. "But she didn't, really, *get* me. She didn't understand the choices I'd made, and she never stopped telling me that."

Gretchen exhaled loudly, as if Allison were merely confirming all that she had come to understand about the world, and she'd prefer it if Allison could pick up the pace.

"I think it helped me," Allison said, "to have to keep explaining *me* to her."

"Great," the girl said. "That's something to look forward to."

Allison hadn't always intended to become a counselor. But in her junior year, her class on "Social and Emotional Development" was taught by Professor West, a magnetic lecturer with an Australian accent and a way of making classic theories urgently relevant to Allison's own experience of the world. As Gretchen swung between confidence and insecurity, Allison could hear her professor's refrain: "at each stage, we are struggling to reconcile conflicting forces." Indeed, Gretchen seemed to switch polarity every few minutes: sometimes oppressed by her overbearing mother, other times neglected and unloved. Both modes caused great pain to Gretchen.

Gretchen's mother was guilty of at least one of her alleged crimes: she wasn't wholly focused on Gretchen. She was distracted. Her husband's company had folded nine months ago, and when Allison arrived to meet with Gretchen, she glimpsed him, shuffling in sweatpants around their house. He looked sweaty and anxious, as if he'd expected that Allison had come to foreclose.

But Gretchen's mother was also worried about black eyeliner and new friends, and in particular about a boy.

"How are things with Jack?" Allison asked, careful to keep her voice light.

Gretchen shrugged. "I thought they were good," she said. "But for like a week I thought I was pregnant, and now he's not calling me back."

"Okay," Allison said. "Number one, condoms."

"I *know*," Gretchen flung her blonde hair.

"Like *every time*."

"Okay, okay."

"Number two." Allison held Gretchen's blackened blue eyes with her own. "What does Jack like most about you?"

"I don't know," the girl said. "I guess my boobs?"

Allison didn't know why she had lied to Gretchen about the value of having to explain oneself to her mother. As if Allison's mom had done her a favor by misunderstanding her. Questioning her judgment. Allison had married the wrong man, too young, and too easily chosen not to practice clinical psychology, instead counseling the neighborhood "wastrels," as her mother called them. And then there was Chad.

"So you can't have a baby," Allison's mother had said in the wake of the fourth miscarriage. "It's a good sign: your genes are incompatible with dipshit. Your body's rejecting the dipshit infection you keep trying to catch."

Allison had tired of defending Ray, had tired of ovulation meters and being terrified each time she used the toilet. She did not respond.

"Your body is taking a pretty clear stand," her mother had said. "It's chosen not to be the body of a mother."

It was impossible not to hear the wistfulness, the wanting, in her mother's voice.

This was something she would not share with her client: the likelihood that at least once, Gretchen's mother, like Allison's, had considered the unchosen choice, the places she might've gone had she not been Gretchen's mother. Sixteen was too young for that kind of empathy.

Maybe thirty-seven was too young.

Because it would've been nice if Allison's mother *had* been on her side. It would've been nice to have shared the agonizing unrelenting *waiting* of the adoption process. To have had her mother's blessing. To have rejoiced, together, when the call finally came. Nice if she'd loved Chad with warmth and pie crust, the way some grandmothers did.

"It's not *me*," her mother had rasped, when Chad

was getting them both a cup of hospital coffee. "I'm just worried about other people being unkind to you. I wish I could protect you from that."

Like Ray, her mother cast these anxieties in hypotheticals. "Don't you wonder, what if, if he looked more like us?" Ray had asked Allison, more than once.

Allison had not wondered, had not worried: she loved Chad; she was the only mother he had known, just as he was their only son.

She could not conceive that anyone's mother would ever call Chad a dipshit. Gretchen's Jack, on the other hand, inspired much less confidence.

"Gretchen," Allison said, "I'm not your mother. But if I were, I'd be very sad to think you were choosing to spend this much time with a boy who doesn't seem very invested in *you*."

"He's not good enough for me, yeah, you sound just like my mom, Dr. Loudermilk."

"That's not what I said," Allison said. "I said he's not good enough *to* you."

The girl's blue eyes like water, offering nothing but reflected light. Finally she said, "Whose side are you on?"

"I'm on yours," Allison said. She tried one of her standard lines, hoping she hadn't already used it with Gretchen: "Tell me," she said, "what are the three things you most want the world to know about you?"

She was surprised to find Ray already at home when she returned. "No late meetings tonight?" she asked. He only shrugged and poured her a glass of wine.

Her session with Gretchen stayed with her as she hurried to get dinner on the table. Maybe she was losing her touch for this kind of work; maybe she thought too much like a *mom*. Sometimes she and Ray would watch a movie that she remembered loving when she was younger—teens who outsmarted their teachers, or kids at boarding school who constructed their own family unit in the absence of those pesky parents—and Allison felt frustrated by the petulant, self-centered youth.

"So selfish," she muttered as she peeled strips of bacon for the split pea soup.

Ray snorted in recognition. "You saw Diana today?"

"No," Allison said. "My client."

He grinned, weighing his hands like Justice. "Your selfish sister; a selfish, troubled teenaged girl." He held his hands level with each other. "You can see my confusion."

"I think my client wears more eyeliner," Allison said, giggling. She clapped a hand over her mouth. "Sorry."

He kissed her. "I like it when you're mean," he said. "Good girl gone bad kind of thing."

She took her time kissing Ray back. His mouth was warm and malty. No wonder he was relaxed: after not being home for dinner in weeks, today he'd gotten home early enough for a beer. The force of the kiss pushed her into the counter, and for a moment she thought they might just skip dinner.

But she ended the kiss. "Later," she whispered to Ray. Then, she grated cheese and sliced an avocado for the tomato soup, and chopped the bacon into the split pea.

Chad materialized from his room in time to set the table. She sliced a round of sourdough and handed him the bread plate.

The machinery of soup night continued to hum. This was comfort, not routine, Allison told herself. It was a shame her mother couldn't experience the warmth of Allison's family.

But just as she'd felt off her game with Gretchen this afternoon, Allison struggled to draw Chad out during dinner. Her questions about his new friends were met with monosyllabic teenage answers. When she mentioned Walter Chen, he bristled with anger she hadn't expected.

She sipped her wine, and ladled a second helping of soup into Ray's bowl.

"So, what did you do after school with Marcus and Andre?"

Chad shrugged. "Mostly video games."

"With your dad?"

"We, uh, didn't see each other," Ray said.

"Oh, I thought—since you were home early…"

Ray slurped his soup. "Delicious," he told her. From the kitchen she heard the dog's feet padding on the linoleum, the tiny jingle of his collar.

"We went over to the playground after," Chad said, without looking up from his soup. "Must've just missed you."

Allison had a mental image of her son and his friends at the grade school playground, swinging and climbing the molded plastic rock wall, before realizing that she was off by several years. They were now the teenagers who hung out near the play structures, the tall, rowdy boys who made other mothers bend closer to their young ones. How had this happened so quickly? *It happens to us all, Allie,* her mother would've said. *Planned obsolescence, just like those gadgets you all think so highly of out there in California.*

Pitch-perfect: she almost laughed at how clearly she could hear her mother's voice. After four months it was undiminished. Did her sister, Diana, hear it too?

It killed her that Diana hadn't been there: not for the first, not for the worst, and not for the end of it, either. It should've been her sister, not Chad, sitting with Allison in the hospital. Taking notes when the doctors provided their plainly horrific reports. Keeping their Mom's spirits up. Rubbing the neuropathy oil into her feet. Walking her to the toilet, in the weeks before the catheter. Making the hardest, worst decisions. Getting the condo ready for sale. Packing boxes and bags for Goodwill. Yet Diana hadn't come, hadn't called, hadn't thanked her. Allison would've been relieved to share her grief with someone else who'd known Linda Marchese. What the hell was a sister for, anyway?

Chad talked about a movie he and Marcus had watched, listing the ways the book that preceded the film had been superior. She nodded, agreeing that this was often the case. But she couldn't help remembering that the book was beloved by Chad and Walter, that they'd written their own stories using the same characters. Those adventures now lost at sea; she wondered whether they'd return to port—as Walter and Chad, too, worked to reconcile their conflicting forces.

"I've been thinking," Ray said, using a crust of bread to clean out his empty soup bowl. "Maybe we should get a lawn service."

"What?" Allison said.

"I met the MacAvoys' gardeners today," he said. "They seem like nice enough fellows."

She cleared her throat. "You always said you *liked* doing it yourself."

Ray shrugged.

Allison considered her husband's reversal. Maybe he was shedding an old skin, like a teenager trying on black eyeliner. She took another sip of wine.

But after dinner, Ray kissed her with the urgent passion that had surfaced earlier. And once again the gears meshed neatly. "God, I love you," he breathed into her neck, and she exhaled.

Two on Two

After school, they met at the courts in East Palo Alto. Chad took the bus and followed Marcus's directions to the park. He noticed the trees at the edge of the fields—birch and oak, a couple of scraggly redwoods—and the missing basketball net. Just a metal hoop on the backboard, which was all you needed. A playground structure was a hive of little kids, climbing and clumping along the metal towers. He decided not to dwell on how poorly the structure compared with the bright new plastic wonderland in his own neighborhood. A threesome of teenagers huddled on a picnic tabletop, their feet resting on the attached benches. Something about their huddle made Chad zip up his hooded sweatshirt to conceal his Paly tee, even though the October air was warm.

Andre pulled a basketball out of his schoolbag, and started dribbling. The familiar rhythm of rubber twanging on asphalt.

Marcus had a finger roll that was pure photocopied MJ but you couldn't call him on it because how was it a diss to say his shot looked like the greatest one ever? Andre's shots clanged off the rim almost half the time, but the other half went in as violent and laser-guided as a cruise missile.

Just as Marcus won the second round of HORSE, one of the picnic table guys ambled over and asked if they wanted a fourth.

"Sure," Marcus said. "Two on two." He pointed to Chad and himself. There it was again, that zing of unfiltered dopamine at being chosen to play on Marcus's side. Attention from Marcus felt like sunshine, like vitamins.

"Jameson," the guy told Andre, and they exchanged a smooth-flowing multipart handshake. A flicker of a maybe: if Chad had known these guys as long as he'd known Walter, perhaps such handshakes would come naturally, instead of needing step-by-step instructions.

The game was fast and hard. The ball was hot in his hands but never with him for long. Andre guarded Chad with sharp elbows and shoves even after he got rid of the ball.

At some point a couple of girls appeared on the other side of the chain-link—one in the tank top from Kevin Hernandez's party, and her friends—their fingers laced through the fence.

Jameson's elbow in his ribs. The ball in Andre's hands, then a shot through the net-less rim. Both of them cheering and taunting Marcus and Chad.

He turned the ball over again, a bad pass that rolled out of bounds.

"Come *on*, Loudermocha," Marcus called. "Step it up."

It was a long walk to the ball. He muttered to himself all the way there and back. *Loudermocha*: if anyone but Marcus Johnson had invented this nickname, Chad would've been sure it was an insult. Darker than milk, but sweet and expensive. The go-to drink of a white lady.

As soon as he picked up speed, Jameson was on him. But Chad found Marcus with a clean pass just out of Andre's reach, and Marcus put up one of his arcing jumpers. It was a moment of beauty that pulled them even.

The girls at the fence giggled about something, testifying to their lack of interest.

He and Marcus exchanged a look. *We got this.*

Chad's stance wide and low, getting a pass in the chest that took his breath for a moment, recovering and posting up.

Then: his eye searing with pain, a staticky glitch in his brain: *Wait, what?*

Darkness.

On his back, then. Above him the sky, five worried faces. The girls had joined the circle; when had that happened?

"Shit," said Marcus. "I think you broke our Palo Alto."

His head fuzzy. He reached up to touch the thing that had landed on his right eye.

"Don't," a chorus of voices urged him.

"You're gonna have a helluva shiner, man," said Jameson, in a tone suggesting this was the nicest compliment he had bestowed on anyone, ever.

Chad knew only that his mom was going to kill him. He tried to say this, but all that came out was "Mimughhh."

Marcus pulled him gently to standing, and stretched Chad's arm over his own shoulders. "Let's get you home," he said. "Get a steak on your eye."

"Some prime rib in the freezer, I bet," said Andre.

Marcus glared. "Don't get pissy just 'cause we were about to beat your ass. Leave it on the court, dude."

Andre snorted, and almost under his breath muttered, "Sorry," as Marcus and Chad shuffled away.

As it turned out, there was no meat in the freezer at all; Chad held a bag of Trader Joe's dumplings to his eye and hid in his room. Put on some Fugees and tried not to worry about how he was going to read more of Thomas Hardy when he was already four chapters behind.

He'd made it through most of the Fugees disk when he heard the front door open, and his mom— humming again—moving in the kitchen. "Chad," she called, "Dinner."

He left the bag of now-thawed gyoza on his bed and shuffled in.

"Your father is hung up at work," she told him. "I got one of those pre-roasted chickens." She looked pleased by the novelty.

"Great," Chad said, trying to tilt his face away from her.

"Chad," she said. "Look at me."

He met her eyes slowly.

"What *happened*, sweetie? Are you all right?" She

put down the carving knife. "Was there a problem at school?"

"Nothing," he said, although he had not yet seen himself in a mirror. "Basketball, got elbowed. Looks worse than it is."

"Did you ice it?" She already had the freezer open.

"Mom."

She gave the bruise a sorrowful look. "I'll call the doctor," she said.

"You don't need to call anyone," he said crossly. Nothing good came of calling for help; you just roped more people into feeling bad with you. Even if you just needed a ride home. He knew this.

She pulled away, hurt. *Please don't cry please don't cry.*

"I'm fine," he said, hoping this would be enough. "It smells good, Mom."

She reached across and squeezed his hand. "Thanks for saying that," she said in her wavery almost-holding-it-together voice.

Over the weekend the swelling went down, and the bruise faded into his skin. Although his mom offered to write a note, it was unclear how the small ridge around his eye socket could be said to justify his being quite so far behind on Thomas Hardy.

Often you could fake it with these British guys: raise your hand early and say something vague about the costs of war, or the rigid class system, or "that scene in the carriage," and then you could count on the teacher to take it from there. Chad's Brit Lit teacher responded particularly well if you mentioned the frustrating limits on women's roles in society, perhaps making an analogy to corsets. Her eyes lit up and she jumped right in, without even pausing for her usual request for you to give a specific example, please, from the text. This could keep the discussion moving, even when the book itself still rested in his bedroom, under his basketball shoes.

But today they were having a test. He would be forced to craft a five-paragraph essay on themes in a book he'd barely looked at. Chad wished he'd let his mom write her note.

Thesis statement: Thomas Hardy writes douchey stories about which I do not care.

There are many things I would rather do than read Thomas Hardy's novel. One example is playing basketball with my friends. Even when this results in getting a black eye, and not being totally sure whether the injury was intentional (current thinking: 50-50), then laying low for the rest of the weekend, even then, basketball is better than Hardy. Another activity preferable to reading Thomas Hardy is playing video games. Almost any video game will do, either with or without my friends or my neighbor Scot. Playing Sonic the Hedgehog by myself is better than reading this novel. I played Sonic the Hedgehog for four hours yesterday, and it almost distracted me from wondering whether my friend clocked me in the face on purpose. Sonic the Hedgehog is not a cool game, but it was better than Thomas Hardy. Another action more enjoyable than reading this novel is doing absolutely nothing. You might call this "staring into space" or "having an introspective moment" or even "mourning my Grandmother" but you would be overestimating me.

"Are you okay?" Kara asked in the hallway after class.

"Thomas Hardy challenged me to a duel," he said.

Kara gave him a half-smile. She wore a bright

aqua shirt with sequins, but her supersized anime eyes looked tired, as if she were hoping the shirt would compensate. "I had a rough weekend, too."

He looked up.

Kara lowered her voice. "My parents," she said, "are fighting again."

"Parents," Chad said, drawing the word out with empathy.

"Right?" She shifted her weight, causing the pattern on her shirt to ripple like fish scales.

"They weren't fighting about Thomas Hardy, I hope."

She chuckled, and gave him a grateful look, like she was glad for the chance to emit a happy sound. Chad felt warmth spreading out from his chest.

"Sorry," he said. "Are you okay?"

"My mom kind of hates it here and she feels like my dad didn't tell her the truth about what it would be like. So they argue when I'm watching TV or they think I'm asleep, and then in the morning it's all rainbow unicorns, everyone's Sweetie and Darling."

They moved automatically through the hallway, and she told him more about her parents. As they reached the Bio lab, Kara's voice caught, and in that pause he could've said something warm and empathetic; he could've revealed something about his own situation—offered something in return for what she was giving him. He could've put a hand on her shoulder. He could've made her laugh, again. Couldn't he? Or would she be one more person he couldn't hold onto?

"Yo," Kara's lab partner called, with a jut of his chin toward Kara. "We're doing frogs."

On each bench was a metal tray, coated with plastic

that was cratered and pitted from the scalpels of a thousand prior students. Their own dissection kits stood ready, waiting to make the first cut.

Ambushed

Diana hated that they'd ambushed her, pretended it was a regular dinner date, sprung for a sitter. She was outnumbered. Across the table, Arthur and Tommy held hands: a united front. In the chair next to Diana there was only her handbag.

They'd tried to butter her up with Pinots Grigio and Noir, starting light and harmless and then deepening. The bouquet was oaky with top notes of blackberry, but the finish was bitter.

It was Tommy's job to keep her wineglass full, while Arthur told an anecdote about staging a Presidio apartment. He'd been stymied by the instructions for an IKEA shelving unit; after an hour of struggling, he'd decided that what he lost in stylish storage he would gain in verisimilitude by leaving the unit partially assembled, Allen wrench abandoned, just as he often positioned half a lemon on a kitchen cutting board. "It gives the suggestion," Arthur said, "of lives in progress; you can see yourself there."

"It gives the suggestion," said Diana, "of sellers who may have a problem with commitment."

Arthur and Tommy chuckled, then they lowered the boom, and it was only later that she recognized the Presidio apartment and its unfinished shelving as an icebreaker.

"It's well and good for you to have this big idea," she told Arthur. "You're not the one whose body gets swollen up, and who has to go on leave from your life for a semester."

Tommy poured olive oil into a saucer for the bread no one was eating.

"We talked about this four years ago," Diana said. "When we decided to have Molly."

"I know we did. But that was before. Now Molly's not just a dream we have, a maybe thing: she's real."

"So real that you want to change the whole deal." This was immensely unfair; she had *just*, only now, reclaimed her life: in Barcelona she'd held her own at the conference podium and with Xander Klein, and returned from Spain to the sweet warmth of Molly's embrace. How could Arthur, allegedly her best friend, want her to throw herself away again?

"Think about Molly for a minute, D. She could end up one of those warped little brats who doesn't know how to share."

"She shares at preschool," Diana said. "Her teachers tell me she's exceptional at sharing."

"Please, every kid at that school is exceptional. You know what I'm talking about. Molly needs to share *us*."

"She's always the star of the show," Tommy added.

Diana refrained from pointing out the irony of Tommy raising this concern—he, who had been asked to leave the San Francisco Opera chorus because his broad gestures in the background were distracting from the soloists, from *opera singers*. She looked intently at Arthur so that he understood she had thus refrained. She said, "So, get a dog."

Tommy made a *shocked/appalled* face that could have been interpreted from the rear balcony, but he stuck to the script and topped off her wine.

"I don't want a dog," said Arthur. "I want a family."

"You've got one." Diana spread her arms. "And we love you dearly."

"Think about it, please," Arthur said. "Just think about it?"

"I *have* thought about it, boys. I've thought about how glad I am that we had Molly when we did, because I'm too old now for midnight feedings and prenatal yoga and all of it. I was too old three years ago."

"You're not old."

"You're six months older than I am, Arthur. I work with eighteen-year-olds, and I have seen the absolute pity in their eyes when I quote from a movie that was released before nineteen eighty-six. Trust me, you're old."

"Let's get back to the eighteen-year-olds," Tommy said, leaning forward. "Could you describe them in more detail? Any water polo players?"

This was what it had been like, before. Joyful, subversive, and slightly buzzed. Back when Arthur had squeezed her hand as he got his tattoo. Late night shenanigans followed by a 2 a.m. diner breakfast, getting shushed by the people in neighboring booths.

Somehow along the way they had been transformed from the shushees into shushers; Diana hadn't felt it happening. To realize now how long it had been since the three of them had sat together, laughing and drinking, made her throat tighten. "How is this not enough for you?" she said.

Arthur hooked a calamari ring and dipped it in Sriracha-infused aioli. "Of course it's enough," he said. "If it had only ever been us, it would have been enough. If we try and it's even harder than last time and it turns out it's just the three of us and Molly, of course that's enough."

Diana drummed her fingers on the white table-cloth. She was mentally drafting a counter-argument.

"It's not to fill a void," he said. "That's not why I'm asking."

"You're *good*," Diana said. "I hate that you're so good at this."

"*Thank* you," Tommy said, giving Arthur's leg a proud squeeze. "He's always been a good closer." And this was true: Arthur had a gift, even now when the shine was off Bay Area real estate, he was closing deals.

She hated it.

"You have a sister," Tommy said, oblivious to Arthur's signal not to pursue this line of argument. "Don't you want that for Molly?"

Did she want Molly to be constantly defined in comparison? To be judged against (and then by) a sibling whose compass had a different polarity than her own? She did not. Her daughter was a singularity. The absolute child, not a subsequent and therefore relative one. Diana sipped her wine. "Thanks, Tommy," she said. "I think in soccer that's called an 'own goal.'"

Rossmann

But it hadn't always been like this, with her and Allison. There had been a time when Allie had cared for things other than an orderly house, a nuclear family.

Allison was someone who kept an earthquake kit in the pantry and diligently monitored the expiration dates on her canned goods. She had a case of bottled water and a set of flares in the trunk of the car, next to her reusable shopping bags. (In Diana's trunk: a Thomas Guide of maps of Santa Clara County, a gift from Allison when Diana moved to Palo Alto; three "just-in-case" diapers that were now two sizes too small for Molly; and a bag of clothes that she had intended to drop off at Goodwill six months ago.)

This was the thing about her sister Allison: she was like a human NPR tote bag silently rebuking you for failing to pledge your own support, flaunting her position on moral high ground, and making you feel guilty about wanting another loop of calamari for yourself instead of donating it to some worthier cause. Adopting a black son as if her maternal ease transcended race and culture, a constant reproach to the way Diana could be undone by much smaller concerns. Counseling other people's children as if to say, *I have this all figured out.* Insisting that Diana attend various block parties and events that flaunted the picket-fence perfection of Allison's life. Already Diana dreaded the upcoming "Big Game Barbecue," a weekend timesuck for a football game her sister didn't even have a stake in.

No, it hadn't always been this way. The sisters had once been allies. Only two years apart, they'd shared a common language, nearly the coded burble of twins. They had adventured together: down the shore, daring each other to swim further out; exploring the woods behind their house in Cherry Hill; playing every role in their self-designed "radio shows." Somewhere, Diana knew, there was a cache of cassette tape recordings; she wondered whether she would recognize the youthful voices playacting at melodrama.

And when their parents' marriage crumbled, they had clung to each other, resolving not to befriend the woman who'd replaced their mother in their home. Then, it had been useful not to be alone.

"Maybe," she allowed, causing Arthur's and Tommy's eyes to spark.

Arthur eagerly refilled her wineglass.

On the other hand, Diana remembered, Allison had betrayed her: she had not only become friendly with their father's new wife, she had begun to imitate their stepmother's way of smoothing things over, avoiding conflict, anticipating messes and stationing herself with hand-wipes for the inevitable cleanup. Once Diana had returned from something—science camp, maybe—to find the two of them reorganizing the linen closet. "This will make so much more sense," Allie giggled to their father's new wife. "I don't know why we used to keep the pillowcases next to the wash-cloths!"

Because, Diana had thought, *that is where Mom put them.*

But her disloyal sister was giddily stacking towels and sheets, laying down new contact paper, joyfully reordering the world.

"Just think about it, D.," Arthur implored her.

One child was an anomaly; two was a definite pattern. It would be harder to persuade the world, or even only Xander Klein, that she was anything but a woman with children.

For a few hours in Barcelona, she and Xander had indeed persuaded each other. It had been reckless, she had known even as they took the elevator up to the hotel room. It had been reckless and irresponsible and wonderful. Not at all something that would've happened in her sister's just-so life.

Won't You Be My Neighbor?

Chad knew this: if you were hoping to accumulate social capital, pretty much the worst mistake you could make was Trying Too Hard. If you happened, further, to be the only black kid in school—but woefully unable to impart an iota of secondhand street cred, or to respond to amplified music in a manner that appeared soulful or particularly rhythmic, then you were not doing yourself any favors. But your peers just might forgive you if you saved them the indignity of watching you Try. Better to Shrug It Off, lean indifferently against the wall. Turn down the Striving, up the Ironic Distance.

At Paly, Chad had learned this lesson, but somehow his mother continued, always and in all ways, to Try entirely Too Hard. Her theory was: good neighborhoods didn't just *happen*. Palo Alto, as far as Chad could tell, was pretty much one continuous good neighborhood, with only East Palo Alto, where Marcus and Andre lived, contributing anything more than misdemeanors to the police blotter. But what his mom was after was good neighbors. And so she organized block parties, potlucks, and boozy nomadic rituals known as "progressive dinners." It was a kind of torment.

Over time his mom *had* backed off a little: it was possible to overwhelm people. So she'd scaled back her welcome baskets, and explained that potluck didn't have to mean homemade. Chad watched her pretend not to notice when all the neighbors brought takeout appetizers and supermarket cupcakes. Watched her mouth tighten into a pinched knot when Chad's dad complimented Irene MacAvoy on a tub of "heirloom" potato salad that still bore the Draeger's label ($11.99).

By and large, though, people went along with his mom's neighborhood deal. You might've expected them to mutiny, to say, at last, *enough* with the Halloween costume contest, especially once Chad had outgrown dressing up.

It went without saying that Chad himself had never won the contest, not with his mom anxious to appear impartial, and that was fine with Chad. Still, he'd been a convincing Ghostbuster, wearing a backpack he and his dad rigged up with a portable fire extinguisher, and another year a serviceable Darth Maul. One year he'd worn a Niners uniform, and all night people said, "Hey, Jerry Rice!" when they opened their doors to him, and each time he explained that he was dressed as Steve Young, pointing to the number eight on his chest.

He had been hoping that she might've lost interest in these things—this might've been one small blessing of his mother's damp-eyed grieving. They'd still been at Grandma's bedside when she might've been orchestrating Fourth of July fireworks, and then, when she was too consumed with mourning to plan the annual back-to-school block party, no neighbors had stepped in on her behalf. She had not mustered the energy for a Halloween party. But alas for her son, Allison Loudermilk was back. Chad had been roped into preparations for next weekend's Big Game Tailgate, to mark the annual football game between Stanford and Berkeley, despite his own indifference to the matchup.

Brightly, his mom explained their task at the craft store: to stock tables with football-themed activities for the dozens of neighborhood kids. Chad could just hear his grandma saying, "So, put out some coloring books."

But there he was pushing the shopping cart, and reaching up for supplies on high shelves. Fabric glue, and stacks of felt squares in Berkeley blue and gold, Stanford Cardinal red and white. The basket of their cart a riot of Big Game colors. Allison stopped to scrutinize a packet of iron-on footballs and helmets.

There was a small crowd in the scrapbooking aisles; Chad steered around them. Two girls he recognized from Paly were scooping up pastel paint pens. They were seniors, cheerleaders: celebrities.

"Hi," one of them said in his direction.

"How *are* you, girls," his mom said, so loud it drowned out Chad's own pathetic *Hi*.

From the deeply grateful way the girls were looking at his mom, Chad realized they were "at-risk" clients of hers. Someone, somehow, had decided that these gorgeous long-limbed girls with their shiny straight hair and shiny straight teeth were in some sort of moral or emotional jeopardy, starving or cutting themselves, and that maybe Allison could help. It was a trip, his painfully sincere mother being BFFs with all the girls who wouldn't even make eye contact with him. He kind of hated his mom for this. Their hair was so shiny.

He tugged at the thighs of his jeans.

His mom said, "Do you both know my son, Chad?"

Crap, crap. His throat closed up and he bleated, "Hi."

The girls nodded coolly back.

They're the ones at risk, Chad tried to tell himself. Chill the heck out.

"Do you, um, go to Jordan?" The girl with darker hair named the local middle school.

"I go to Paly," he said. "I'm a freshman?"

They blinked, and one of them played with the ends of her shiny hair.

"Oh, Chad, I forgot to get safety scissors. Could you go find some for me?"

"Sure." He wasn't sure who his mom was trying to rescue from whom. He drummed his hands on his thighs in double-time to the music the store was playing: one of those songs from the seventies that told a story, about a boy who fell off a levee or a girl who ran away from her one-horse town.

His mom caught up with him as he was tossing four packages of scissors into the cart. "Sorry if I embarrassed you."

He looked at her carefully. Was she messing with him? Son, I know those girls' darkest secrets, and you don't even know their names...sorry if that's awkward for you? Sorry they assumed you were still an eighth grader? Sorry you're pushing a cart full of toddler art supplies for a party I'm forcing on everyone within a half-mile radius?

"It's cool," Chad said, Ironically Distant.

In the parking lot, he put the bags into the trunk and closed the hatchback. The lower portion of the back windshield was covered with stickers, displaying his mother's allegiance to Human Rights, to Earth Day being Everyday, and to Rutgers, where she and his dad had gone. Unlike the cars parked on either side, she did not have an American flag flying from the radio antenna. These flags were everywhere now, like the battlefield poppies in that poem from Brit Lit.

His mom already had KCBS droning out of the speakers when Chad sat down and buckled up. "How's Walter liking his new school?" she asked.

"He likes it all right," Chad said. Probably this was true. He hadn't talked, really talked, with Walter since their Confirmation a month ago. Yesterday, Chad had called Walter to make plans for the Big Game shebang.

"Sorry," Walter said. "My cousin's getting married." Walter had something like a hundred cousins, and many more "friends of the family" who were also called cousins, so this was an untestable alibi.

"It would be cool if you were there," Chad said. "Can you come after?" He hated how desperate he sounded.

"Afterwards I have tennis. My mom's new mission. Thanks a ton, Michael Chang."

"What's she watching, ESPN Classic?"

"Asian excellence is timeless."

"No doubt." A needle had slipped into a groove, and Chad could feel the rhythm and ease return.

But Walter said, "Let's do something soon, man."

So he swallowed all the things he'd saved up to share with Walter, and now he had nothing to say to his mother. "They wear uniforms," he said.

She gave an understanding murmur.

He felt she might be trying her counseling tricks on him, leading him into confessing his loneliness or something, just like those girls must've admitted their eating disorders or crushes on teachers or, maybe, addiction to hair-shininess-products.

"Well, if you see him, tell him I say hello."

Chad shrugged and looked out the window.

They passed the house his mom called "the old Wilmot house," although Chad himself couldn't remember any Wilmots ever living there. Apparently they'd moved to Florida when he was still in preschool, and since then the house had changed hands several times.

His mom had told him that the Wilmots had a daughter a few months younger than Chad; they'd played together often, while the two mothers talked. He wondered what life might be like if the Wilmots still lived there, with a girl he'd known his whole life just down the street. They might've built a treehouse where they acted out adventure stories; she could've been like a sister to him. He could imagine it, a shadow life running just behind his own, always out of reach.

Somewhere back there, too, was the life he might've had if Allison and Ray Loudermilk—"nice and well-meaning folks," Marcus called them, "but nevertheless white,"—hadn't adopted him.

"Your father and I love you very much," Allison said, as if she'd felt the shadow's breath on her own neck.

The Place You're Supposed to Laugh

"Sheesh. I know."

Allison lifted her hands from the steering wheel: *That's all I've got.* She laughed, a braying sound that was Trying Way Too Freaking Hard not to miss Grandma Marchese. They pulled into their driveway and she yanked up on the parking brake.

"You need a hand inside? I was going to take the dog out." You were not alone when you walked your dog. That was something.

His mom exhaled loudly. "This stuff can wait. I'll keep you company."

Together, they walked up the street, lingering for a moment at the Wilmot house. He ruffled the back of Red's head with his hand.

Chad was doodling in the margins of his World History notebook when Mr. F. announced it was time for this week's "Friday Fun Fact." *Fun* was relative; you had to sense that even Mr. Farris understood this. It wasn't fun like a pool party or a day at the Santa Cruz Boardwalk, it was fun like Friday morning in World History.

This week's Fun Fact came with a visual aid. Mr. F. tapped the smart board to reveal a black-and-white portrait of a dark-haired girl, maybe sixteen, in a flowy dress and pearls. The girl wasn't smiling but she wasn't sad either, she was just looking straight out like: What's up. Just a level, direct gaze. It was kind of refreshing given all the unreadable gigglers at Paly.

"Countess Anastasia," said Mr. Farris. "When her family was murdered by the Bolsheviks, her body was never found. She just disappeared." Mr. Farris bounced a piece of chalk in one hand. "So, who *were* the Bolsheviks?"

Chad watched Kara Stevens take notes. Her hair was done in a new way, with her bangs sort of braided back from her face and then held in a barrette. She bit her lower lip when she concentrated. He had to give her credit; a month ago when she'd first arrived at Paly, she would've raised her hand to tell the whole class what she already knew about the massacre of the Tsar, and about how the family was in captivity for a month before the firing squad, and she probably would've said Ana-STAH-sia in some melodramatic voice that the other girls would imitate later in the hallways. But not today. Maybe she'd learned the benefits of flying under the radar.

She looked up then, and caught Chad staring. She looked straight back at him, with steady eyes just like the Countess. He turned quickly toward Mr. Farris. Smooth, he told himself. You are so not smooth.

He shifted in his seat.

He imagined being in his room with Kara Stevens. Just talking at first, and then, not. Her hair would smell like Texan sunshine and the tips of it would graze his skin.

When he looked down at his notebook he didn't recognize his handwriting. The boy who'd been moved to the seat next to Chad when Walter Chen was transferred caught his eye and mouthed, "*Loser.*"

For a moment he wished he could time travel back to Moscow, 1918, and blend in with the Bolsheviks for a march across Red Square. Just one among the many, goose-stepping toward a shared goal.

After school he and the guys did some browsing

at the music store; Marcus bought a Fugees live disk, and they walked back to Chad's house. For three blocks Marcus extemporized about Lauryn Hill.

Among her many merits were her luminous beauty and her ferocious independence. "Remember her with her arms all full of Grammys, right? That was the public saying, you've been anointed. Don't let us down. Don't take up with any tattooed thugs, don't get pregnant again until we've seen you take some vows, and you can keep doing some *occasional* rapping—as long as you don't let the balance shift too far away from that melodic shit we pipe into Starbucks."

Chad nodded in agreement with Marcus, thinking of Hill's performance on MTV's *Unplugged*, strumming her guitar and singing lyrics so raw she might have been making them up on the spot, her voice on the ragged edge of tears.

"She didn't play along," Dre said.

"No sir." Marcus shook his head, admiring.

The little dog on the corner yapped at them as they passed.

Chad was ready to discuss it further—what this public anointment had signified to, say, Lauryn's ex-bandmates; what other musicians and actors had received such an anointment, historically, and whether they'd played along; and, maybe, whether a plush neighborhood in Palo Alto was in any way analogous to an armload of Grammys. He shot a glance at Andre, but before he'd made up his mind whether to speak, they were already almost home.

Scot MacAvoy was picking up the newspaper from his driveway, dressed in a SIGGRAPH t-shirt and shorts. He didn't appear to see them approaching.

"Hi," Chad said. "What's up?"

Scot looked up and offered a distracted, *Hey.*

Now they were close enough to see the dark circles under Scot's eyes, the twitchy way he looked at them for only a few seconds before turning back toward his own house.

Chad said, "You want to come over?"

Marcus held up his CD. "You cannot say no to Lauryn Hill."

"Oh, yeah, she's hot," Scot mumbled. It might have been the least enthusiasm anyone had ever used to deliver that sentiment.

"Stop by if you want," Marcus said. He sang in an imitation of Lauryn Hill fronting the Fugees, "You're just too good to be true; can't take my eyes offa you," waggled his hips, and then bellowed, "I love you baby, and if it's quite all right, I need you baby."

Scot gave a queasy smile. He carried his newspaper gingerly as he walked back inside.

Red rushed them at the front door, and followed them into the living room. "Must've been some party," Andre said. "That guy is way hungover."

Chad collapsed into the couch, and Red collapsed onto him.

Marcus said, "That, or he's pissed we're bringing down y'all's property values."

The Loudermilks spent Saturday morning on last-minute Tailgate prep. When he walked outside, Chad found a cart with a laptop, a digital projector, and a long spool of extension cord, but there was no other sign of Scot or of Mrs. MacAvoy. Chad used zip ties to hang a bedsheet screen from two trees.

His dad wheeled his grill into the cul-de-sac. He'd gotten home from work late last night, to another microwaveable portion of a long-cold dinner, and looked like he was dragging. While Chad was watching his dad clean the grill, his aunt Diana arrived.

"Chad," she said, shaking his hand in her formal, disengaged way. "How's it going?"

He swung his cousin Molly, in her toddler-scale Stanford cheerleader's uniform, into the air. "Nice outfit," he told her after he'd set her down.

"It's from Daddy and Tommy."

"I'm so glad you could make it," his mom said to Aunt Diana. "Things won't really get started until two."

"We can't stay long," Diana said.

"Of course not."

"Don't start, Allison. I have to pack for a guest lecture at UCLA. Oh, and also, write the lecture." She passed Allison a small bundle of fabric. "They're selling these on campus."

"Thanks." It was a cheap white t-shirt that had been screen-printed with a crudely drawn bear and a cartoon pine tree glaring at each other. *Big Game 2002*, it said, *This time it's personal.* His mom pulled the t-shirt on over her outfit and showed it off with a game show hostess flourish. "So for UCLA, do you need someone to watch Molly?"

"I hired one of her teachers from the daycare. She'll just take Molly home with her after school, and I'll be back the next morning."

"Okay," his mom said in her dubious-but-willing-to-suspend-disbelief-though-only-up-to-a-point voice. It was weird to hear that *I know better than you* tone used on someone else, as if she were suggesting that Diana finish her homework before playing video games.

"She loves her teachers," Aunt Diana said.

"I didn't say anything."

"People are on waiting lists to get spaces at her day care. People wait for years."

His mom snapped a loose thread off the cheap t-shirt. "Dad says hi," she said.

Diana accepted a Coke, and looked at Chad. "How's he doing?"

"Chad begged off this time," his mom said. "Had a sleepover that he couldn't get out of."

Diana nodded solemnly. Chad thought she might have winked at him.

"But Dad's okay," his mom said. "Hadn't seen him since the funeral, so."

Diana flinched a little at the word *funeral*. "It's so nice that you guys do stuff like this," his aunt gestured to include the party tables and the grill. "I don't really know my neighbors."

His dad looked up from cleaning off the grill rack. "Hey, Diana, so glad you could make it."

"She can't stay," Chad's mom said quickly.

Chad's dad nodded and returned his attention to the grill. His aunt was always on her way somewhere: always slingshotting away from his mother.

Molly reappeared, hand-in-hand with Mrs. Abdelnour from across the way. Mrs. Abdelnour was holding a lemon. "Your little one tried to climb my tree for this," she told Diana.

"Fruit," Molly said excitedly.

"It's a lemon," said Diana, making a face. "Too sour to eat."

Undeterred, Molly reached for it.

"You can try it," his aunt offered. "I don't think you're going to like it, but let's find out for sure."

"I'll wash it for you, Molly," said Chad's mom.

Mrs. Abdelnour made a face. "What would you be washing off?" she asked. "I don't spray my trees." To Chad she said, "When we moved here there were orchards all around this neighborhood. You could smell the apricots and prunes."

He nodded: this was part of Valley lore, the fruit trees giving way to the empires forged out of garages. "A lot has changed," he said.

"I miss them," she admitted. "The trees softened the sound of the train whistle. It's more shrill now, I think." Mrs. Abdelnour tore into the lemon rind with her thumbnail, baring the flesh. Molly bit into it eagerly, then made the bitter face they'd all expected.

"Hypothesis proved," said Aunt Diana. She thanked Mrs. Abdelnour for donating the materials for the experiment. "We need to get going."

"Not yet," Chad's mom said. "Molly, let's see if we can find the sweetness in this and make ourselves some lemonade." She pulled Molly in her cheerleading skirt inside.

"Jesus," said Diana. "She is too much." To Chad, she amended: "No offense."

By the time his dad got the grill going, Aunt Diana and Molly had gone. But before long, there were forty or fifty people in the cul-de-sac, and he could hardly hear the music his mom had chosen.

Chad teased her for the low-tech sound system.

"Mom, I could've set up a playlist on my laptop."

"Next time," his mom said. "For the holiday party."

Ray looked up from the grill. "You don't have a laptop."

"Scot gave me his old one."

"That was generous of him," said Allison.

"Goddamnit," Ray yelled. Chad and Allison spun toward him. "Lost a dog," Ray called, poking at the coals. "Just burnt up on me."

It was probably for the best Chad couldn't hear the music; knowing his mom it was all Joni Mitchell all the time. Nothing said Football-Themed Barbecue like Joni Mitchell. He watched his mom survey the crowd, the greatly diminished cooler of beer, the clusters of her neighbors chatting animatedly. Manufactured or organic, regardless, it was a successful showing. His mom looked content as she tickled the bare feet of someone's three-month-old son.

Kids crowded the craft table to make their felt collages, and Chad's dog Red ran under their legs. Red allowed himself to be chased away, then flopped onto the asphalt to permit his belly to be scratched.

Marcus showed up and sat on the curb with him. Andre had a game, and Chad didn't exactly mind that he couldn't make it. He showed off the new laptop while plates of food sat forgotten beside them. Earlier, the sun had glared off the laptop screen, but by now the sun had nearly fallen out of the sky, and it was easier to see.

The plates were made of bamboo, not paper; Chad's mother didn't do "disposable." She had placed three plastic bins near the cooler of drinks: one to recycle the cans and bottles, another for the bamboo, and one for composting the food waste. The bins were clearly labeled. Later, after they'd set off some mild firecrackers and lit a few black snakes that would leave streaky trails on the sidewalk, after everyone had gone home, Chad and his parents would scrape off the food and wash the bamboo plates, stack them neatly in the pantry for the next neighborhood event. His parents would chat about which neighbors seemed to be healthy after difficult diagnoses, who was struggling with their children, whose job prospects still hadn't recovered, and who might have to sell and move next.

The MacAvoys arrived, and Scot was immediately pressed into service to improve the sound system amplification. One of the recruiters handed him a beer bottle, which Scot accepted with a shrug.

"Dude still looks wiped," said Marcus. "His wife's hot, though."

Near the grill Chad's dad and Irene MacAvoy were standing close—keg-party-close—and Mrs. MacAvoy was laughing. Laughing the way Chad's mom would laugh when his dad was riffing hard.

It didn't quite compute: his dad charming the wife of a guy he couldn't stand.

But then, horribly, it made perfect sense.

Chad's dad made jokes about his own house looking like the servant's quarters for Scot's, jokes like Chad's line to Walter Chen about First Class and Steerage—things that turned out to be less funny once you said them out loud, leaving awkward silence in the place you were supposed to laugh.

Chad searched the street for his mom.

Two families had surrounded Allison to say good-night and thank her, almost as if they'd been waiting for a Scot MacAvoy sighting to take their leaves. Chad watched his mom embrace the neighbors, nodding as if she truly believed they would do more than exchange friendly waves from the ends of their driveways until the next event Allison put on. This was maybe what enabled her to keep up the effort of Trying So Hard: she believed it would, eventually, win people over.

Chad's thoughts were a maddening jumble. Should he find his mom and tell her what he feared about his dad and Mrs. MacAvoy? But what if his dad was just being polite? Chad powerfully wanted to believe this was true.

"I got to hand it to that guy," said Marcus, pointing out the jerry-rigged solution for the sound system. "He had zip ties and duct tape just ready to go."

"Scot's a regular MacGyver," Chad said.

Marcus looked at him, confused.

"It was a show."

"Dude," said Marcus. "You're my first white friend. Don't make it weird."

"Ha-fucking-ha," Chad said, as if he'd never heard that one before, as if *Loudermocha* wasn't just an update of "Oreo." When Chad looked back toward the grill, he saw his dad standing between Scot and his wife with his hands in a protective position, like the guy in a heist movie saying, *Let's not go crazy and kill the hostages before we've tried to negotiate.*

Scot shifted his beer to his left hand. He said something to Ray that was too quiet to hear, and then:

Scot punched Ray, hard, in the right cheek.

What the freaking fuck.

Scot's punch had spun Ray around, and he lost hold of his grill tongs. Scot laughed, a sort of angry bark, and then Ray hit him back.

Scot fell. His beer bottle smashed against the curb. Mrs. MacAvoy covered her eyes.

"Oh SHIT," Marcus said.

Chad wanted to move. Closer to his dad, to know what the hell was going on; closer to his mom, who had been restocking a condiment platter and now stood rooted, alone; but also, as far away from both of them as Chad could possibly get. But his legs were numb and he doubted that he could get up from the curb without stumbling.

Chad's dad sprang on Scot, and the two men grappled on the ground.

From the broadcast speakers came a brassy blast of the Stanford band playing "All Right Now."

Chad levered himself off the curb. His dad was scrambling to his feet, looking down at Scot with his face flushed with ugly anger. Scot's wife was crying, *Please don't hurt him.*

Chad pushed through the thinning crowd in time to hear his dad say, "treat her with the respect she deserves," before he kicked at Scot's midsection.

Scot rolled away so that Ray's foot only grazed him. "Look," he said as he got to his knees. "Just because she fucked you doesn't mean she loves you. Don't make an ass of yourself over it."

Chad froze; he'd lost confidence in his legs again.

Abruptly, he recalled the view from the back of Mrs. MacAvoy's car, the way she'd leaned over to buckle his dad into his seat. *It's a misunderstanding,* his dad had promised.

He remembered, too, the feeling that Mrs. MacAvoy and his dad spoke the same language. The evenings neither of them were around. All the dinners his dad had missed.

Chad remembered begging Mrs. MacAvoy to do him this favor. Leading her straight to his dad.

Fuck.

His eyes swung through the crowd, looking for someone whose gaze could steady him. He couldn't see his mom. Where he'd expected her to be, a group of neighborhood women now huddled, studiously pretending to reverse-engineer the potato salad.

At once Chad could taste sour, bilious potato salad, hamburger, soda. Potato salad was *revolting*, he realized. He would never eat it again.

Finally he saw his mom, or he saw the back of the white t-shirt Aunt Diana had given her. His mom's shoulders were hunched and he guessed she was crying, or trying like hell not too. Chad felt like he'd been sucker-punched himself; he swallowed hard to get the acid taste out of his mouth.

He tried to catch his dad's eye, but Ray was staring at Mrs. MacAvoy.

Scot's wife had one hand over her mouth. She shook her head firmly at his dad. *No*—what did that mean, no more of this fighting? Not here? Not now?

Scot's voice was smaller now. "What the hell did you think was going to happen?"

Chad didn't hear his dad's response, or the CD that had started to skip when Scot collided with the table, or the wet smack of bamboo plates landing in the bin. He simply stood there.

Jesus Is Not A Bean Counter

Time had stopped and restarted at the moment the Big Game barbecue went wrong. Chad felt as if the hours and days since the party had been marked on a new calendar, ticked off on a new clock; subject to new laws; there was nothing that did not feel different now.

Possibly this was because he had spent those hours and days at Marcus's house, not at his own. He hadn't planned, or packed, for this. A Walgreens bag on the couch held a new toothbrush, a Cool Wave Speed Stick, and a ripped-open three-pack of tighty whities; only one new pair remained inside. In a second bag, he kept a notebook and new pen. He had failed another quiz on Thomas Hardy.

His mother had called and spoken with Ms. Johnson, whose side of the conversation went: "Yes, he had some dinner. Chicken with broccoli...[long pause]…Yes, okay, I'll tell him." Her voice sounding warm and gentle, leaving lots of space to listen. Ever since, Marcus's mom had been solicitous, letting her hand linger on Chad's shoulder and filling up his milk glass before he'd noticed it was empty.

He remembered how his dad looked, throwing the punch that sent Scot reeling. He saw Scot on the ground, and Mrs. MacAvoy looking like a mother whose two kids were fighting: her loyalty divided, her disappointment equally distributed. His own mom standing there, frozen.

On the way to church on Sunday morning, Marcus asked whether Chad guessed his parents would divorce. When he was with Marcus and Andre, Chad felt like an outlier, not so much for having white parents as for having parents who were still married to each other.

Chad shrugged. The bus lurched around a corner, and he slid into Marcus's leg. His friend braced himself against the seatback—which held his mother, who was performing exactly the same bracing maneuver. There was no mistaking them for anything but family.

"I'd be pissed," said Marcus.

"I'm not *not* pissed," Chad assured him.

Marcus shook his head. "They sold you a bill of goods, man," he said. "You can't be plucking a kid out the streets and saying you have a nice family now, and then fourteen years later yank the wool out from under him."

"Shut up," Chad said.

"Get you all situated comfortable in the suburbs, and shit."

"*Dude.*"

"Popped collars, khakis, the whole nine. All bull-shit, going *poof.*"

Chad glared at his own feet.

"On the other hand, this could go down good for you," he said. "Munificent folks like your parents, feeling guilty; you could score serious presents out of this."

"Shut the fuck *up*, Marcus."

They rode in silence the rest of the way.

The sermon that morning focused on a verse from Matthew, about Forgiveness. Marcus elbowed him, hard, but Chad said: "Big deal, every third sermon is about forgiveness."

Marcus's mom nudged him from the other side and said, "You boys hush up."

The pastor read the Bible passage, in which Peter came to Jesus and said, "Lord, how often shall my brother sin against me, and I forgive him? Until seven times?" And then, there was a parable: a king had showed compassion to a servant, and had forgiven his debts, but then had been appalled when that same servant was not as patient with his own debtors. The pastor said, scornfully: "Forgiveness is not a matter of mathematics; it is a matter of heart." From the back of the church, a man's voice said, "Yes, yes." The pastor raised one hand to acknowledge the man and said, "Like most of what's in our hearts, it doesn't add up properly, it's not a matter of keeping a SPREAD-sheet. Jesus is not a BEAN counter.

"People SAY they forgive. They SAY they 'bury the hatchet.' But, they almost always keep a MAP that marks the SPOT where it's buried so they can dig it up later. We say we forgive but what we really do is put our resentment in cold storage so we can thaw it out when it SUITS us."

Next to him, Marcus's mother nodded vigorously.

The pastor said, "Now, true RECONCILIA-
TION takes two people, though an injured party can
FORGIVE an offender even without reconciliation.
We can forgive someone even if they don't ask or even
WANT to be forgiven."

Right then Chad knew that this was what would
happen: his mom would forgive his dad without Ray
even asking. She would smooth things over inside
herself so that she remembered why she loved him,
and then his dad would feel that forgiveness in every
hug and kiss—the weight of it. The load would be
too much for Ray. Chad saw that it would be Allison's
forgiveness, not his dad's affair, that broke apart his
family.

The pastor cited Ephesians 4: 31-32. *"Be kind and
compassionate to one another, forgiving each other as Christ
forgave you.* We understand who we truly are before
God: we are wretched and small. Only PRIDE and
self-righteousness lead us to think otherwise. God is
kind, compassionate and abounding in love. This is the
heart that He calls us to imitate in Him."

Marcus leaned tight into Chad and said, "Hate the
game, not the player."

"True that."

The choir had been steadily building throughout
the sermon, occasionally chiming in with an "Amen,"
or repeating the pastor's last phrase, and now they
burst into joyous song that began just where he'd left
off: "Imitate in him," they exulted, "Imitate the heart
in him."

After church, they went home for lunch, walking
from the bus stop through the straight and even streets
of the Johnsons' neighborhood. In Chad's neighbor-

hood the streets all curved, branching into courts and cul-de-sacs, but here the streets were on a predictable grid. "What's a cul-de-sac," said Marcus, and Chad said it was sort of like a dead end. "Shit," Marcus said, "we got plenty of those."

"Why'd you say *streets* before," Chad said.

"Huh?"

"You said my parents yanked me out of the ghetto."

Marcus held up his hands. "You're right," he said. "No doubt your birth mom was finishing up her doctorate in philosophy, and she only just took off her diamond shoes long enough to hand you off to the Loudermilks."

"She died," Chad said. "In childbirth. I don't know much about her."

"We could google that shit," Marcus said. "You could find out who you are."

"I know who I am," Chad said. He winced to hear his voice crack.

"Yeah," Marcus said, smirking. "Me too."

Chad wondered what Marcus's own rap of self-proclamation would say.

"Also," Marcus added, "who the hell dies of child-birth anymore?"

This reminded Chad of the woman in the Thomas Hardy book, cast aside by her lover who was then undone by grief for her and the son she died deliv-ering. It was hard to imagine his birth mother's life bearing much resemblance to the book, otherwise, but Chad had no way of being sure about that.

Later, they met up with Andre, and somehow used up the daylight until it was time to go back to the apart-ment. Marcus fell asleep quickly, leaving Chad to lie awake and wonder whether this feeling of newness, of having restarted the clocks and reordered the world, would last.

After world history on Monday—which was itself truncated by another Shooter Drill—he began to think of ways to play with this distorted time. What if, for example, he acted as if the last six months hadn't happened?

On the way home he took a detour and before he knew it, he stood on the Chens' front step, psyching himself up and trying to erase the desperation from his face. He had thought he'd have more time to prepare— he'd expected the walk to Walter's house to take longer. But he'd hardly even seen Walter since he'd been trans- ferred to the protective custody of his academy, and especially since he'd begun tutoring fifth graders in Mandarin after school. Chad supposed this program was Double Happiness for Walter's mother since it was effective both as community service for gilding college applications *and* as an educational instrument for Walter, whose pronunciations, according to his mother, were lazy and embarrassingly second-genera- tion. So, three months after Walter had left Paly, Chad had begun to think of Walter as having moved far away. That Walter's house was still a six-minute walk from his own was mostly unbelievable.

But here it was, the same pseudo-Spanish bungalow in which Chad had spent hours of his childhood and early adolescence. Standing on the porch he could picture everything inside: the den where he'd watched *Scooby-Doo* and played *Mario Bros.*; the kitchen where he and Walter had sat at the counter, spinning themselves dizzy on the well-oiled high stools until Mrs. Chen, citing injury statistics, curtailed the practice. And upstairs, Walter's room, where the two of them had created their own comic books; planned their future private detective agency; and written programs on Walter's computer. Their only interruptions came from Mrs. Chen, who would lean in to remind them *there was no need to yell when they were right next to each other, or cackling isn't polite, boys,* or *I don't know what the rules are at Chad's house, but at our house we don't appreciate that sort of behavior.*

What sort of behavior? Well, cackling, perhaps, or using words Mrs. Chen found inappropriate, or getting unseemly satisfaction from having neutralized a cartoon turtle in *Super Mario,* or wrestling. Yes, wrestling was more or less guaranteed to rouse Mrs. Chen from even the darkest corners of the house, and to tell them horseplay was better suited for the out-of-doors. This was how they had come to discover the Sunks.

The Sunks was their name for a spot in the park—a hollow bowl of grass where no trees grew. Had there been more than two of them, or had they been different boys, it would've been perfect for touch football, long enough to take a few well-executed plays to traverse. Instead, they rode their bikes to the Sunks in order to duel with twig lightsabers, or show off Matrix-style kung fu skills. Chad would've preferred to tell Walter about his parents there, in the spot in the middle of the Sunks from which you could see a whole IMAX screen of sky. In that place, staring up at the clouds, he would not have minded crying.

He swiped his eyes with the sleeve of his sweatshirt and rang the bell.

Mrs. Chen opened the wood front door but not the screen. She stood there looking at him through the crosshatched wires, patently disappointed. Chad didn't know whom she might have been expecting: a blue-blazered boy who wanted to take Walter out for an afternoon sail? Someone whose parents had raised him properly? Someone whose family owned a house instead of renting? Chad could only assume—*hope*—that Walter had been as lonely as he had for the last few months, at least until he'd met Marcus and Andre—when he kept his elbow out of Chad's eye, anyway.

Mrs. Chen just went on looking at Chad. He stared back, giving her his best apathetic washout. He didn't want her to sense how much he wanted to be allowed inside, how much he needed to talk to Walter.

Finally she opened the screen and said, "He's in his room."

Inside, the air carried a familiar astringent, almost-pine smell. There was antibacterial soap in the bathroom and a canister of sterilizing wipes on a table in the front hall. Chad was a little surprised that Mrs. Chen hadn't hosed him down with Purell on his way inside. There was probably still a child-safety lock on the door to the back patio, where Mrs. Chen had forbidden Chad and Walter from playing: *Don't even breathe* on the cement, she'd warned. In the living room, he saw the foam rubber corners still on the coffee table and the piano bench, from when Walter's sister had been learning to walk. She was six now; Walter's mother must've figured, better safe than sorry.

"He's got another half hour of homework," Mrs. Chen said, "but he can stop the clock while you're here."

"Okay."

"And we'll be leaving at five for tennis," she said.

"Got it," he said.

"There's no need for that tone."

He bowed his head and said, "Sorry, Ma'am." Let her hear *ma'am* whichever way she liked. He did not look back on his way into Walter's room.

The decor inside was meant to motivate: felt pennants from Stanford, Princeton and Harvard; the *Time* magazine cover naming Dr. David Ho the Person of the Year for his breakthrough AIDS research on protease-inhibitors. While a few framed certificates honored Walter's own accomplishments, the rest of the room provided a vector.

Walter's computer was in front of the bay window, blocking out the view. Walter himself faced the screen, blasting away as he moved down a hallway of doors from which various thugs and blast-worthy mutants emerged. Weird that Walter wasn't allowed to play the victim in Paly's Shooter Drills, but instead came home from private school to practice being the Shooter.

"Nice one," Chad said as Walter dispatched a scar-faced nasty.

Walter did not turn.

"Hey," Chad said, louder.

Walter remained focused on the screen.

At last he saw the wire around Walter's neck: earphones, of course—how else to prevent Mrs. Chen from perceiving and interrupting the digital multiple homicides in progress?

Chad crossed the room, placed his hand on Walter's shoulder. "Hey," he said again.

In a fluid sequence of mouse clicks, Walter paused

and exited the game, and brought up a window with a half-written essay on—based on the words that jumped out at Chad—*Great Expectations*. The cursor blinked patiently after the words "Estella hopes." Walter shrugged his earbuds into his collar, and then looked at Chad. "Jesus," Walter said.

"You didn't have to go all Code Red there. It's just me."

"Hey."

"You mind?" he thumbed toward Walter's well-made bed.

Walter shook his head.

They both looked at the ground, at Walter's computer screen, at the blue pinstriped bedspread. "*Great Expectations*, huh?"

Walter shrugged. "Not-so-Great Expectations, the guys call it. I *liked* it, actually, but Father Bob is sucking the life clean out of it."

The guys, Chad thought, and could envision Walter sipping tea with a pack of blue blazers, all chuckling drolly. Club chairs and ambient pipe smoke. "That's good," he said, "Father Bob."

"No, his name really is Father Bob."

"That's some fine establishment you've hooked up with," Chad said.

Walter rapped his fingers on an SAT study guide. "What's new at Paly?"

He considered telling Walter about the new girl, Kara Stevens, but decided to wait until he'd shared his other news. "You know my mom's Big Game party?"

"Sure." Walter's eyes snapped back toward the computer screen.

It made no sense that it would be so hard to talk

to Walter. Chad had never had to think about what he was about to say before. Now, his head was so fuzzy he couldn't remember whether he'd mentioned the Big Game out loud, or only imagined it.

"I was sorry to miss it," Walter said, only that wasn't something Walter would say, it was a robotically well-mannered private-school kid talking.

Chad attempted to wave away Walter's apologies. "I don't care about that," he said.

"Whatever."

"I mean, I wanted to tell you something about the party."

Mrs. Chen stood in the doorway. "No party today," she said, "Tennis lessons in ten minutes."

"Ma—" Walter said, but she was gone. He made a face at Chad. "This tennis thing came out of nowhere."

Chad nodded.

"Maybe later you can tell me about the Big Game? Oh man, did your mom do some insane Martha Stewart crafting again? Like all the kids crocheting toy footballs out of their own hair or something?"

It was easy for Walter to laugh at Chad's mom for Trying So Hard. Mrs. Chen, whatever her flaws, had never been humiliated at her own party when the whole neighborhood found out at the exact same moment she did that her husband was sleeping with someone else.

Walter was still grinning at him, anxious to hear about his mom's foolishness.

Instead, Chad just said, "Scot came."

His friend's face shifted to an approving, *no shit* nod. "MacAvoy.com, nice. Usually a no-show at the neighborhood functions." Walter grinned again. "Did he do the crafting?"

Chad bit down, hard. "He did not."

"Walter," Mrs. Chen called. "Is your tennis bag packed?"

"Yes, Ma." As he spoke, Walter busied himself with a duffel bag, tossing in socks and shorts.

"Anyway," Chad said. He glared at the pennants and picture frames. He thought that he would like to punch smug Man of the Year Dr. David Ho right in his protease-inhibiting face.

Walter struggled to get the duffel bag zipper to close, biting his lower lip with concentration. "So, I guess I'll see you," he said.

Dismissed. Might as well have been smacked to the ground, the way his dad had improbably pummeled Scot MacAvoy at the party. Two days later, in post-Big Game time, it hadn't started making any more sense. Chad said: "You're just going to do this, then? Just roll over and become the guy your mom wants you to be?"

"I don't know what you're talking about, man." Walter's voice was dry ice.

Chad flicked his eyes toward the tennis bag, meaningfully.

"Whatever," Walter said.

"Don't you whatever me. Whatever you." Chad's voice echoed in the small room.

"Is everything okay in here?" Mrs. Chen's eyes measured the angle at which Chad leaned above Walter. "Chad, I think it's time for you to go."

Sanctuary

On Tuesday morning, when she should've been finalizing her grant proposal, Diana instead sent Arthur a list: *Ten Only Children Whose Lives Were Not Ruined by Lack of Siblings.* They were Franklin Delano Roosevelt, Lillian Hellman, Ada Byron, Cole Porter, Leonardo da Vinci, Lauren Bacall, Albert Einstein, Joe Montana, Charles Lindbergh, and Indira Gandhi. She added that she had left off Isaac Newton, because he was a verifiable asshole, though she could not be sure whether this was correlated.

She was mad at herself for wasting time constructing the list, this on top of the time at her sister's before the party Saturday; she was furious because she was still thinking about Arthur and Tommy's proposal. Worse still, she was thinking about it *in her office*, a sanctuary *separate* from her personal life, where she was Professor Marchese and no one else. Where she had a talk to write, a trip to prepare for, and a grant proposal due in a week.

When her sister called, Diana didn't even bother with politeness.

"Ah, Christ, Allison, I'm swamped. UCLA, remember?" She continued typing as she spoke.

"Am I on speakerphone?" Allison's voice wavered and sounded distant, but Diana did not have time to troubleshoot her sister's emotional state.

"Headset," Diana said. "Cordless."

"Okay. Well, you're swamped, then, too bad."

"Yeah, I mean, maybe if I had some notice. What're you doing tomorrow?"

Allison took a moment, probably checking her color-coded calendar. "Tomor—"

"No, shit, tomorrow's no good. I'll be in L.A. How's Thursday?"

"Thursday's Thanksgiving, Diana."

So when Diana returned from UCLA, her sister would be busy herself with the preparations for her perfect holiday feast, crimping the pie crusts, making cranberry sauce from scratch.

This was another problem with siblings: only children did not get distracting phone calls in the middle of the day; only children could power through and finish their proposals, submit them well in advance of the deadline, so that they would be admired for both their promptness and the luminescence of their scientific vision.

She glanced at the collage of photos above her computer monitor: Molly at various stages, sometimes with Arthur and/or Tommy. Sometimes Diana believed her life boiled down to the question of whom she was letting down at the moment.

The next assault on her professional ramparts came in the form of an email from Xander Klein. His messages had begun soon after her return from Barcelona, and they were not without temptation. It had seemed conceivable that an hour in bed with Xander could transport her back in time: return her body to its pre-motherhood form and her mind to its pre-motherhood laser-sharp focus on her own pleasure, on physics, on her own goals and ambitions. Anyway it had been worth a shot, for she had known that the hour would be electric, would stretch like saltwater taffy into nothing but their bodies and the heat.

But Diana was a realist. She had drafted, and deleted, a dozen responses to Xander. She had written enough recommendation letters for unexceptional students to have developed a fluency in innocuously faint praise: "I enjoyed your entertaining presentation and our brief chance to speak. Be well."

She drafted something frankly sexual but stylish: "While in Barcelona I learned the local term Madrugada. It means *dawn*—not just the time of day, but the delirious, uninhibited sensation of having been up all night."

When she began to type out Madrugada, an extravagantly polysyllabic, sensuous word, her computer anticipated that since she had begun with capital-M, she would most likely continue with "olly," and offered in a discreet dialog box to complete the word for her.

She stared at the ludicrous phrase on her screen.

While in Barcelona I learned the local term Molly.

Delete. Do not Send. Do not Save as Draft.

She forced her thoughts back to the grant proposal,

where she had tried to make a compelling case that her research would answer vital questions. This was always hard for her—*vital* wasn't on her radar, really. What motivated her were *interesting* questions: funny or unexpected ones. Her last two papers reported her calculations on the phenomenon of breakfast cereal tending to clump or to cling to the insides of a bowl. And it was Molly who'd first posed the question. Molly's bowl was printed with colorful ladybugs and butterflies, and she'd wondered why her Cheerios were crawling up after the ladybug. Diana had said something about surface tension and then scribbled a note on her palm. The Cheerios effect, as she'd named it in her first paper on the subject, was fascinating, but it would've been hard to make a case for *vital*. She couldn't imagine persuading the DoD or NSF that it was worthy of their closely held money. If there were some way for the military to build an autonomous spy Cheerio that floated in the breakfasts of terrorists and transmitted key information about their plans back to the oatmeal bowls at headquarters, Diana wasn't the one who would pursue this application.

This was a common knock on physicists, that their heads were too fogged with abstraction for them to see the potential implications of their ideas. The whole, *Oh, I didn't know the giant bomb I was building to test my theories would actually be used on people,* or *How is it possible that the dinosaurs I created from this ancient DNA would be anything other than passive, lovable pets?* Arrogant ignorance, or ignorant arrogance, or something. This reputation pissed Diana off. It wasn't as if unintended consequences were somehow unique to physics—you could write a beautiful book, and some sick asshole might still go assassinate John Lennon.

John Lennon, incidentally: only child. (His killer, on the other hand, had a younger sister.)

The department secretary dropped by with her mail. "Thanks," Diana said. "You didn't need to—I could've come to pick this up."

"It's not a problem," the secretary assured her. "That's what I'm here for, Professor."

How many times had she asked to be called Diana? Uncountably many. But the secretary's day involved performing mundane tasks for the faculty: She made copies and coffee; she arranged platters of cookies in concentric circles for the weekly seminar; she could control a fax machine that flummoxed most of the professors; she patiently reminded callers of professors on sabbatical who had not managed to set their voicemail message appropriately before departing. So although Diana would've preferred the informality of a mutual first-name basis, it might've been necessary for the secretary to pronounce *Professor* with some grandeur, to allow the flourish to excuse the faculty's utter ineptitude.

"Nancy," Diana called when the secretary had almost reached the doorway.

"Yes, Professor?"

"Diana, please." She leaned forward, elbows on her desk. "I was wondering, and I don't mean to pry, but... how many children do you have?"

"Two sons and a daughter, Professor."

"Do they get along well?"

The secretary appeared startled. "They do, most of the time. My boys do like to one-up each other, but both of them look after my daughter."

"How old are they?"

"Sixteen and fourteen, that's my sons," she said. "And Jilly's just seven."

"My daughter's almost two," Diana offered.

"That's a great age." She sighed.

"Would you like to see a picture?"

Nancy eyed her with suspicion. What's the big deal, Diana wondered; wasn't this how people spoke with each other?

"Here," Diana said, gesturing to the wall behind her desk, "here she is."

Nancy approached, bent across Diana's desk to see clearly. "She's beautiful."

"Her big thing now is putting all her stuffed animals down for naps, covering them with dish towels. I've got little towel-covered puppies all over my apartment. I never even knew I had so many dish towels. Most of them were gifts from my sister.

"Anyway, now when we're playing she'll just decide, *Bang*, it's naptime, and she'll kind of push my shoulder and say, 'Down.' If I hesitate, she gives me a look like, No, seriously, make with the lying down, and then she drapes a towel over me."

She nodded warily.

This had been too much, Diana sensed. "Thank you," she said. "For bringing my mail."

"You're welcome, Professor." The secretary's footsteps in the hall outside were quick, like falling rain.

On the top of the mail stack was a flier about bomb scares, cautioning faculty to be mindful of their envelopes and packages. In this department, years ago, an unmarked package had blown three fingers off an assistant professor's hand. But professors' hard-wired absent-mindedness was problematic. The flier noted that interdepartmental envelopes had been found on the elevators, bulky and unmarked; bits of circuitry had been left in restrooms and caused daylong evacuations. A month ago, the bomb squad had been called in to investigate an abandoned briefcase in the hallway. Men in blue suits and Darth Vader helmets crouched, prodding it and listening with stethoscopes, until the department chair approached and said, "Ah, yes, there it is."

The next piece of mail explained that Diana's only female colleague had lost her tenure appeal, and would be leaving the University.

A few years ago, Diana had attempted to serve as a sort of mentor, making sure this colleague knew the department's rituals and offering her own field notes—which colleagues held grudges, who required extra ego-stroking, and who was better left to his own devices. But as the woman had struggled, Diana wound up feeling the way she felt in the ladies' room when she heard the familiar sound of peeling adhesive tape from the next stall: equal parts *Sorry, babe, I've been there,* and *I'm glad as hell that's not me.*

She did feel guilty, though, when no one sat next to her colleague in department meetings. It reminded her of grad school, of a student who'd been the star of her lab group poker nights. After he'd failed his quals, each of the other students took pains to separate themselves from the diffusing stench of his failure, and afterwards the lab had felt empty even when all eight of them were present, typing and peering at their screens.

She stared now at her own blinking cursor. An electronic chime alerted her to an email arriving from

Arthur: another invasion of her professional zone. No doubt he'd already constructed a rebuttal, all the ways a sibling would enhance Molly's life and improve her future prospects. Diana rubbed a temple with her fingertips and tried to keep her focus on the proposal she was writing. *The broader impacts of the proposed work—*

When her students had caught dotcom fever, they'd fled from the major, and from the University itself, in that heated frenzy. Unaware of how overmatched they were, the Dean urged the creation of classes in Entrepreneurship, Innovation, and Market Leadership. Her department chair stood his ground, averring: This is a *Physics* department, not an incubator for half-fertilized eggs. They held themselves nobly above the madness, and lost half their majors to the engineering school or Google. They would come back, the chair was sure, now that the emperor had been fully revealed, but Diana feared they'd return with a taste for finery and a prospector's heart-pounding thirst for gold.

In her first year on the faculty, she'd been invited to a party at a Stanford housing co-op. She'd nibbled strange tofu canapés as she wandered through the party looking for the student who'd invited her, finding him at last in a crowded hot tub. Hey, he'd said, it's my professor, and he'd waved a small pipe enticingly. Two girls had moved apart to make room for Diana in the water. But Diana stammered some version of *I made a mistake / I don't belong here / Excuse me please*, thinking only: *I am too old for this.*

"Aw," the student had cried after her, "but my band's playing later!"

She would be in college for the rest of her life, and she was already too old. Too old for co-op parties, bean burritos, ramen. Too old to be up until dawn, to watch the sun rise over Barcelona. Too old to tear down the walls she'd erected around the sectors of her life. Too old to groom students for startups, to train them to innovate when they couldn't yet integrate properly. Too old even for Arthur and Tommy's new plan. Just: too old.

The phone rang, again: her sister Allison's number appeared on the LCD screen. Another attack on the fortress, emotion heaving one more assault on reason. Diana let it go to voicemail.

Feet Fail Me Not

The six-minute walk home from Walter Chen's house took longer, in the new stretched-out post-Big Game time. Chad moved without observing the flowers, birds, or neighbors. He did not swing the plastic bag of toiletries and notebooks he'd brought from Marcus's place. He was thinking: *Tennis.* He was thinking: *Whatever.*

He should've gotten Walter outside. Maybe at the Sunks he could've explained what happened with his parents, the ruined Big Game party, and his fear of what might come next. Maybe there, in the park, Walter would've been his old self. Chad was trapped in a slow-motion catastrophe, and the Chens were well-stocked with emergency supplies. Walter wouldn't have made it political, like Marcus had. He wouldn't have been waiting for Chad's white parents to slip up; he'd known them longer. Maybe at the Sunks, instead of making fun of Allison's arts and crafts, or tendency to Try Too Hard, Walter would've understood that she'd been hurt, hurt in a way Chad himself couldn't fix.

Not that Chad wasn't angry at her, too. All that energy spent Trying So Hard, when his dad had only wanted things to be easy.

When he walked inside the house, Red nearly knocked him over. "Good boy," Chad said, as the dog followed him into the kitchen. The note from his mom said she had an evening counseling appointment and he was on his own for dinner. There was an annotated flowchart detailing the provenance and final preparation of a casserole she'd made. Everything short of a map to the oven was provided.

Red had other plans, anyway: prodding Chad with his muzzle, *let's get out of here.* Chad hung the Walgreens bag from his doorknob, and grabbed a leash and the bag the morning paper had come in, and they left.

At the playground on the corner, Red dropped his nose to the ground and began hunting for his perfect spot. Chad let go of the leash and watched him.

He had not asked for a dog. But he had come to love Red: the way he nestled on top of Chad's feet when he sat on the couch or at his desk; the way the dog trotted toward him to welcome him home.

He wondered whether his dad had given him the dog as a way to forgive himself somehow for Irene MacAvoy. Chad couldn't quite imagine what had led her to sleep with his dad. She appeared, anyway, to be the opposite of Trying Too Hard: her thing was Not Giving a Fuck.

He could hear the Caltrain whistle, those four blasts as it moved through the railroad crossing. Red finished up; Chad bagged it and tossed the package into a trash can with graffiti on the side: THRILLA, it said in one place, and MONSTER JAMS in another. More people announcing themselves to the world, just like Jay-Z. I was HERE, I am SOMEONE, I am WORTHY OF YOUR NOTICE.

Though Chad had worked hard for inconspicuousness, he was starting to understand the impulse toward self-proclamation. He could feel the urgency of crying, I AM HERE.

I know who I am, he had told Marcus. He had tried to sound sure.

But.

That night he'd pulled out photo albums, and the baby book in which his mom had noted every inch he'd grown; the order that his teeth had broken through his gums. Who he was at each month, each year of his life. *Chad has no interest in rice cereal, but prefers to feed himself Cheerios. At 7, Chad learned to ride his bike without training wheels.*

In the Bible he'd carried dutifully to his Confirmation classes, she had filled in a family tree inside the front cover. Anyone looking at it would know exactly who he was: from Allison (nee Marchese, sister of Diana, daughter of Linda) and Ray Loudermilk. These were the well-labeled branches of his tree. But underneath, another mother, another father: the roots, the hidden, the uncharted.

This was, also, who he was.

After class on Monday, still in shock from the weekend, he'd told Mr. Farris how much he'd liked the poems he read at the September 11th assembly. *Pack up the moon*, he said, *Dismantle the sun. Pour away the ocean and sweep up the wood. For nothing now can ever come to any good.* It was the first thing anyone had said at the assembly that made any sense at all to Chad.

Mr. F.'s eyes sparked, and he said, If you like *those* you've got to read *this*. He thrust upon Chad a gray-green paperback called *Leaves of Grass.*

In the book, Chad found a prototype for Jay-Z and Eminem: Song of Myself. The Myself in question, though, was not subject to the whims of high school social strata; not some boy whose dad had sabotaged his family; the Self was larger than this, the Self transcended.

For every atom belonging to me as good belongs to you.

The real magic was the way this Self was rooted and aloft at the same time: the Self could be particular and detailed, and also an inclusive universal *ME.* *Born here of parents from here from parents the same, and their parents the same.* It was great, he told Mr. Farris, but I'm not sure I understand all of it yet; and Mr. F. said, "Likewise," and that Chad could keep the book.

The sky was streaked a pale pink, the world growing dimmer and soft-focus. A single bird swooped down from a tree, and altered its flight plan when Red barked.

Chad reached down to scratch Red behind the ears. "Good boy," he said. "Good boy."

He wasn't going to over-analyze any connection between getting adopted after your mother died and being picked up from the animal shelter. Not going to overthink it. But man, he loved his dog.

On his way home with Red, he passed the MacAvoys'; Scot was sitting out front. With some effort,

Chad decided not to think about the fact that his dad and Mrs. MacAvoy were both unaccounted for.

"You hungry?" Scot said, and didn't wait for an answer.

They walked quickly, without talking, to the pizza place by the train station. Their slices were delivered on paper plates that soon became translucent with grease.

Chad hadn't realized how hungry he was until the slice had disappeared. Scot bought him another. "Least I can do," he muttered between mouthfuls.

"How are you, um, doing?" Chad asked when he'd polished off the second slice.

Scot cocked his head, a Red-like gesture of curious bemusement. "I'm okay," he said. "Thanks."

"Are you getting a divorce?"

Scot peeled a piece of pepperoni off his slice, and ate it. "Not that I'm aware of."

This was confusing. Chad had thought the point of being married was to, you know, forsake all others. If the others weren't forsaken, why stick with it?

"How are *you?*"

It surprised Chad, the way Scot was peering at him. "I'm okay," he said.

"No, you're not," Scot said. "But you will be."

Chad made a face. "If you say so."

From the kitchen came a crashing sound, and a shouted conversation in Spanish. The patrons at another table looked alarmed. "Please tell your mom how sorry I am about the party."

"I don't think you're the one who ought to be apologizing to her," Chad said.

"Maybe I'm not the only one," Scot said. "But I am sorry."

Chad took a long drink from his soda.

"I was angry," Scot said. "But I shouldn't have got in your dad's face like that. Not in public. I was mad at him, not at you and your mom."

And not at your wife? Chad thought, but couldn't say it.

"Nothing's a dealbreaker, Chad, unless you want to break your deal."

"Okay," Chad said numbly.

"Anyway, I *love* Irene. I shouldn't have needed that kind of shock therapy." He began tugging at a second slice of pepperoni. "But sometimes disruption is a virtue."

Maybe Scot had been able to forgive his wife by putting all the blame on Chad's dad. Which was crazy, thinking of his dad as some suave seducing guy, like in a matador costume or something. Getting punched for it, and punching back.

Chad wouldn't have minded punching all four of them.

Scot nodded toward the arcade game in the corner. "You have any change?"

When he'd first started hanging out with Scot, his mom had asked him nervous questions. *Why is a grown man spending his time with children? What kind of adult plays video games all afternoon?* But it was almost like the terms "grown" and "adult" didn't apply to Scot. His mom's worry struck him as quaintly sweet, now. Hiding under your desk while your family imploded.

Pouring quarters into the slot, Chad felt himself relax into the sweet oblivion of blasting cartoon aliens. From the speakers came screaming guitars and the unrelenting refrain of "Hot-Blooded."

It was hard not to take the digital explosions personally.

In Chad's peripheral vision Scot was throttling aliens with abandon. How could he just take his wife back? He'd made it sound easy, natural. So different from the way Chad's mom loved his dad now: sadly, like he was a favorite dish that had chipped, or a floor that warped—and no amount of wishing or swabbing with lemon vinegar could recover its former condition. In the last few days she had seemed weary of the struggle, tired of cutting her lip on that chipped glass. Yet next to him, in pretty much the same position, Scot was almost energized.

Chad wasn't sure what all this came down to, whether it was about the quantity, or the quality of love, or whether it was something like fatigue.

His mom's flowchart to a casserole dinner, Chad realized, was intended for his father, not himself; since Chad had been living at Marcus's for a week, she didn't expect to feed him. She was willing to cook the dinner and draw the map to the oven, but not sit across the table from his father. Screw him, Chad thought. Let him get his own pizza.

On the walk back to their houses, Scot asked Chad how school was going. Chad almost told him about "Song of Myself," but chickened out and talked about the program he was writing for his computer class instead. Coding, Scot would understand.

"Picture a young man, a boy, much like myself. Picture him in college." Scot grinned, remembering. "Berkeley. Bean burritos, ramen, my mattress on the floor with a batik tapestry tacked to the wall. I'm a cliché but I don't know it. I spend most of my time blowing off class, writing code, and playing games online. In the CS building we have a couple of servers dedicated to... well, let's just say, media. Everybody had uploaded their entire CD collection, and movies. Now this is Computer Science at Berkeley, so what that means is a whole lot of Monty Python skits and *Star Trek*."

Chad gave him a dubious look.

"We used those servers as a twenty-four-hour entertainment hub," Scot said. "We ripped CDs. Created our own *Greatest Hits* albums for bands that hadn't released them. Made video mashups for our girlfriends—or, again, more precisely, for the girls in our classes we were mooning over but unable to make eye contact with. Just like in high school when we used to spend hours making mix tapes for our crushes. You know that feeling you have at the end of a movie, that there was maybe twenty minutes of good laughs but the rest was just filler—we could collect just the laughs. *The Best of Fletch*, say, or *The Best of Major League*. We could make *The Best of Everything*."

Maybe Scot was telling him that he'd simply edited out his wife's betrayal, and preserved his own *Director's Cut: The Best Of Irene*. On the other hand, he was a businessman. "Are you pitching me?" Chad said. "Is this what comes after Latte?"

Scot grinned. "I know you're thinking, MacAvoy, you reminiscing blowhard, get to the point. And this is it: we have got a framework to make this sort of library available to everyone in the world. All we need is bandwidth, and anyone who wants to can look up a performance by Baryshnikov, or the trash compactor bit in *Star Wars*, or a video their grandkids made that afternoon a thousand miles away."

It wasn't a bad pitch, Chad figured. Even now, Scot was thinking about markets. Maybe his mellow, easygoing mien was an act: Scot seemed laid-back, but he was the guy who'd thrown the first punch.

Chad and Walter used to have conversations like the thing Scot was rehearsing. Exchanging only punchlines, or even random quotes from the movies they'd watched over and over again, without context or elaboration. He wondered how long it would take him to get to that kind of shared ease with Marcus and Dre.

At home, he refilled Red's water bowl. The casserole dish still sat on the counter, its complex instructions unfollowed. In the living room his mom sagged, exhausted, on the couch. He'd been disloyal to her and her casserole by eating pizza with Scot MacAvoy. His stomach clenched with self-censure. But even his mom was calling a handful of potato chips dinner, eating in front of the TV, getting crumbs all over Grandma Marchese's afghan. Nothing about this felt right.

She was half-asleep as he told her the broad outlines of his day.

Under normal circumstances, he could've mentioned seeing Walter; then, she would've spoken in her annoyingly soothing therapist's voice about friends drifting apart. She might've helped him make sense of Scot's Zen calm at the Space Invaders console, his puzzling lack of either anger or sadness. Instead, she only said she was so glad to have him back at home, and sank further into her mopey couch coma.

In another moment she had fallen asleep, and Chad pulled the afghan over her. In his room, he put on his headphones and turned up the volume until he could feel the bass in his ribcage.

Too Young

Diana sat in her car, gathering her strength. The bungalow where her sister and Ray lived had a large picture window in front; Diana strained to see inside, but the evening light made the window a mirror. For all she knew Allison was in there, watching Diana try to get up her nerve. She rapped an anxious rhythm on the steering wheel.

She didn't have a plan. This was not like her. Other than a vague sense, derived from movies she'd seen parts of in conference hotel rooms, that a woman in Allison's position might be buoyed by lip-syncing to Motown songs and guzzling pints of ice cream, Diana had nothing. What was worse: she didn't have any ice cream in her freezer, or much uplifting R&B in her collection.

Allison's neighborhood was nice: sweet midcentury bungalows to house nuclear families. Even with the

out-of-scale addition on the house next door, this land-
scape was suburban perfect: it was what Arthur and
Tommy craved. Two kids, two dads, and an avocado
tree. They continued to send articles and statistics to
support their case for trying for two. Diana had deleted
Arthur's latest email without even reading it; the subject
line, *Exhibit 19*, was more than enough.

When Diana, at last, rang the doorbell, Allison
didn't look thrilled to see her.

"Listen," Diana said. She held the screen door
open with her foot. "I know you've got this virtuous
one-car family thing going on. So I am picking you up."

Allison's shoulders lifted as if to say, *well, how much
worse can things get?* "Let me leave a note."

"At the risk of repeating myself very soon: Fuck
Ray."

"A note for *Chad*," Allison said, disappearing into
the kitchen. "I'll be back by ten, right?"

Diana waited in the doorway. Even now, Allison's
house was perfectly in order; a framed photograph of
her and Ray flanking Chad could've been an advertisement for the portrait studio, or for tartar-preventative
toothpaste.

Allison locked up. "It'll be great to see Molly."

"She's spending the night at Arthur and Tommy's,"
Diana said.

"Oh."

The traffic was bad on El Camino, and worse on
Page Mill. Other drivers were impatient, unwilling to
indulge red lights or slower cars. Diana stopped to let a
pedestrian cross, and the car behind her honked.

She turned on the radio. Allison winced a little, and
Diana turned it down. The radio voice went on about

the stock market, about trends to watch in 2003. There was some discussion of what might be the next bubble to burst. People expected collapse now. They'd learned that the universe couldn't expand indefinitely. Next to her, Allison gripped the armrest and sighed, sinking too deep into her thoughts.

"Slug Bug," Diana said, and whacked Allison's shoulder.

"Where? I didn't see anything." Her sister turned to look for a Volkswagen Beetle, the way they'd tracked them as children.

"It was going the other way."

On her salary, Diana would never have been able to live so close to campus without the University's subsidies. Even in the caved-in housing market, she would never be able to afford Allison's cul-de-sac, even if this had been something that she wanted. No: Diana loved her apartment, loved the staff that kept things green outside, the manager who sent someone to repair flaky appliances. This was Allison's first visit in the eight years Diana'd been there.

Diana put out hummus and chips, with a stack of cocktail napkins, and tried not to see her apartment as her sister would: sparse, poorly lit, not especially clean. There was a stack of physics journals in the corner, listing toward a ficus that had died from neglect.

The wine was red and dry and it had legs. She poured two full glasses, handed one to Allison, and tilted her own, watching the wine tears slide back down into the bowl. She wondered whether standard thin film theory—the wine's viscosity and surface tension—

could model the patterns of wine tears. There might be a paper in it, she thought. "Cheers," she said, and they clinked glasses.

Allison took a long drink. "I know this makes me naïve," she said, "but I never thought Ray would be such a cliché."

"The next door neighbor, even." Diana agreed. "I guess he's never been an overachiever."

After placing her wineglass on the coffee table, Allison picked at something stuck to the surface. Tidying up, improving Diana's poorly cared-for surroundings. She couldn't curb this impulse, even now. "Have you ever...? With a married...with somebody's husband?"

Diana's mouth was dry. Finally she said, "Not with yours."

"I'm such a fool," Allison said.

"You're the best thing that ever happened to him," she repeated one of their mother's honored refrains. "And he knows it. Maybe he resents you for it, sometimes. But he loves you."

"Do you remember our wedding?"

"It was beautiful."

"Ray told me that day, 'I will choose you again and again.'" Allison sniffled.

Kleenex, she should've got Kleenex. Diana jumped up for a roll of paper towels and stood them on the coffee table. She pictured the family portrait that her sister had framed and hung. "He's choosing you now," she said quickly. "He didn't leave. Yes, okay, he fucked around. Men do. But he never, ever said he was leaving you. Men say they're leaving their wives, even when they aren't."

"How could they have kept it a secret?"

"Maybe secrecy wasn't the point."

Allison exhaled loudly. "With all due respect," she said, "what the fuck do you know about it?"

"What?"

"You don't know anything about Ray. You don't know anything about me. How often do we even *talk*?"

Diana curled into the couch, as if the cushions might protect her.

"I left three messages that you never returned. Two emails. Why do I have to work so hard to tell you my bad news? You know *nothing* about this, Diana." Allison reached for her wineglass, nearly knocking it over. Droplets of wine sprayed onto the coffee table surface.

"Here." Diana handed her a napkin.

Allison stared furiously at it. "*Now* you give a shit, Diana?"

She relaxed a little. Anger made sense, and her sister's anger was easier to witness than her pain. She knew Allison would find a way to reconcile with Ray to provide stability for Chad. Even if she did it simply to spite Diana and their mother. She would fold her sadness into increasingly small squares, as she was doing now with the blameless napkin.

Diana, for her part, was angry too. What business did a schmuck like Ray have, cheating on the perfect wife? She didn't want to discuss Ray, any more than she wanted to consider Arthur's latest salvo in the let's-have-another-kid debate. Or Xander Klein, who'd been sending needy little emails since Barcelona. She needed all these men to leave her alone. Men were goddamned exhausting.

What they ended up talking about was their parents' marriage, and why they thought it hadn't worked. Diana had a list. Number one: they were too young.

This observation in itself was unassailable. Their mother had been seventeen, their dad nineteen. Their grandparents had disapproved, urging patience and caution. Neither set had attended the wedding, of which their mother had just one photograph, taken at an odd angle: the two of them wearing stunned expressions that said, *What now?*

"Also," said Diana, this was number two: "Mom never wanted to be married."

"I don't believe that," Allison said. Her voice trembled with the ferocity of her grip on this article of faith.

"If she wanted that life so much," Diana said, "why did she abdicate so easily?"

Shrugging, Allison scooped hummus onto a pita chip.

"When other kids' parents divorced, how many of their dads kept the house?"

Her sister allowed she didn't know of any others.

"It was the *dads* who moved to crappy condos," said Diana. "Or to Florida with their secretaries."

"Oh God, remember Joel's dad moving to Manhattan with his hygienist?" Everyone in school found out about this reconfiguration via the postcard reminders of their next dental appointments, offering referrals now that the office had moved. The hygienist had signed them herself, with a heart over the i's.

Diana held up three fingers. "It was our fault," she said, "for not being bright, or beautiful, or helpful enough."

"That's ridiculous."

"Nevertheless, I believed it for years." Diana

drained her glass, and made a face at the empty bottle. She moved to get up for another, but Allison stopped her.

"So was it Mom? If it wasn't us?" She bit her bottom lip. "Did she drive him away?"

"It was Mom, and it was Dad. I mean, Dad *was* an asshole." Diana leaned back into the couch.

"And, according to you, Mom didn't want to be married anyway."

Diana licked hummus from her finger. "Consider this," she said. "I'm sixteen and, huge surprise, no one's asked me to the Prom. Because I'm sixteen and I can't conceive that anything will ever be so heartbreaking as the implicit rejection of sixteen-year-old boys, I am moaning and saying, 'Mom, I'm pitiful, how will I ever fall in love and get married?'"

Allison smiled sadly.

"And Mom says, 'Let's think about what you really mean when you say "get married." Maybe you mean, 'I want someone to take care of me.' In which case, Mom says, I should consider committing a felony, because the state of New Jersey would be happy to provide three squares a day and a roof over my head for the foreseeable future."

Allison drew air through her teeth.

"Then again, Mom says, maybe when you say 'get married' you mean you want a companion to snuggle with. In which case you could achieve that with a kitten."

"Really put the Prom into perspective for you, then."

"This is what I'm saying."

"I can just *hear* her saying that." Allison laughed.

"She once told me, 'The secret to being a mother is *not holding a grudge.*'"

"To Linda Marchese: Long may she wave." Diana set her glass down with a clank.

"May I add one to the list? Dad fell in love with someone else," Allison said.

"QED."

The lovely, streamlined second wife had none of Linda Marchese's rough edges. Where Linda prized a brutal honesty, her replacement was all silken, like a layer of protective wax after their mother had sanded them down. It wasn't hard to see the appeal this might've had for their father, who preferred to feel robust and invincible.

Allison said: "I could never be sure whether Dad changed when he met her, or whether he became more like himself." She offered to make them both a cup of tea, hopping up before Diana could try to provide for her. The tea kettle was out on the stove: a gift from Xander Klein after he'd watched Diana fill her mug with boiling water from a saucepan, spilling most of it on the counter. Allison found a sampler box of herbal and turned quizzically back to Diana. "What's with all the honey?"

"Molly," Diana began to explain, then stopped. "Hey, how are they doing?" Diana remembered her sister's visit with their father in September, remembered the passive-aggressive way Allison had told her she was going. In case there was anything Diana wanted her to relay, she said.

"They're fine." Allison's voice tightened. "They're fine, and Mom is gone."

"I hear her voice in my head all the time," Diana said.

"I miss her."

Diana reached for her sister's hand. Her skin felt cold to the touch.

"Was Mom right?" Allison asked in a whisper, as if the power of the words was proportional to their volume.

"She was happier without him," Diana said. She thought her sister would be, too, but the thing about Allison was that she'd built her life as a reproach to their own mother's choices, as a counterexample. Look: marriage can last; homemaking can be fulfilling; rearing a child can be so straightforward that I will offer guidance to others. So Diana knew Allison would steer her at-risk marriage through the rough seas, back to calm water and predictable winds. Her only hope was that Allie might find time for a revenge affair herself, a torrid evening with a handsome loner just passing through town, before she pardoned Ray and spackled over the holes in the walls of her perfect house.

Try Harder

To top it all off, Ray's train was delayed. Halfway between Burlingame and Belmont, the brakes *whooshed* and the train ground to a stop. The man across the aisle continued talking on his cell phone for another few minutes, and only after ending his call did he appear to notice they'd stopped, saying to everyone and no one, "What the hell?" His fellow passengers offered only a collective shrug. As they sat, Ray looked out the window at a strip mall bodega, watching people enter empty-handed and depart a few minutes later with their bags. The man across the aisle grumbled to himself.

For five years Ray had actively resented the industry he worked in. And then that industry had foundered. His annoyingly youthful and confident clients no longer needed print and media campaigns to fuel their businesses; their businesses no longer existed. Enter

Southwest Airlines and Sammy's Salmon.

And then, rapidly: Exit Southwest Airlines and Sammy's Salmon. The pitches had fallen flat. Ray no longer had "it." He could feel the Goldsmith & Wong bullpen pulling away from him. The guy at the next desk hadn't even bothered to shred his last set of notes, as Ray was no longer potent enough to be a threat.

It was possible that he had never had "it" to begin with—that the inexperienced instant millionaires of the Valley simply hadn't known any better. That they'd hurled money at Ray's campaigns only because the money was there, and there was so very much of it, and they might as well spend it. This was a hard idea to hold onto: that Ray might have been as undeserving as the dotcom boy geniuses, and not an advertising wizard after all.

At the height of it, Goldsmith & Wong had scored a plum: a Super Bowl ad for a company whose "product" was the addresses of websites. Not the service of building a website, or the software to do it, just your choice from a list of website addresses the company had secured, for a fee.

The Super Bowl was Budweiser, Ford, U.S. Steel. And now it was the website address dispensary, too, whose ad had featured babies and live animals and had barely made any sense at all.

Making sense hadn't mattered then.

They told themselves it was Dada, it was hip and edgy, and this was the kind of thing clients had come to expect from Goldsmith & Wong's "vibrant intellectual community."

And now, to Ray Loudermilk, nothing made sense at all.

A voice came through the train's speakers to tell them the reason they were still not moving: a "fatality emergency," elsewhere on the line. This meant some poor schmuck had wandered or fallen or parked himself in the way of another train. They would be sitting there, watching the bodega customers, until the EMTs and police had done their horrible work. *First responders*, everyone said now. A phrase they hadn't known before last year.

Lucky Ray would have more time to think, here in the Best Place on Earth.

He could not be sure whether his afternoons and late nights with Irene MacAvoy had contributed to his own foundering, or only distracted him from its painful progression. But now he'd lost her, too. Worse: he might well be losing his wife.

In the weeks since the disastrous Big Game party, he had been penitent.

When he tried to atone with flowers, Allison pushed him away. "Be yourself," she said.

This wounded him a little. But he came to understand this as one more example of how very well she knew him. And what he heard her saying was, "Try harder."

With these words she had swept the easy options off the table: there would be no weekend getaway, no Napa spa treatments, no shopping excursions with a flushed Allison emerging from a series of dressing rooms wearing increasingly flamboyant outfits. This would not be repaired with a jaunty montage. He would not produce an advertisement for himself in order to persuade her. He would not claim to be New and Improved. Irony was easy; Irony was cheap. And

Irony, he knew, was no longer as effective as it had been.

He reasoned that Allison was giving him an opportunity; not to explain—she had cut him off each time he had attempted this—but to prove himself, to demonstrate that his offense had been a one-off. He was not sure how to do this, other than *not* to have another affair, ever; and he wasn't sure that this would be enough.

And so he tried: he bought more flowers, and he took the car for service before the date she'd marked on the calendar; he struggled to learn the rules of Chad's new video game, and to remember enough algebra to help him with his homework so that Allison could read her book. He asked questions about her mother even though he knew the answers, because he knew Allison longed to talk about her. He brought her a cup of tea in the evening. This was the least he could do, to the milliliter.

When Diana came to pick Allison up for dinner or a movie, she stared Ray down: *Not buying it*, her eyes said. He suspected she was not an advocate for his cause. But he had never been able to talk to Diana. She gave you so little to work with. She was like her father in that way: not trying to be secretive, just not interested enough in you to bother. Listen, Ray had wanted to say, it's not that I'm so fascinated in what physicists do, I'm just making conversation here, you know: we're family. If he'd had the chance, he would've readily told Diana they were not so very different: "I don't think I deserve her, either."

Allison would not sleep with him. Or rather, she would *only* sleep; she did not cuddle or spoon or welcome any other kind of bedroom advance. One night last week, he had reached to smooth her hair onto the pillow, and she had allowed this for a long moment before giving him a small sad smile that made him pull his hand away. She had purchased a bathrobe, and she encased herself in it before and after showering. An inviolable armor of blue terrycloth.

When her face turned toward him, he was sanctified, absolved. She was beautiful: this was something he had not forgotten, exactly, but he felt it more keenly now.

In three weeks, Ray had only seen the MacAvoys once, when Ray was picking up his takeout dinner and they were eating at a corner table. Irene was laughing at something Scot had said. Ray ducked his head and left quickly, scrawling an absurdly large tip on the bill.

His stomach lurched, on the train, realizing that without Goldsmith & Wong he'd struggle to pay for the next month of meals. He wasn't fired—not exactly; the partners had called it a "leave of absence" to "find his voice" again. It sounded luxurious, to have enough cash tucked away that he could do something like taking a "leave of absence" from his paycheck.

Sitting on the train, he wondered whether he'd ever be able to fix things with Chad. His son, too, had pulled away, toward Marcus and Andre—away from Ray and what he'd done. The mess he'd made.

He was half an hour late to pick up Chad. He explained about the train delay, but Marcus's mother—"Ms. Johnson," he'd tried, but she insisted on "Paula"—only blinked at him and told him the boys were on their way back from the park. She wore her nurse's uniform and white shoes, and there was a sack of fast food on the counter that her eyes went to every few minutes, as if she were calculating how long Ray might be standing in her kitchen and whether the food would still be hot when he left.

"So, you're Chad's father."

"That's right."

She made an *mm-mm*ing sound.

He had encountered this before. You looked at Ray, you looked at Chad, and you figured Ray was in over his head. He and Allison knew parents who sent their adopted Korean kids to Tae Kwon Do, or their Chinese children to learn calligraphy and subtle dipthongs that their white parents couldn't pass down. It was less clear what should be done in the case of a family like the Loudermilks, though there were a neverending multitude of things that ought not to be attempted.

The adoption books devoted most of their real estate to when and how and why to tell kids they'd been adopted, in what way to make the big reveal; this had never been a concern of Ray's, whose son knew the truth as soon as his eyes could focus.

Marcus's mother watched him carefully. Like Allison, she wouldn't let him off the hook. He didn't know whether his whiteness, his boldness in adopting Chad, or his adultery had most deeply offended Marcus's mother. But when he said, "We do our best," he could see in her raised eyebrow that she was thinking, *Try harder.*

Ray opened his mouth to explain himself, but she held up her hands. "At the end of the day we all family, Raymond."

"Thanks," he said.

She kept her eyes on him for a long beat before they darted back toward her food.

Outside Marcus's apartment building, Ray used the keychain remote control to unlock the car he'd retrieved, at last, from the station. "You were late," Chad said as Ray hustled him into the car.

"I'm sorry about that," Ray said. "My train stopped."

Like all his other apologies to his son, this sounded flimsy.

"You were late, too," Ray said.

"We were just over at the park."

"Back at Addison? That's quite a hike."

"They have parks here, Dad. There's a playground with basketball courts just down the street."

Of course there were parks in East Palo Alto; he didn't know why he'd assumed the boys would trek back to Chad's old elementary school, except that was Ray's own mental picture of Chad playing with friends. "I'm sure it's very nice."

"There's a parking lot, too. But you'd probably want to lock the car." Chad had noticed the beep of the keychain remote, catalogued it. Implicit in the noticing was the fact that Ray rarely locked the car when it sat in their own driveway; sometimes, he neglected to lock their front door.

He exhaled loudly. "Chad, it didn't mean anything. I had a rough day at work, and—"

"Whatever." Chad stared out the window.

Ray downshifted as they approached a line of

speedbumps. Despite his care, the final bump rattled the car's undercarriage. Shit, car repairs were the last things he needed. His hands tightened around the steering wheel.

He winced at the crowds at Mi Pueblo, realizing how late it had become. It would be more economical to stop here than to wait for the high-priced tacos in downtown Palo Alto. More flavorful, too. "You hungry?"

Chad shrugged.

His own middle had felt tight since the meeting at Goldsmith & Wong. He thought wistfully of the sack of fast food on Marcus's counter.

He decided to try honesty. "I, um, really did have a shitty day today."

"Right, the train."

"Before that."

Chad looked toward him.

Staring into his son's brown eyes, Ray choked on the words *leave of absence*. His stomach felt as if it were dissolving itself in digestive acid. He had let Chad down once more. He was the man in his underwear fighting with the neighbor's gardeners, the fool in a fistfight at the block party, the dad with the ill-chosen gift who'd skipped out on confirmation. He was exactly the kind of man he hadn't intended to be. Chad's eyes were steady on his, and Ray didn't know what would be worse, if his son's response to his job loss was a familiar sadness, or if Chad's eyes didn't even flicker at the news.

They drove in silence along the avenue: outside, East Palo Alto's bodegas and apartment buildings gave way to the bungalows and uniform green lawns and unironic picket fences of Palo Alto. Every third house had a palm tree.

On one or two lots per block, someone had razed the charming old bungalow to build a larger, charmless version of that house. Many of these augmented new boxes bore FOR SALE signs, as the bubble had burst at just the wrong moment for people who'd sunk their cash into architects and contractors. A week ago, Ray would've thought they'd deserved this retribution; now he was more than a little anxious about making his own rent.

He saw a hand-lettered sign on one now-vacant property:

NO COPPER PIPE
PLEASE STAY OUT

He shivered.

Chad's voice was muffled by his sweatshirt. "Dad, I was wondering, how did Mrs. MacAvoy know where to drive? That day we came to get you, she knew without me saying."

Ray considered this.

"Were you two already—"

"No," he said quickly.

Chad looked down at the floor mat.

"She knew where I was because she saw what I did to get in there," Ray said.

Chad turned toward him.

"I sort of took a baseball bat to Scot's car."

His son grimaced. "To celebrate the Southwest Airlines pitch," he said flatly.

"It was more like a wake, actually," Ray said. He remembered the pained looks on the faces of the Southwest execs, the way they pushed back from the conference table to put more distance between themselves and the horrendous job he'd done pitching the team's campaign. Which *wasn't quite what they'd had in mind, gentlemen.* Was Southwest Airlines the beginning of his downturn, or had he already been losing his grip, his "voice"?

He doubted anyone had ever said no to Scot MacAvoy. "He doesn't deserve what he has," he told his son now. "He doesn't realize how hard it is for other people."

Chad nodded as if he'd solved a puzzle: familiar, pathetic, lust. Ray didn't know how to tell him that was only part of it. "So you smashed up his car?"

Ray took a deep breath, deciding how much to admit. "It was such a rush," he said finally. "I felt like a warrior for justice." This came back to him, a muscle memory: the metal and glass no match for his rage. The alarm shrieking throughout, each whack a new exhilaration. Banishing forever the image of Scot taking Chad for driving lessons, riding shotgun with his eager apprentice.

"Chad," he said, "it was so simple for him to be your friend. The way you want to hang out with him." Ray's hand wrapped tighter around the wheel. "I wished it was that easy for me."

His son stared back at him, an impenetrable unblinking stare. *Please*, Ray thought, *accept what I have offered you. It is all I have.*

Ray had slowed down, realizing how close they'd drawn to their own driveway, when this conversation would end, when Scot MacAvoy's capacious ark of a house would once again loom over him. When Chad would disappear into his room, a den of safety and

mysterious computer games Ray didn't understand.
By tomorrow night he'd be back at Marcus's. Ray had
wanted to postpone that moment when he encountered, instead of his wife, either a Post-It note with
instructions to reheat a casserole, or a distracted,
distant ghost.

Seismic

Little earthquakes happened all the time. Just for a moment, Chad's house would sway; it was usually over before you could even think to yourself, *It's an earthquake.* Some were rollers, longer but gentle, and some quakes shook and rattled. The last really big one had been in 1989, the night of the World Series game at Candlestick. Chad had been a toddler: his mother dutifully recorded the quake on a page in his baby book called "What's going on in the world." At their house, according to her detailed entry, pictures had fallen, and some bottles in the kitchen broke. His mom had written that little Chad had slept right through it, untroubled.

Now, they were in the library, where the internet was slow but unsupervised. Andre had headphones on; he'd found a site that streamed European concert videos of his top five bands. Marcus and Chad both had reports they were supposed to be researching.

Scrolling through websites, Chad felt calm in a way he could not feel at home, with his parents' uneasy détente making everyone hyper-aware of each others' relative positions: if Dad was in the kitchen, then Mom was doing laundry; when she came into the kitchen, he almost immediately moved to the living room. No one bothered anymore to pretend there was a reason for the movement—that snap of the fingers and murmured *Oh, where is that thing I needed*—just moving away from each other, like a stream of water in a river separating around a rock.

Chad hadn't forgiven himself for his own involvement, for asking Mrs. MacAvoy that morning to bring his dad home. *Here*, Chad had basically said. *You seem to be looking for a way to fuck up your life. Have you considered adultery?* Trapped in the backseat of Mrs. MacAvoy's car, unable to re-route the collision course they were on.

He was taking the dog on lots of walks, to the point where it sometimes felt like Chad was the one talking Red into it, and he was hanging out with Dre and Marcus; spending his hours anywhere but home.

Now, at the library, they looked at earthquake statistics. Damages, lives lost, commuters whose cars had fallen when the Bay Bridge collapsed in '89. The census of disappeared dads.

"Don't I *wish*," Marcus said. "If my dad was one of those guys, he would've disappeared *because* of something." He ignored a whispered *Quiet, please* from one of the other patrons. "Mom says that's what uncles are for." He asked Chad, "You got uncles?"

"My dad has a brother. He still lives in Jersey. And I've got Arthur and Tommy, Molly's dads."

"You got three white dudes," Marcus said.

"Actually," Chad said, "Tommy's Puerto Rican."

"Fanfuckingtastic." Deadpan, unimpressed: Marcus was a hard guy to wow.

Eight computers were lined up, with a sign that said, PLEASE LIMIT YOUR COMPUTER USE WHEN OTHERS ARE WAITING. The other library patrons disregarded this request, spending hours trolling job websites and uploading resumes.

Near Chad, one guy was talking on his cell phone, in flagrant violation of another posted sign. "A year ago I was a millionaire," he said, "and now I'm praying that fucking PetSmart will get back to me."

The person on the other end said something, and the guy snorted. "Yeah," he said, "like, will code for food."

They hadn't seen it coming, somehow: they sat at the library terminals like trauma victims, still light-headed and disoriented from the blast. But I'm a millionaire, their Patagonia fleeces and Tevas protested. I'm a *content provider*. How was it that the world had turned so upside down?

Listen, Chad almost told the PetSmart guy, I can relate.

After the quake in '89, they'd postponed the World Series for ten days. After the hiatus, Chad's team, the A's, had swept. He watched with his dad as, onscreen, Dennis Eckersley celebrated making the last out. Even his moustache was jubilant. This was the last time they'd won the Series; you had to wonder whether the rumbling earth had jinxed them.

"Dude," Marcus hissed, "what's your birthday?"

Chad told him.

"Are you sure?"

"Sure I'm sure."

"I know that's what your white adulterating parents told you, but—"

Chad gave him a dark, sideways look.

Marcus held up his hands. "Okay, we'll just put your alleged birthday here, and, um, where were you born?"

"In a *hospital*, Marcus."

"Okay, which hospital?"

"St. Francis." Pasted into his baby book was an official photo: eyes still squinty, a slightly conical shape to his head. There was a picture of his parents holding him in a bucket-shaped infant car carrier, preparing to take him home.

"That's in Jersey?"

Chad nodded.

Marcus typed, peered at the screen, typed some more. "So, it looks like no one's looking for you," he said. "I mean, your real parents."

Chad rolled his eyes. He was trying to play it cool with Marcus. Certainly he wouldn't give him the satisfaction of knowing how Chad had been poring over his baby book and childhood photos since Marcus had started needling him. He kept up the front: *I know who I am*. I know who my family is.

"I know, I know. You've *got* parents. I got it. I'm just saying."

"The woman died," he said. "My mom's my mom. And don't give them my real email address, either," Chad said. "Use Bob at bob.com."

Marcus, unaccustomed to having his ideas rejected, refreshed his browser sulkily. "It's like you don't see the beauty of your setup."

The Place You're Supposed to Laugh

"So tell me about the beauty of my setup, Marcus."

"The beauty is, you can choose who you want to be. How black you want to be. How Palo Alto you want to be."

"Anyone can do that," Chad said. "You can change your name to Aragorn the Strider, if you want to. That guy—." He nodded toward the man at the next terminal. "He can be the manager of PetSmart."

"Okay, then, how 'bout your dad." Marcus appraised the hue of Chad's forearm. "The dude was black, or at most Dominican."

Marcus was jazzed to go on a quest for something Chad wasn't looking for. "My dad is Raymond Loudermilk."

In the silent moment that followed Chad could feel the tenuousness of their connection, and sense how easily Marcus could disappear from his life.

Andre took off his headphones. "Are you fools done with your *bibliographies* yet?" He said "bibliographies" in such an absurdly baroque tone that Chad pictured the word in ornate calligraphy, hanging in the air.

"I'm starving," Marcus said. "Let's bounce."

They walked to the mall, which was fully decked out in metallic holiday splendor. Silver tinsel bunting decorated storefronts, and the speakers played synthesized Christmas carols. They bypassed that cheesy place where the waiters embarrassed themselves by singing— Chad wondered how many of them were really content providers and tech wizards, and not singing waiters at all.

Marcus led them to the FroYo stand, and afterwards

they browsed in the bookstore. Andre planted himself in the magazine racks, devouring the British music trades. Marcus and Chad left him there, then noticed the security guard hanging four steps behind them.

Marcus spun around. "Something I can help you with, Officer?"

The guard pointed to Marcus's half-eaten FroYo. "No outside food or drink," he said.

Chad watched Marcus swallow hard and glance pointedly around the store, at the women with paper coffee cups, the kids in strollers with Cheerios and puffed rice scattered across their plastic trays. Marcus said, "Certainly, I'm so sorry, Sir," and handed the FroYo bowl to the guard, who muttered, craning his neck for a place to put the container.

Marcus walked quickly back to the DVD section. Chad hurried to keep up. There was a large cardboard display for *Buffy the Vampire Slayer*. The cardboard blonde Buffy stood in a fierce stance, though her eyes were wide with fear of the invisible vampire she was planning to slay. "Nice," Marcus said, approving of her tight tank top and sinewy arms.

"She's aiight," Chad said, his voice a near-perfect echo of Marcus's own. He had been practicing.

"You watch *Buffy*?"

He shook his head. "My mom thinks it's too violent." Why had he admitted this? It was like some part of his subconscious *wanted* him to get rejected by Marcus, the same way he'd been dropped by Walter.

"Shit, Negro," Marcus said, amused but not unsympathetic.

"But have you seen *Firefly*? The same guy writes it. It's pretty brilliant."

Marcus looked dubious.

"Also there's a superhot chick."

"Now you're talking." Marcus nodded. Smoothly, he slid a DVD case under his shirt.

Chad's tongue felt glued to the top of his mouth. *What the hell?*

"Fuck that guy," Marcus said, a small nod toward the memory of the security guard.

"Yeah, but—"

"What, you got a problem?" His voice trailed off for a moment and came back low: "I'm pissed."

"And this helps?"

"Find out," Marcus said, eyeing the fearsome cutout of Buffy the Vampire Slayer.

Chad shook his head. What happened then was a whirring internal calculation of what he'd lost and what was owed to him. His family was self-destructing. A $15.99 DVD, weighed against this, was nothing. A pittance. And there was a towering stack of them: no one would miss just one. Walt Whitman made his own case: *This is the meal equally set, this the meat for natural hunger; It is for the wicked just the same as the righteous.* He was hungry. Also, having already disappointed Marcus by declining to go on an electronic quest for his parentage, he wasn't eager to double down on wuss-dom. Andre would happily close ranks, and Chad would be two friends lighter.

He coughed quietly as he reached for the disk and tucked it into his shirt. It slid down an inch into his pants, caught securely by his waistband. Against his skin the plastic felt cool. Chad gnawed on the inside of his cheek. "Okay, man, let's go," he said to Marcus.

"Nah, we got to *browse*," Marcus drawled. "Looks

bad if we tear out of here right now."

The security guard was stationed near Andre in the magazines, watching the store exit. A white guy came in and walked right past the guard with an oversized chocolate chip cookie. The guard didn't even blink.

"I'm gonna look at some poetry," Chad said.

Marcus made a face like, *Who's shitting whom here.* But he said, "My girl Emily Dickinson gets it done." He locked eyes with Chad. "I'm nobody, who are you? Are you nobody, too?"

They watched each other for a long moment.

Marcus slid another disk into his pants.

Chad found several editions of Walt Whitman's *Leaves of Grass*, and flipped through "Song of Myself" in each. One version contained annotations that explained Whitman's references and similes. He might've taken notes on these, if he hadn't felt Marcus's insistent glare on his back.

In order to anticipate an earthquake, the experts monitored known faultlines, measuring tiny vibrations. There were distant early warnings. But Chad had realized that there were fault lines you couldn't see, cracks you didn't know about, and that they could wreak havoc with your footing.

On the cover of a book by Fernando Pessoa, a photograph seemed to make this point: a man in a business suit was in a kind of ecstatic backward fall, as if he'd been tripped, or possessed, or shot. A young boy in the foreground had turned in surprise as the businessman flung his arms into the air. Chad opened the book to see a numbered series of short paragraphs: *"Although I am constantly looking for myself, I am afraid to find me, to not have the chance to discover I am somebody else."*

Chad's nerves resonated as if plucked like guitar strings. He powerfully wanted to sit down and spend time with this book. It was too important, and also too big, to steal.

He chose a few other books at random, thinner volumes that kept easy company with his pilfered DVD.

His gut pressed against the books and DVD. Looking down, he could see the rectangular outline under his shirt. A matching shadow on Marcus's belly was a mark of brotherhood.

"You gonna buy that?" Marcus said to Andre.

Andre shook his head and smoothed the magazine he'd read back into place. "Already read it," he said.

The guard stood six feet away. Chad was conscious of his lumpy shirt, the sound the plastic made as it unpeeled from his damp skin each time he moved.

At Marcus's cue, the three of them fell into step just behind a woman with two large shopping bags. The alarm beeped as they passed, startling her. She spun back and said, "Oh dear, most of these are already gift-wrapped," thrusting the bags at the approaching security guard.

The guard made a face, and said, "Just a minute, boys."

"Oh dear," the woman was saying. "I just knew that girl didn't get all those tags."

Possibly, Walter Chen's mother had been right about Chad: he might've been a bad influence after all. Marcus mouthed, *Run.*

They slowed down on the other side of the mall, breathing hard outside the Mrs. Fields.

Chad was sweating, his heart pounding. All he

wanted was to get home as quickly as possible, to cocoon himself in blankets. He had a queasy feeling he would never watch the *Buffy* DVD.

"Um, hi," Kara Stevens said. "Fancy meeting you here."

"Hi," Chad gasped. Kara wore a shirt he'd never seen before: striped, like Picasso in old pictures. The stripes wrapped around her middle and got wavy higher up. Even if he weren't hyperventilating with panic, she would've taken his breath away.

She twisted the ends of her hair. "You guys holiday shopping?"

"Just call us Santa's elves," Marcus smirked. How could he be so infernally calm even now, when their stolen goods were burning a hole in Chad's gut?

Andre pulled Marcus's sleeve and they left Chad alone with Kara. As usual with Andre, Chad wasn't sure whether this was an act of kindness or cruelty.

His ears thrummed with the sound of his own heartbeat. Damn that Edgar Allen Poe, he had it right. He could hardly hear Kara when she said, "I liked your CD."

He felt the DVD pull away from his skin. Wincing, he tried to adjust his pelvis to keep it from falling. "Really? That's, um, that's awesome," he said, twisting awkwardly.

Kara's lovely face was askew with uncertainty. Clearly he was freaking her out. "I hadn't heard most of those bands before."

Inspired by Scot's new product idea, he'd burned Kara a disk and labeled it "Winter 2002 Mix," but it was really *The Greatest Hits of Chad, Winter 2002* edition. It was the Songs of Himself. When he'd presented it

The Place You're Supposed to Laugh

to her, he'd felt like one of those frogs they'd flayed, his bared heart twitching. And—galvanic tremble— she had listened to it! But this was not the moment to discuss it further. Each time footsteps sounded behind him, Chad tensed, sure he was about to feel the guard's hand on his shoulder. "I'd better catch up with my friends," he said.

"Oh, um, okay," she said, still quizzical.

And that was how Chad ruined his fraction of a chance with Kara Stevens. He could only watch as she receded, without even a glance backward.

Then, Marcus appeared, a defeated look on his face, the guard from the bookstore close behind. "Just a moment there, son," the guard said to Chad.

Rules of the Game

The guard left them in a backroom to sweat. "This dude watches too much *Law & Order*," Marcus muttered.

Andre said: "Question is, is he the good cop or the bad cop?"

"Both," Marcus said. "Had to go change his outfit. Maybe put on some glasses so we won't recognize him."

"Lucky for America guys like this are on patrol," said Andre. "Just think if he hadn't been trailing us through the damn place."

Chad was furious with Marcus for getting him into this, but grateful not to be alone in the bookstore's back room. The movie playing in his head was of Kara retreating outside the store.

"Whoever comes back in here, we both know who he's going to find: the three politest, most decent and remorseful little African American boys he's ever seen." Marcus contorted his face into a sorrowful mask. "You're doing great," he told Chad, "you look like you about to shit your pants."

"I *am* about to shit my pants."

A knowing smile. "Your parents didn't give you the talk. Why would they?"

"Marcus—"

"Keep your hands where they can see them. Smile like you tap dancing. Yes, *suh*. No, *suh*."

"Is all this before or after you steal shit from them?" Chad did feel remorseful; he regretted more than anything that he'd allowed himself to be persuaded into walking out of the store with contraband. The loot sat on the small table in the back room, looking small and unworthy of the drama unfolding around it. He had thirty dollars in his wallet that could've covered both the poems and the DVD. "Listen, why don't we offer to pay for the stuff, we'll say we just forgot."

Andre stared at him, blinking.

Marcus's voice was low and resolute. "He comes back in here, you duck your head. Don't look him in the eyes 'case he takes that as a challenge. You say, 'Oh my goodness,' you are 'so sorry, Sir,' and that is all you fucking say."

Chad nodded. He felt like the least street-smart member of a heist crew, the one whose naiveté would be the operation's undoing. First to fall and die in the ringleader's arms when it all went south: *You were the best of us, Johnny.*

The guard returned. Chad's throat tightened; he looked at the pockmarked linoleum floor, the metal file cabinet in the corner, the mini-fridge and microwave combo with a note taped up that said DON'T EAT IT

IF YOU DIDN'T BRING IT. He knew better than to make eye contact with Marcus or Andre—his nerves were so taut he would probably giggle or in some other way screw things up. He focused on the row of mismatched mugs lined up next to the coffee maker.

While Chad was avoiding eye contact, the guard was explaining that petty theft was a serious crime, punishable by fines or community service or "incarceration." Chad's stomach flipped. Your first offense, the guard said, was your best chance to avoid jail time. He explained all the reasons they'd made a big mistake, taking things out of his bookstore without paying for them first. Running away, to boot. Chad heard Marcus swallow hard.

He wondered whether his dad had felt this scared during his own night of "misunderstanding."

The guard continued to describe their dystopian prospects. If it happened again, even their best-case scenario was a fine and JD. There was a process, he said, for getting one's record expunged, providing one didn't make the same mistake again. But until that time had passed without incident, they would be marked men. And whichever way things went from here, they would be on a mall watchlist.

Chad was in a calamity of his own making. His face was warm, and he felt tears slide down his face.

The guard placed a hand on his shoulder. "It's all right, son," he said. "You didn't know, before, did you? But now you do."

"Th-thank you," Chad managed.

Having judged them suitably educated, the guard released them to Marcus's mother. She looked tired and irritated.

She offered the guard her own apologies and gratitude, which he accepted with a magnanimous wave of his hand. You could feel, in this gesture, the guard's sense of social responsibility: that he'd followed and watched them in the store simply for the opportunity to offer moral instruction. He was but a humble teacher.

Chad swiped at his wet eyes, pissed at himself for crying in front of the guard, for giving him exactly what he'd wanted.

Marcus's mother marched them silently through the mall, back to the bus stop. "I can actually walk from here," Chad said.

"You going to listen first," she said coolly.

"Yes, Ma'am," the three boys said together.

"That was some boneheaded fool stupidity," she said. "You are all three better than that."

"Yes, Ma'am," they repeated.

"The thing is," Andre said, "Chad here has parents that don't see color."

He felt that arm in his chest again, the alienating beigeness of his life.

She gave Chad a look so hot it annealed him. "I don't see thieves when I look at y'all, either," she said slowly. "Did it matter, in that store, what any of your family sees?"

They shook their heads.

"You damn lucky that man decided to lecture you instead of all the worse things."

"We know," said Marcus. "He told us all about the worse things."

"You don't know shit, boy," she snapped.

Chad trembled at the fury coming off her in waves.

"I hope and pray for you boys," said Marcus's mom, "but the game is rigged. And the only way you get a say in changing the rules is, you live long enough to stay in the game."

They ducked their heads in penitent accord.

She nodded toward Chad. "And *this* one don't even know the rules."

Andre stifled a chuckle. "Forget poker, he don't know Go Fish."

Marcus's mother grabbed both Andre and Marcus by the arm. "You think you're running some hustle, here? You think *you're* the ones going to win the kitty when you bring him to the table?" She dropped their arms, and Marcus rubbed the place she'd been gripping. "Don't hustle a hustler, fools."

"No, Ma'am."

"Your parents love you," she told Chad. "I don't doubt it. But they can't teach you what they don't know."

If Only

If you wanted to play *if only* it was easy. If only Allison hadn't been so distracted by grief, so busy with her clients, she might've noticed the signs: Ray's moods, his work hours, his doing pretty much every single thing on those checklists in the magazines and pamphlets.

If only they'd never come west. It seemed unlikely that she would've hosted a picnic in November, if she still lived in New Jersey—especially while wearing shorts and Tevas and a vulgar Big Game t-shirt. And back east, she was almost sure, her husband would not have punched an internet mogul whose wife he claimed to love, bringing an abrupt end to her 2002 Big Game Tailgate barbecue.

If only she hadn't agreed to meet him for coffee at a place that was playing a succession of eighties songs "curated" and distributed by the café management. A stack of CDs next to the register, Allison's youth packaged and shrink-wrapped for only $9.99.

"I'm so goddamn sorry, Allison. I never meant to hurt you." It was not the first time he had said it, but it was the first time he had sat still and looked her in the eye while he did.

If only she hadn't been watching the Atlantic, bare feet crossed on the arm of her lifeguard chair, when two guys about to be seniors at Rutgers crashed onto the sand below her. If only she hadn't gone out with them after her shift, and found out one of them was smarter and funnier than he thought he was (and that his friend was the inverse). If only, if only, if only, then she never would have met Ray Loudermilk.

Or maybe she would have: maybe she would've sat next to Ray on the train, or met him at a campus party, or bumped into him in a music store when she reached for Supertramp while he was grabbing Springsteen. There were people who talked about destiny, who said that one way or another it was meant to be. And truly, Allison couldn't imagine loving anyone else the way that she loved Ray.

And their story started down the shore, when he'd made her laugh.

Somehow he'd convinced her to attend a party at his friends' rented house, and they sat on the dock overlooking a lagoon. Fireflies darted nearby: a fleeting gleam in the dark. Ray offered to get her something to drink.

"A glass of milk would be lovely," she said. When he made a face, she asked, "Is something wrong?"

"No, no, it's just that—most girls say a margarita."

Allison gave him a look that said, *simultaneously, I pity you for the smallness of your world if it so easily encounters its outer borders, and I am not most girls.* It was not an easy look for an eighteen-year-old to pull off, but Allison had practiced.

She scratched a greenie bite on her ankle, and Ray fished an ice cube out of his drink to relieve the itching.

They were married within a year. Ray started working in Manhattan, and Allison went to graduate school after finishing her BS.

Allison had never liked the term "miscarriage." It sounded like clumsiness, like carelessness. Especially so if it became a habit. All those ideas of daughters and sons, merely misplaced.

Still, she couldn't deny that Chad made her feel that something had clicked back into place. She stood with Ray at the hospital nursery, peering through a lemon-scented window at their son. Wrapped in a standard-issue blanket, Chad was nut-brown and squinty. There had been forms, and interviews, and waiting—so much waiting—and now there was a beautiful, perfect baby boy. *Oh, there it is*, Allison thought, as if she'd found an earring on the floor without having felt it loose itself from her earlobe.

She felt breath rush out of her lungs. "I love you, Raymond. I've loved you since I was nineteen." Goddamn this ridiculous café for playing the same music she'd loved then. From the speakers, XTC melted into Talking Heads.

A bicyclist clomped into the café. Allison watched as he unstrapped his helmet, and walked to the counter in the peculiar mincing gait produced by cycling shoes. She recognized him from Chad's elementary school PTA, and returned his wave. Palo Alto was that small sometimes: you couldn't get away from your neighbors even when you wanted to.

The corners of Ray's mouth lifted. It wasn't quite a smile—she couldn't remember the last time she'd seen him smile—but it was hopeful. He let a long beat pass, then said, "It's over. With Irene. It's over."

This was the least he could say; it was what her sister would call necessary, but not sufficient. It was also almost impossible to believe that it had been Ray's decision to end things with Irene. She felt disloyal to Ray for thinking it, but Diana was right: Irene had been out of his league. Allison traced the grain in the wood tabletop.

"Really. I fucked up. It wasn't serious."

"She lives *next door*, Ray." Don't shit where you eat, her mother would've said.

"I know there will be awkward moments."

She sucked air through her teeth. "Awkward moments, Ray? Are you delusional? What the hell were you *thinking*?"

"Allie, please. People are looking."

"Oh. Is *this* an awkward moment?"

Was the worst part that her mother had, after all, been right? Over and over she'd warned Allison and Diana—*Girls, men lie. Men run, and with the other side of themselves they say they love you. I think maybe they don't even know they're doing it. It doesn't matter how beautiful you are, or how clever—because trust me, you girls are beautiful and clever beyond measure—men can't help themselves. Men are made for running.*

Her mother never said, "running around," or "running around on you;" she left it at "running."

For the first time, Allison felt something like relief that her mother had died.

If only she had been a different wife, a different person, instead of doggedly, bullheadedly herself.

Even as a child, Allison possessed a quiet competence that led authority figures to trust her implicitly, and got her elected secretary of every club to which she belonged. From the time she was twelve, she had no shortage of babysitting jobs.

(The winter she was sixteen, she agreed to babysit for a family down the hall from her mother's post-divorce condo. "Who?" Her mother pursed her lips to indicate she had taken no notice of the three boys. She had never known her neighbors. "Is she going to pay you per kid?")

Her sister Diana possessed a different sort of competence, a louder sort that announced itself and dazzled people. Diana was, for Allison, a hard act to precede. They'd both scored well on standardized tests, and overheard their parents at cocktail parties saying their daughters were "going places," that "the sky was the limit." But while Allison had thought they were climbing together, pacing each other to avoid dehydration or altitude sickness, she found at sixteen that her fourteen-year-old sister had outpaced her, and had already claimed the thinnest, driest air for herself.

Quiet competence was easier to take for granted, to betray.

"It wasn't your fault," Ray said now in the café. "I mean, there wasn't anything you did, or didn't do."

Her throat squeezed shut. "No?"

"Allison, you were—you are—a terrific wife. You're so smart, so beautiful. I mean it. I don't know where

I'd be without you. I'm not saying I wasn't jealous of the time you spend with Chad. Of your connection."

"You're not saying that."

"No."

"You're his father."

"He's just—the way he looks at me, Allie, with those huge dark eyes, it kills me. Honestly, it scares me." Ray looked nervous now, saying it. "I feel like he sees right through me."

"He's fourteen, Raymond."

"And these new friends do it too," he said. "Marcus and Andre. What was wrong with the kids in Palo Alto?" Ray tapped his French fry in a pool of ketchup. "He needed to bus these guys in to hang out with?"

She gave him a long cold look. Shook away her memories of Chad's black eye, of the call from his friend's mother about an incident at the mall. She told herself this was only teenage trouble. Hadn't she herself had friends who used a five-finger discount at Wawa? And wasn't acting out, shoplifting or rough-housing, kind of a natural reaction to everything else that was going on?

She remembered Paula Johnson's voice on the phone. "All due respect," Marcus's mom said, "loving him isn't going to be enough."

She told Ray, "Let me tell you something about your big what-if. If we didn't have Chad, I wouldn't be sitting here talking to you right now. But we made a promise to him."

Allison had done her best. Been the best wife she could be to Ray, and the best mother she could. She had sacrificed herself on the altar of family, over and over. Early on she lost the ability to be embarrassed by what she got wrong: her own stained, unfashionable clothes at school drop-off; her imperfect handmade cannoli for the bake sale among all the professionally knotted pink boxes.

She had been happy to learn which lotions were best to prevent ashy skin; she had found a barbershop that could tame Chad's unruly curls into a fade. They'd stretched to rent here, because of the school district. Palo Alto schools were at the top of every list—test scores, college placements, opportunities from AP classes to a fine arts studio. The only knock against them was the profound lack of kids who looked like Chad. For this, too, Allison adjusted: she found a soccer league in neighboring East Palo Alto, and hoped that Chad would make friends on the team. But when he hated the sport and begged not to be forced to play a second season, she acquiesced.

She'd surged with hope at an elementary school open house, smiling warmly at a black woman with braids. Allison eagerly arranged a playdate, which was when she learned the woman was the nanny to one of Chad's white classmates.

So she'd accepted that they were a sort of island, the three of them. She could provide Chad with this family, this love. If only.

Ray shrugged heavily. "It's just hard."

"Be patient, Ray."

"I know, it's just—everything." He sagged into his chair.

"Be patient," she told him as gently as she could.

She'd counseled teenagers whose sexual adventurousness astounded her; wait, she should have told them, *you don't need to try so hard yet. Save that for when you're both exhausted, and there's a gorgeous willing woman right next door.*

They sat in silence for a long moment.

"This is nice," Ray said. "You and me, having coffee. Talking."

Allison gave him a weak smile.

"I'm sorry about the party."

"Nobody's said anything." Even Mrs. Abdelnour had kept her distance, continued to wave from the end of the driveway.

"Maybe they didn't notice."

"Raymond. People notice everything." Especially an ugly brawl in the middle of the cul-de-sac.

"They don't. You'd be surprised."

She shrugged again. "Okay."

He sat up straighter, almost proud: "The night I wrecked MacAvoy's truck, no one saw a damn thing."

She shook her head. "I think I would've noticed that, Raymond."

"You were at your father's." He raised his eyebrows.

She could picture Mrs. Abdelnour watching from her picture window, remembering this scene later, when Allison asked after her azaleas. Thinking to herself, *That poor woman has no idea.* She took a deep breath, grateful the music had slowed to Roxy's "Avalon."

"It isn't fair," he said. "That asshole doesn't deserve to be Chad's hero."

She shook her head. "You know what your problem is, Ray? It's that you think you know what your problem is."

"I didn't have a plan, Allie. I'm not like you. Not everyone's prepared for any goddamn thing. Some people don't keep an earthquake kit in the kitchen and a set of flares in the car. Other people just *throw away* those little envelopes of extra buttons that come with shirts, instead of filing them by the Dewey Decimal system. And that doesn't make them terrible people."

She bit her bottom lip. "So it was the extra buttons that pushed you into Irene's arms."

"This isn't about Irene."

"So it's not *my* fault, and it isn't about *her*." She looked pointedly across the table.

Her sister Diana would've left ten minutes ago. But Allison was still here. She did believe that under this swaggering vandal, poisoned by envy, he was still the boy from down the shore.

She sipped from her latte. Most of the vanilla syrup was concentrated at the bottom, so the drink was becoming steadily sweeter. "I get that you wanted to hurt Scot. I don't understand how Chad and I were acceptable collateral damage."

He closed his eyes for a moment, as if he could picture the storyboard of their love story. The wrinkles between his eyebrows uncreased themselves. Finally his eyes opened, those blue eyes boring into her. "I love you, Allison. I loved the nineteen-year-old Allie Marchese I met down the shore, and I loved Allison Loudermilk who had so much love in her heart that she found a son to share it with, and I love the woman who repossessed my fucking tackle box to organize her extra buttons."

"It's a little wordy, Raymond," she said carefully, "but I love you, too." She let her hand fall into his.

Ray gave her fingers a light squeeze. "I was starting to think I'd lost my touch for pitches," he said.

Her face must have shown her confusion.

"There's something else," he said. "While we're confessing and all."

Allison pulled her hand back onto her own lap.

"They're calling it a *leave of absence*," Ray began.

On the road just past the café, Allison pulled up to a stoplight next to an enormous SUV that dwarfed her own hatchback.

She had read studies saying a small, nimble car carefully piloted was safer than a large one, but if it came down to her against one of them, she didn't know how far nimble was going to get her. She shot a glance at the SUV, and she saw a woman waving frantically from behind the wheel.

Perhaps from her elevated vantage point, the SUV driver could see some problem with Allison's car, or wanted to alert her to a deranged, armed drifter lying in wait across the backseat. Allison reached across the car to unroll the passenger window.

The woman stopped waving, but continued to grin at Allison. "Hey," she shouted. "I'm from New Jersey, too!"

"No kidding," Allison said, startled. It took her a moment to remember the Rutgers sticker on the back window. "Where in Jersey?"

"Mendham."

"Cherry Hill," said Allison.

Their exchanged facial expressions meant how about that.

The light changed, and they kept grinning at each other, and then Allison said, "Take it easy," and they drove off. Half a block later Allison realized she'd wanted to be in the woman's lane so she could turn right, and instead she'd gone straight, into a dead-end street.

She pulled over and felt, suddenly, hot tears at the improbable gratitude she felt toward the woman from Mendham, New Jersey. She blinked back the tears, and a sob escaped from her throat, a naked wail that echoed through the car.

Certified Organic

Those inclined to irony might find it in the Palo Alto Farmers Market assembled on asphalt, where there had once been an apricot orchard. Each weekend from May through December, the workweek parking lot filled with vendor stands and umbrellas protecting bins of trucked-in garlic cloves, avocados, tomatillos, et al. The University down the street was known as "The Farm," though it hadn't been one since the Stanfords donated their country estate and chartered a college in the 1880s. Stanford grads and especially its dropouts had been transforming the Valley ever since; the fruit came from further and further away.

But there was this: the sun was out, and Diana was walking hand-in-hand with her best friend Arthur. Tommy and Molly had raced ahead, leaving Diana and Arthur to linger over the produce. Baskets of berries triggered a memory of paying to pick their own ollalieberries in Watsonville. Of the subsequent attempt at jam-making, resulting in a sticky mess. Of their joy, in the noisy chaotic kitchen. This was how she and Arthur loved each other: because of, in spite of, and all the way through the messiness.

Years ago, east for an obligatory holiday visit and to remind herself of winter, Diana had tried to fill her mother's larder with her favorites. Her mother was still in the spartan condo; her fridge stocked mostly with mustard and diet soda cans. Diana brought in armloads of lettuce, filled pastas, crusty breads, delicious cheeses—easy luxuries for them to savor. But her mother stopped short at the December strawberries. "It's not natural," she sniffed. "Things have a *season*."

"They *are* in season," said Diana, pointing out the label on the plastic clamshell. "In Argentina."

Her mother shook her head, and shamed her with the memory of childhood trips to New Jersey's cranberry bogs, flooded in October for the harvest: men in waders waist-deep in a lake of red fruit. That evening in the condo, they sat together nibbling at the lush cheeses and bread, but her mother would not touch the illicitly imported berries.

Now, she suspected that the fetishistic provenance of foodstuffs at the Palo Alto market would've pleased Linda Marchese. Diana and Arthur passed a sheepsmilk dairy stand, each cheese with a laminated index card explaining its making, the rind and/or rub specifics, cave time, and everything short of the names of the sheep who contributed.

"This one is Tommy's favorite," he said, pulling her over. "A quarter pound, please."

She squeezed his hand. "Tell me, what's domestic

bliss like, anyway?"

"Don't take that tone with me," Arthur said. "You always heap your darkest scorn upon the things you're yearning for most."

"I always?" She pretended to be injured. "I do not yearn for that hideous tattoo of yours, I can assure you. That scorn is bona fide."

"Your protestations reveal you," he laughed as a couple and their dog passed.

"Well, if you mean marriage," she said, "I'll have you know I recently turned down a proposal from a very desirable candidate."

Arthur made a face, slinging his bag of cheese over his shoulder. "Are we talking about that asshole from Columbia?"

"We *are*." She had introduced Xander and Arthur, once, resulting in a disastrously chilly evening. Worse than the evening was the ensuing weeks each man spent recalibrating his own standing with Diana: if she chose to spend time with that other *him*, what might that mean about himself? The rapacity of the male ego put her off both of them for a month.

"One Barcelona seduction does not a proposal make."

"He's been emailing me since then," she said. "Told me his therapist says he's almost done becoming the person I want him to be."

Arthur's sour face puckered further. "And who's that? Someone who's not already married?"

"That would help," Diana admitted. "Also someone who doesn't quote his therapist so often. Anyway, I broke it off."

"You broke off your email flirtation with a man you broke up with three years ago."

"I did," she beamed. "Aren't you proud of me?"

He swung her hand lightly as they walked. Stand by stand, they filled their bags: heirloom tomatoes; garlic scapes; a crisp bouquet of celery. Arthur found a baker whose baguettes would complement Tommy's cheese; Diana bought a quart of artisanal salsa.

"About the other thing," Arthur began.

"Shit, Arthur."

"You've been ignoring my emails for a month."

She clenched. Why was Arthur so intent on disrupting the precarious balance of their lives? She swallowed hard and gazed into a basket of apricots, lovingly arranged by the vendor.

"Now, hear me out. I know we're asking a lot from you. If it's the logistics, or the hours, I want you to know: Tommy and I are open to changing the custody terms. We could pull more than fifty percent."

Diana felt a lifting of internal pressure, a lightening. Arthur's offer was permission to pull back, to stop pretending her maternal efforts even came close to "domestic bliss." To reprioritize, return her research to its central place.

"You promised you'd think about it, D."

"I am thinking. I am literally never not thinking."

"It could be really great," Arthur said. "There's no one else I want to do this with."

"Me neither," she said.

At one corner of the market, a guitarist began to perform. His voice was reedy, his strumming plangent. This was the last farmers market until May, he reminded them, so he wanted to send them off with a song. Two little boys danced in a circle.

"Wait," Diana said. "What did you mean about not

doing it with someone else, are you guys considering that?"

Arthur hesitated. This was the "Sorry, Diana, I kissed your boyfriend" look: guiltily exhilarated, a little relieved. The look that meant he hadn't wanted to tell her, but was glad she knew. "That would be another option."

She imagined this: some other woman. A woman whose ovaries were ready, a woman who didn't need to publish to stand for promotion to full professor, a woman who knew how to cook. A woman who wasn't Molly's mother. "I don't want you to do that either."

He exhaled hard. "D, I love you, but you can't dictate the terms of our family." Arthur left her staring at the apricots, with the singer and his guitar.

Thirteen years ago in Cambridge, they had found each other. Diana was in graduate school, startled by unprecedented uncertainty. Putting up a brave front in classrooms filled with confident men, who did not blush if they gave the wrong answer, who only shrugged off hard problem sets, who did not experience each exam as an opportunity to question their very identity as smart and capable humans, she sought refuge, as she always had, in the swimming pool. The satisfaction of slicing through the water. But she was uneasy about leaving the research lab for too long: what if she missed an important conversation; what if her faculty advisor interpreted her absence as a lack of commitment; what if someone were alerted to the fact that she didn't belong at MIT, at all? She half-expected to return from the pool and find her bags already packed, the desk cleared, the whiteboard wiped clean, a lab full of grad students claiming they'd never heard the name Diana Marchese.

She burrowed into herself, into her work. Ignored letters and calls from her sister and her parents, or issued replies whose vagueness and brevity caused the recipients to wonder whether Diana had written a computer program to simulate human communication. She found a kind of groove, academically, and cleared her two-year research milestone in just fourteen months. When she stood in the doorway of her advisor's office, she noticed that he turned his chair all the way to face her, and took his hands off his own keyboard: most of the time, he did not fully acknowledge the presence of grad students. She was moved nearly to tears by his attention.

One day her apartment mailbox held a thick envelope with Allison's return address—Diana's own name and address in extravagant penmanship.

Inside the envelope she found an invitation to a party Allison was throwing for their father and his second wife, to celebrate their wedding anniversary. With the invitation, her sister had enclosed a gift certificate for ballroom dancing lessons.

"What the hell, Allie." *Don't you have a new baby to care for?* Diana wanted to say. She felt sure that if she ever had an infant at home, she wouldn't be planning fancy parties or hand-lettering the envelopes. Not that these were things she was likely to do *without* an infant, either.

"Ha! Mom was right, all it takes to get you to call me is an engraved invitation."

"Does Mom know about this, though? A party for Dad and *her*?"

Her sister sighed. "She knows about it, Diana. She's coming."

"She's *coming?*"

"I have been trying to tell you about this for months. Yes, she's coming. Also, she picked out the band. Which is why I sent the other thing."

Diana made a harrumphing sound she had learned from their mother.

"It's only a couple lessons. You can spare two hours so you look semi-graceful at the party."

"This is some DEFCON TWO control freak behavior, Allison."

"I can never remember, with DEFCON, is it the higher numbers that are more serious, or the lower ones?"

Diana had swallowed hard. "You remember *every-thing*," she hissed into the phone. "Don't try to bullshit me."

"Don't you think Dad would like to dance with his daughters, without incurring major injury?"

"This was not our father's idea," Diana had said evenly. "Not the dance lessons, not the party, not inviting Mom. This is all you, Allie."

"So do it for me, then."

Diana stalked across the Charles, furious with herself for giving in, getting progressively angrier until she arrived at the dance studio's Back Bay location. A woman with an elaborate updo sniffed at Diana's blue jeans and Chuck Taylor sneakers, and offered a loaner pair of heels. "Feels like upping the degree of difficulty," muttered Diana.

The woman demonstrated a quick foxtrot and then placed Diana's hands into those of a much older man.

The Place You're Supposed to Laugh

Both of them counted out loud as they marched each other around the room.

The woman reminded Diana to relax her arms.

Diana cursed her sister, again, for the passive-aggressive dance lessons, for forcing her into yet another situation where she questioned her own competence, and especially for this old-fashioned gendered bullshit: "In the ballroom, you react to *his* signals," instructed the updo. "Even if his feet or his hands are incorrect, even if his timing's off." She gently lifted the man's hand back into the right position. "Your job is to follow his lead."

Diana wobbled in her borrowed shoes. "Fuck this," she said, kicking them off.

The woman coached Diana's partner. "Remember, you lead with your torso, not your hands. You're not *pulling* or *pushing* her, you're showing her where you will go together." She clapped her hands. "Let's try things with a new partner. Gentlemen to the left, please."

Barefoot and seething, Diana found herself standing before a handsome man with a wicked gleam in his eye. "Lead, follow, I don't care," he said. "I have to dance with my brother's new mother-in-law next month, and I don't believe she plans to follow."

"She sounds like my kind of dame," Diana said.

"Do you want to put some shoes on?" he asked. "Just for your protection. This is only my second class."

She chucked the heels into the corner and retrieved her sneakers. "I'm Diana," she said.

"Arthur."

The music began, and they clasped hands.

She was his date for his brother's wedding, and he hers for the anniversary party. "I knew those lessons would pay off," Allison smirked, and Diana let her sister believe that she'd played matchmaker right up until Arthur slipped his number to the head cater waiter.

Arthur's friendship enabled her to relax, to stop monitoring her peripheral vision for the intellectual border patrol who would throw her out of MIT's Maclaurin buildings. She finally felt comfortable enough to join the lab's regular poker game.

In turn, they all moved west: first Arthur—a devastating departure halfway through her PhD—then Allison and her family, then Diana herself. The Bay Area and its hot real estate market pulled Arthur with an almost gravitational force. Allison's husband's assignment to help launch the West Coast office of a New York ad firm had first sounded like exile, then turned out to be lucrative when kids dropped out of college to build corporate kingdoms out of thin air. Suddenly even a schmuck like Ray Loudermilk was spinning straw into gold.

Though the buzz had worn off, and Arthur's properties spent longer on the market these days, this magic was still floating on the air. Diana couldn't help but admire the market baskets of organic apricots. Golden and dappled with red as if they were blushing in the Silicon Valley sun.

She bought four of the perfect specimens, placing them in her bag with care so they wouldn't bruise. Arthur had paused at a pickle stand, eyeing the variety of items the bearded vendor had brined in his artisanal vinegars. Diana squeezed his hand in a kind of apology for herself. She had never become comfortable with following; she was grateful that Arthur was a patient partner.

Together, they caught up with Molly and Tommy, who were deeply absorbed in Molly's best-loved feature of the market: the beekeeper's glassed-in honeycomb slab, where you could watch industrious bees tucking in and out of cells. Diana saw that Molly had already persuaded Tommy to buy her yet another small jar of the bees' viscous nectar, which she clutched as she stared, entranced, at the honeycomb.

The small bear-shaped jars of honey were adorable, if expensive. Overall, the farmers market prices recalled the corner store near campus, back when Diana was an undergrad: as the only independent source of food within walking distance, the store overcharged with impunity. Its larcenous prices were, somehow, part of what she loved about her campus: its separateness from the real world. She only recognized the bubble she was living in when she and Arthur happened to be watching a game show in which contestants guessed the prices of common items, and Diana shouted, "Four dollars!" for something the prizewinner priced at seventy-nine cents.

Standing before the honeycomb, Molly's hand was in Tommy's. Her own protective bubble was actively maintained and insulated by her three parents. Perhaps this was true for most children. Except when something awful punctured the bubble—making everything you loved suddenly more dear.

Diana leaned into Arthur.

"So what can I bring, for Christmas?" she asked.

He looked bemused, no doubt remembering all her culinary disasters to which he had borne witness. "Bring wine, if you must."

"I was wondering," she said, "could I bring Allison and Chad?"

For once, she had surprised him. "Of course."

Comfort and Joy

The soup was different. Chad's uncle Arthur had made it—it was butternut squash, with a dollop of cream floating on the golden surface, and it was delicious, but it was different.

Chad and his mom had brought a pie and an armload of gifts—mostly books and music from the store at the mall, and the Pessoa book for Chad himself. He made a point of carrying his full basket by the security guard on his way to the cashier. *I'm This Guy,* he wanted the guard to know. *I'm not the guy you thought I was. I'm the guy who pays for stuff. With his mother's credit card, sure, but still.*

Arthur and Tommy's place was an industrial loft in South San Francisco, with a large window that opened like a garage door at one end of the living room, and exposed pipes on the ceiling.

Aunt Diana had brought flowers and two bottles

of wine, but no food. "I play to my strengths," she said, laughing.

As soon as she saw him, Molly grabbed Chad's hand to show him her "other room," not the one at Aunt Diana's. She named all of her stuffed animals, pointed out her Dora nightlight, and asked, "Do you have two bedrooms, too?" Chad said he didn't, and she looked at him with sorrow.

At dinner she begged for the seat next to his. She had a great deal she wanted to tell him, all of it urgent. "Sorry," Tommy whispered in Chad's ear, as he rearranged the crumb-catching mat under her highchair. "She's like Spalding Gray in toddler form."

"It's okay," Chad whispered back, and it was. It was noisy and the soup was different, and he felt bad that his dad wasn't here, but it was okay.

Chad resolved not to listen to the voice in his head that sounded like Marcus, running commentary: butternut squash soup, two dudes in a loft, Spalding Fucking Gray; could this Christmas be any damn whiter?

Still: Molly's two dads were two more than Marcus could count on. Chad had made this point when Marcus started up, shutting him down, and he had seen something like admiration in Marcus's eyes; it was powerful enough to make Chad swallow the apology he'd been about to blurt for saying it in the first place. Approval from Marcus was like that.

On the other hand.

While Chad had proven a piss-poor thief, Andre saw his opportunity to fully eclipse him in Marcus's eyes, and he'd carped the diem at the Macy's jewelry counter.

This was strike two, which meant probation. Juvenile detention was on the line if Andre so much as looked funny at someone in uniform. At this point, it was hard to imagine Andre making it through three more years of high school without getting himself incarcerated.

Meanwhile at Paly, the juniors who ran a decent speed and cocaine business had just been written up in the *Palo Alto Weekly* as all-star scholar-athletes. A certain indifference to authority came off in the article as charmingly roguish. They were the type of guys who would always be given the benefit of the doubt.

His mom began to clear the table and package up the leftovers, but Aunt Diana refilled his mom's wineglass and walked her onto the terrace. "Be selfish for twenty minutes, Allie," she said. "I'll do the dishes." On her way to the sink, she tossed a towel to Chad. "You dry."

When he was younger, he'd been a little frightened of his Aunt Diana. There was something imposing about her, something always slightly out of reach. *Chilly* was the nicest word his parents had used, when Diana declined yet another invitation. But he realized now that she reminded him of Grandma—the flint in her, the refusal to soften to make other people more comfortable. He was glad to have a job to do, standing next to his aunt in the sleek, small kitchen.

"You guys have nice traditions," Chad said, and his aunt gave him a puzzled look. He explained, "You and Arthur and Tommy, what you guys do for Christmas."

"This is the first time I've had Christmas dinner in years," Aunt Diana said, and it was Chad's turn to look confused. "I'm usually at lab. It's perfect on a holiday.

No one else is there and I can concentrate."

"Uh-huh," he said slowly, thinking maybe his mom was right about Diana preferring equations to people. *Or anyway people she's related to*, his mom would add.

"My mother would be horrified that we didn't have a ham," she said without looking up from the sink full of soapy water. "I mean, *radicchio*. Christ."

"God bless," Chad said in Grandma Marchese's voice.

Diana smiled at him.

"I miss her," he said.

"Me too."

She scrubbed at a stubborn patch on a serving bowl. "I'm glad you and Allie were with her at the end. I would've just gotten in the way."

Chad felt his brow wrinkle. "Maybe not," he said.

"My mother didn't make it easy to love her."

"No."

Diana handed the bowl to him, a cluster of suds still clinging to the rim. "If you make it too easy, how can you know the people in your life really want to be there?"

This sounded uncannily like something Grandma M. would've said. Chad blinked his stinging eyes hard and fast.

"How's your mom doing?"

"You can ask *her*," he said, wiping a handful of forks dry.

She sighed. "I can, and she'll say she's fine, she's just worried about you, and then she'll make me a pie or something just to show me how fine she is."

Chad grinned. On the counter behind them sat the pie his mom had made for their dessert—its lattice top perfectly golden.

"So how is she." Her voice did not make this a question.

"She's okay." He told her about the weird vibe in his house, painfully quiet as if the way to avoid fighting was to avoid making any sound at all; and how his parents kept out of each other's way, so they were together but rarely in the same space. He told her this seemed kind of like water in a river, around rocks.

His aunt Diana lit up. "That's beautiful, Chad. Like water and a rock. And there's eddies behind the rock, and that makes it take longer for the streams of water to reconnect."

He swallowed hard. "But they *do* reconnect."

"Well, in laminar flow, sure they do. But turbulence is tricky, and random."

"That seems more realistic."

She was smiling, almost proudly. "Bingo. More realistic, but intractably complex. You can't predict or model it without statistics or a lot of simplifications." She swung him a half-rinsed platter to dry.

"Are we still talking about my mom?"

She flicked a handful of suds at him.

From the loft's thoughtfully placed speakers came a sudden flare of music as a new CD began: an urgent blast from a horn section. He heard Tommy and Arthur rushing to turn it down, so that Molly could rest.

"I believe," Diana said, "that moving out of our house was the best thing that ever happened to my mother."

He stared at her, rubbing uselessly at a knife that was already dry. She thought his mom should move out, get an apartment and some gay best friends just like Diana? Spend the holidays alone at work?

"It *is* hard to imagine her making pies for Grandpa," Chad said with a hitch in his voice.

"She was a really good cook, though," his aunt said. "Not romantic about it, but *if you can read, you can cook*," she used to say." She shook her head fondly.

Tommy asked if anyone wanted coffee, and made some anyway when everyone protested they couldn't possibly. Before long all the adults were sipping from warm mugs.

Dessert, too, had seemed impossible, but then it became necessary. Molly emerged, hair tousled with sleep but bright-eyed and surprisingly hungry. The pie his mom had made was delicious.

Molly loved everything except Tommy's rice pudding; this, she pronounced Weird and Lumpy and Not My Favorite. This judgment echoed his Grandma Marchese's reviews of the food at Hotel Carcinoma, making Chad grin madly at his cousin. He looked forward to these hints of his Grandma in Molly as she grew.

He and his Mom had gone out for a tree, strung it with lights, and put out decorations, so that the house looked the way it always did. Leveling the tree was an annual struggle for his dad, and his mom usually turned up the Mormon Tabernacle carols to drown out Ray's mumbled swearing. This year was different, though: his mom paid extra to have the guys at the lot saw off the trunk and entrap the tree in a cheap plastic stand.

"I could've done that," his dad said when he got home. He was visibly struggling to mask his surprise that Chad's mom had spent money on something intended to be thrown away. Probably she would end up re-using the plastic stand, taking it back to the tree lot next winter and asking the guys to put it on next year's tree.

But she told his Dad, "Maybe next year."

This hope was like the sparkly strands of tinsel Chad used to fling upon the branches: lovely and fragile and, possibly, ephemeral. Like the tinsel, it might be limited to the holiday season; then again, Chad remembered that tinsel filaments had shown up around the house well into April, turning up under couch cushions and wrapping themselves around the vacuum cleaner's brush. Hope could linger like that, in forgotten corners. So there was that.

Like Cancer or California

Something remarkable had happened to Allison. Diana listened to her news: one afternoon she'd driven to downtown San Jose and gotten herself hired at the Women's Free Clinic. The clinic director had grasped Allison's hands and said, *Bless you,* when Allison provided her credentials and wondered whether she could be of use.

They were sitting outdoors, in palm-filtered February sunlight. They sipped drinks from the student union coffee shop. Stanford students had returned for the winter quarter; just last week she and Allison had been the only people on the patio. But today, they'd waited in a long line for their drinks, and had to wait for a group of students to vacate a table.

Diana squinted into the sun as Allison described her new routine: a shift at the clinic; meetings with her Palo Alto at-risk clients; sometimes an outing with

Chad. And all at once it had been a week, and then it had been two.

The woman across from her was a whole new Allison, Diana thought. She was breezy and she was hitting every third word hard, as if it were in bold letters or italics. The new job had made this happen. It was probably easier to live with Ray if she wasn't around much, Diana figured. She remembered Chad's line about water flowing around rocks.

"Good for you," she told her sister.

"The moral of the story isn't Woman Gets Job, Is Better. No longer *just a wife and mother*, now with a career to provide true fulfillment."

"That's not what I meant," Diana said.

"It pays the rent," Allison said firmly.

Always the pushing and pulling, everything subject to interpretation, weighted with baggage accumulated over a lifetime of sisterhood. The ways their parents had distinguished them, the different paths by which they'd pursued career and motherhood: the filter of history distorting good intentions into insults. Nothing was just what it was; it was everything that had come before.

"I'm sorry," she said, so Allie would continue.

The San Jose Free Clinic was dealing with a whole different kind of at-risk, Allison said, than her Palo Alto referrals. She felt *needed* now; she was absolutely *vital*. "It's mostly heartbreaking," she told Diana over her coffee. "These girls come in, and they're so...*clueless*. Their boyfriends refuse to wear condoms, and so I'm talking to thirteen-year-olds with STDs. I ask how many partners they've had in the last six months, I used to say year but forget it; they say twenty-five, maybe thirty. So I give them the prescriptions and a pamphlet, and I know they'll be back next week.

"The absolute worst are the ones with *boyfriends*. You ask if maybe they want to be tested, you know, as long as you're doing the Pap, might as well check for gonorrhea, chlamydia, whatnot. And these girls give you their most self-righteous little faces and they say, 'I trust my boyfriend.'

"We go through the whole 'Boys don't have symptoms, he might not even know he has it,' because we're giving the boys the benefit of the doubt, that's clinic policy. You can't just say, 'Boys are sociopaths,' and 'I love you' is so fucking easy to say, Jesus."

Diana nodded: it *was* easy to say. She stirred her coffee, watching the paired-off student couples around her with new wariness.

Allison gulped her tea and continued. "This girl today, maybe fifteen, she takes her prescription slip, and says, 'The real problem is, I can't have an orgasm.' What can you say to that girl? I want to say, Hey, maybe start with one partner. Maybe get to know a man and take some time together. But she won't hear any of that. And if I give her a lecture, I'm going to sound like her mother and she'll never come back. So I say, 'Have you tried different positions, lubrication, oral sex?'"

This was the longest speech Allison had made recently, possibly ever. Diana wasn't sure whether she was more shocked at (a) its volume; (b) its vulgarity, or (c) the casualness with which the vulgarity fell from Allison's mouth. She could think of nothing to say but, "Wow."

Nearby, a skateboarder attempted to leap over a curb, and miscalculated. His board clattered to the ground. A spring, the boy was quickly upright and on the board, ready to try again.

Allison went on. "The girls shave all their hair off, you know, because the boys want everything to look like *Playboy*. So yesterday the no-orgasm girl who trusts her boyfriend comes in with these horrible boils. She's crying and I want to say, Listen, there's a reason you've got hair down there. It's a *filter*, okay?" Allison repeated, stage-whispering *filter* the way their mother used to whisper *cancer* or *California*. "Like hair in your nose, cilia in your throat, you know, it keeps you *clean*."

"Wow," said Diana again.

"I know," said Allison. "I mean, God. The *power* they hand to these boys. Boys don't like pubic hair, okay, boys don't like condoms, okay, these are the conditions. And these girls just fuck up their lives. They don't know they're allowed to find the conditions unacceptable, that they don't have to take this shitty deal."

Diana cleared her throat. "You're right," she said. "That is heartbreaking."

"That's fifteen," her sister said.

"They're lucky to have you," Diana said, meaning it. Realizing she'd skipped lunch, Diana wondered whether she should brave the coffee line again. "You want to split something?"

Allison shook her head, already describing the clinic where she'd found this frank, candid voice. The exam rooms were small, with a décor that was bland and institutional except for a six-inch wallpaper border at the ceiling, brightly colored hearts and Gerbera daisies. Whoever had pasted it up had wanted those six inches of cheer to transcend the water-stained acoustic tiles, the cracked walls, the stirrups covered with fabric booties printed with the Ortho Tricyclin logo.

"It's a lot to ask of a border," Diana said.

Allison said she found the clinic décor weirdly reminiscent of the chemo ward and the wing of the hospital where their mother had spent her last months. Hotel Carcinoma, and her Metastasis Suite. The room service, she said, was horrid. "I had to bring in takeout, and we ate watching the news," Allison said. The TV, she said, was good distraction from their mother's chemo regimen: Taxol, Capecitabine, tamoxifen, each IV bag hung in turn by an earnest nurse in scrubs printed with sunflowers or cartoon characters. The fabric prints as overmatched as the wallpaper border in San Jose. As overmatched as the chemo itself had been.

Diana no longer felt hungry. She had visited Hotel Carcinoma only once, and briefly. She was still nursing Molly, and the hospital discouraged visitors under six from entering her mother's wing. Also she had classes to teach. Those had seemed, a year ago, like valid reasons.

Near the building entrance, a Stanford *a capella* group began to perform. They wore coordinated shirts and jeans, arms swinging to the beat. As they sang, a small crowd gathered around them.

"She had pictures of you both up, in her hospital room. She talked about Molly to all of the nurses. 'Look at my beautiful granddaughter,' she'd say." Allison crushed her empty cup.

I get it, Diana thought. *I should've been there. I'm a selfish jerk. You've made your point, Allison.*

But instead of twisting the knife further, Allison returned to the Free Clinic: "We're understaffed, underfunded, overworked, overwhelmed. We could use a few coats of fresh paint. But the women—the *girls*—who come in, they need us, and we try our best to do right by them. They think what they need is the pill, a mammogram, an abortion. But mostly what they need is to talk, and to have someone listen."

On the mesh table, her sister's cell phone plinked out its mechanical melody. "Sorry," Allison said, picking it up. Her eyes widened; Diana could pick up only the frantic terror in the caller's voice. Into the receiver Allison said, "Oh God. Oh, no. I'll be right there."

Listen Up Close While I Take You Backwards

A TV in the corner of the ER waiting room was tuned to a cooking channel, a nonstop parade of smiling white people tossing bowls of chopped onions and herbs into pans. Chad thought the TV made the room's smells of burnt coffee and Lysol even stronger, somehow, because they didn't match up with the images of sautéing chicken breasts or kernels of risotto becoming translucent. A speaker crackled with each call for a doctor to report to an unseen station. Odd niche magazines with outdated news were stacked on side tables. A zone out of time, with mismatched sensory input: hospitals were thoroughly disorienting. Chad had been here before.

He wondered who chopped all those onions—surely not the charismatic, nonthreateningly attractive hosts of the cooking shows. Some intern whose job was to mince garlic, tear cilantro leaves from the stem, measure out tablespoons of olive oil and pinches of salt into telegenic glass bowls.

He flipped idly through a magazine whose cover celebrated a celebrity couple who'd found love filming a movie that came out a year ago; Chad knew that one half of the erstwhile pairing had since been admitted to rehab, and the other half had eloped with the rock guitarist whose concert she'd attended in hopes of comforting herself after the breakup. Chad hated that he knew this. His cultivated high school invisibility granted him such unwanted knowledge; he overheard all kinds of things. Along with the movie stars, he knew about Paly celebrities. He knew about the girls' lacrosse team captain's romance with a Stanford student. He knew the art teacher was cheating on her husband with the vice-principal. He knew that the members of the water polo team who'd been selling speed and coke had added Oxycontin to their wares. He knew they had a system where kids who wanted these things could send a coded text message to one of the dealers. He knew the school's attempt at a crackdown wasn't having much effect. A shed behind the gym where the burnouts used to smoke was now called "The CASA," and served as the headquarters for a new club, the Committee Against Substance Abuse. Either the administration was completely clueless, or they were being ironic; you couldn't be quite sure. That was high school for you.

The TV chef of the hour announced her intended menu, and Chad's stomach growled. He got Mrs. Chen's call just after school, and he'd been sitting outside the ER ever since. There were no windows in the waiting room, but he'd counted the time in TV meals, and knew six hours had passed.

His mom smiled at the sound of his stomach. "Want to find the cafeteria?" she asked. "I wouldn't mind a change of scenery."

Chad shook his head. He wasn't sure he'd be able to swallow.

He'd heard about Walter's accident without knowing it was Walter, hours before Mrs. Chen's call. The train whistle at noon sounded different than usual, not the four blasts but a single, harsher sound—a higher pitch.

At Paly, he overheard clusters in the quad saying someone had been on the tracks. Not on accident, they said.

I heard it was a kid.

A little kid?

Dude.

I heard he didn't jump, he was just sitting there, like meditating.

Like bring it on, *Mortal Kombat* style. His classmate made the universal gesture of tough readiness for battle, one hand beckoning: *let's go.*

Well, like, he wasn't going to win a faceoff with the Caltrain. That would be hella dumb.

Hey….have you seen Ronald Lee today?

A hush, as the possible fate of Ron Lee was considered by the group.

Yeah, I just passed him in the hallway, man.

Chad heard his classmates take stock of the Last Known Sighting of their peers, a morbid roll call.

Not for the first time, he wondered whether they would notice if he himself were missing.

In the hospital, there were more conversations he

wished he couldn't hear. The whispers of desperate reassurance among those waiting to be seen in the ER: *Everything's going to be fine; Just a little longer; You'll see, it'll be all right.* Recounted tales of how they'd got here, muttered into cell phones: *Fell off a ladder, Heard a weird crack in my knee.* Repeated with each call or new arrival. The nurse responsible for triage sent the direst cases straight back, so Chad only had to hear those stories once.

He shifted in the vinyl-upholstered chair.

Chad thought of Walter, that day in the record store; Walter, being hustled from Bellarmine Academy to tennis practice. Walter, shooting video game zombies. Walter, saying to Chad: *whatever.*

Walter on the train tracks, waiting.

Years ago, they'd invented a game they played in Chad's backyard, a kind of obstacle course that required them to walk the fence like a tightrope, leap from tree limbs, and casually endanger themselves in a variety of ways. They were adventure boys, invincible. Skinned knees were their medals of honor. Together, they would vanquish pirates and other evildoers, belay each other as they climbed into the treetops, and reward themselves with a bike race to the grassy bowl of the Sunks.

Chad closed his eyes, remembering.

He heard the TV cook say, "If you don't have lemons, a lime will do in a pinch."

The doctor who came out to tell them sagged against the wall. The triage nurse beckoned Chad and his mom toward a quieter corner of the room. "I'm Dr.

Huang," he said. Numbly, Chad shook his outstretched hand. "I'm sorry. We've done everything we could."

The Chens were there, then, with blank eyes and curved spines, and Chad and his mom hugged them both. The four of them walked out to the parking lot together, but there was nothing to say.

The funeral was at the church where Chad and Walter had graduated from Sunday School to youth group to confirmed young congregants. The minister had known them since the days of backyard adventure. Just last fall, he had presided over their confirmation ceremony.

It was the worst thing that could happen, the thing your parents had been holding their breath against since they first cradled your delicate neck in their palms. Since they first dared to dream they might one day have a child to hold.

It was the kind of pivotal tragedy that everyone in your high school would remember as a landmark, making them conscious of their own mortality. For some, it would be the thing that made them more reckless, because they would see what being careful got you.

Mrs. Chen had always been brittle, but she held herself now as if anything might break her—as if she had no more capacity to bend, but could only shatter. She accepted condolences with a nod, winced when people touched her arm. Her husband shook hands, repeating *Thank you for coming* in a robotic voice. Walter's sister huddled with an aunt or older cousin.

In the narthex, on the poster of a thermometer monitoring the church's fundraising drive, the magic

marker mercury had risen several degrees since confirmation. There was a large box collecting donations
for kids in group homes and foster care. This was the
shadow life Chad could've had: opening presents from
strangers; wearing t-shirts other people got tired of.
This is the meal equally set. But for what the Loudermilks
had given him.

Salvation.

At their confirmation service, the minister had told
Chad and Walter: "You are now part of this community, a full member in our congregation. You have made
a mature statement of faith, and sealed the covenant
created in your baptism. You are all, now, united more
firmly to Christ."

Chad had watched his mom nodding, her eyes
maybe glistening a little. She craned again, looking for
his dad.

To the congregation, the minister had said: "The
grace bestowed to these young people in their baptism,
long before they could appreciate the teachings of
Christ and their own faith, is now complete."

At that, his mom definitely dabbed her eye with a
tissue.

"But the word *foundational* means we expect you to
keep building on that, and we are prepared to help."

This was the moment that, at Marcus's church, the
congregation would have signaled their willingness to
help with a warm "Mmmm, yes," or a solemn "Yes, we
are." But at Chad's own church, the minister did not
receive a response, except for the flapping thunk of
someone's program falling to the ground.

This had only been four months ago.

Today, the minister read Bible verses and described

Walter's broad outlines—diligent, responsible, academic promise—without mentioning his mischief, his eye-rolling, the way he wore cargo shorts and Tevas under his choir robe. Chad struggled to focus on the minister's words.

The choir sang, and the organ played, and Mrs. Chen's head remained unbowed. Chad's parents sat on either side of him, which made him feel nothing so much as trapped, forced to listen to all six verses of "Abide with Me."

What had Walter been thinking, cross-legged on the tracks as the train bore down? It was cruelly unknowable. What might he have hoped he could change before he'd decided the only possible option was to stare down the southbound engine? What might Chad have been able to do?

The church altar was filled with flowers: a platoon of wreaths on easels, cascading ribbons with hanzi; and a few tall arrangements with florist's cards impaled among the lilies. One of these was from Chad's family; his mother had tensed when she saw how it stood out from the Chinese wreaths. Later, driving to the funeral banquet, his dad reassured her that the Chens would appreciate the flowers regardless.

Chad's grandma hadn't wanted a funeral. "Pour the ashes into the ocean," she said, dusting her hands. "No muss, no fuss." Chad's mom, though, organized a service at a place near Grandma's apartment: not a big Catholic to-do, but *something*, with a lunch reservation afterward. Chad's mom being Chad's mom, probably she'd been hoping to rebind them in some way, with shared stories of Grandma Marchese and a nice eggplant parm.

But Chad's grandfather and his wife had theater tickets in New York, so after some brief recollections, they were off. Aunt Diana made a string of excuses for not staying longer herself, finally saying, "Mom didn't even want this, Allie."

The lunch reservation was trimmed from the private room his mom had booked to a table for four, where Chad and his parents ate with a woman who'd once worked with Grandma Marchese. She remembered Chad's grandma as a "pip" and a "beauty," and wished they'd stayed in better touch. Chad watched his mom listen to the woman's stories and resolve that it was for this woman that she'd insisted on having a service. "Tell me more," she said, again and again.

For Walter's funeral banquet, the dim sum restaurant was packed, pervaded by the salty aroma of pork. Red paper lanterns hung from all the light fixtures. Tables laid out with towers of steamer baskets, troughs of rice, a lagoon of vegetables labeled Buddha's Delight, and carving stations for roast pig and duck. Chad didn't think he could eat, but soon found himself holding a plate piled with shumai.

With the food and the lanterns, it might've been a wedding banquet, except for the fact that everyone was wearing dark clothes and somber expressions. Like the least joyful, lowest-energy wedding ever. Also, there was no cake in evidence.

He shook hands with Walter's grandparents, and an assortment of cousins who remembered Chad from various events. "It's been a while," they said, and he felt this stab him sharply: he had allowed Walter to drift, had accepted the distance between them. Had let tennis and blue blazers keep him away. There was no bravery in him. He set down the plate of dumplings, untouched.

A Chen uncle presented him with a small glass of plum wine. The uncle's face was already flushed red with alcohol, though Chad knew from his and Walter's experiments that this didn't necessarily mean the uncle had drunk a great quantity of wine. It had taken only half a beer for Walter to blush brighter than a sunburn. "It's not fair," he'd told Chad. "Look at you, your face will never give you away."

Remembering this now, Chad let out an involuntary chuckle, and the uncle who'd given him the wine nodded approval. He raised his glass toward the man and took a large gulp.

His parents were seated at a table with other families from church, parents of kids who'd been in elementary school and junior high with Walter. None of the kids themselves seemed to be at the banquet, but the parents had come to pay their respects. Possibly they too were a little bit frightened of Mrs. Chen.

His father had his arm around his mother, and she wasn't shrugging it away like she usually did. Chad didn't know whether this was real affection for his dad or an unwillingness to make a scene, to have her refusal of his comforting arm become a topic of someone else's conversation.

Chad took another glass of wine off a passing tray, placing his empty glass smoothly in its place. It was a slick, movie-star move, and he glanced briefly around to see whether anyone had noticed. He met the eyes of a girl in a cluster of cousins, and gave her a confident nod. She offered a cautious smile back.

O Lord, thank you for the courage in a glass of plum wine.

Walter's dad used a microphone to thank everyone for coming. Mrs. Chen stood beside him, solid and unsmiling as ever. Walter's little sister gripped her mother's hand. Six years old. Chad wondered what she would remember of Walter. Or whether she would feel a difference in her parents, before and after. How would she tell herself the story of her family?

Another man was talking now, an uncle or great-uncle, perhaps. He was recalling for the room a ceremony from Walter's first birthday, when he'd reached for a celery stalk rather than a pen or a yen note. The way they had all swelled with pride at this portent of his future industriousness. And then year-old Walter had dropped the celery to toddle over to his mother and embrace her. "Love," said the man. "Even as a baby, Jiahao chose love."

Who the hell was this dude even talking about? Walter chose to be known to the world as Walter, not as Jiahao. Walter chose love? Walter chose adventure. Video games over *David Copperfield*. Salty over sweet. Pretty much anything over a stringy stalk of celery.

"Hi," said a South Asian boy who'd sidled up next to him. "Are you Chad?"

Chad allowed that he was.

"I'm Sri," the boy said. He seemed to assume that his name would be familiar, and it pleased Chad that Walter hadn't mentioned Sri to him, but had obviously told Sri about Chad. *I know who I am*, Chad thought firmly. Walter and I were Frodo and Samwise.

"You go to Bellarmine?" Chad guessed.

Sri nodded.

"You like it?"

"It's all right," Sri said. "It's school."

"I hear you."

"Walter talked about Paly a lot. He missed it, I think."

Chad said, "He only went there a few weeks before his parents pulled him out."

"I think he missed public school in general. You know, having teachers who aren't priests, picking your own clothes, *girls*."

"What even was that? 'He chose love,' that guy said. Never even went on a date." This, to Chad, was maybe the saddest of all—for Walter to have died without falling in love, without kissing a girl, without—"Actually he was kind of seeing this girl from Notre Dame."

"What? No."

Sri gave a nod. "Yeah, we had this mixer right after he started at Bellarmine, and the two of them hit it off."

"Mixer?" Chad was uncomprehending. He looked around for his plate of dumplings. Which table had he left it on?

"Like a dance, but no one dances. There's music and punch and lots of standing around awkwardly."

"Sounds like a funeral banquet."

Sri shook his head, pointing to the silent ceiling speakers. "No music."

"*That* would be a playlist," Chad said. "Songs for an untimely death."

"Walter said you guys liked Neutral Milk Hotel," he said.

He allowed that this was true.

"I fucking love them. And Apples in Stereo."

"Right on." Chad was warming up to Sri despite himself. "Hey, so is the girl here? From the mixer?"

"No," Sri said. "I don't know if she knows."

"Jesus," Chad said.

"It's like a gift, though," Sri said. "Now she can be forever haunted by the tragic loss of her first love. It's like permission not to commit."

"That's an interesting take, Sri."

The boy shrugged. Suddenly, he stood up straight and gave his half-drunk wineglass to Chad. "Hello, Father Bob," he said to a silver-haired white man.

"Good afternoon, Srikumar," the man said. "I'm sorry for your loss."

"This is Chad," Sri said, forcing Chad to juggle both wineglasses to shake hands with the priest/teacher.

It was all maddening: that Sri existed, that Sri was funny and a little bit wicked, that Sri had good taste in music, that Sri knew about the mysterious girl from Notre Dame, whose name Chad had never heard. He felt heat rising in him.

Across the room, Mrs. Chen accepted the kindness and sympathy of a line of people. He decided that she had always wished to be a martyr, and had now achieved this. Fuck her, Chad thought. She pulled Walter away from me. Maybe if he'd stayed at Paly—

He was utterly furious with Mrs. Chen.

Probably this was not how you were supposed to feel toward the mother of a dead teenager.

Unable to locate his abandoned plate of shumai, Chad returned to the banquet table. He popped a wonton into his mouth while he waited for a grandmotherly Chinese woman to finish her selection. She gave him a smile before taking the last soup dumpling.

Chad swallowed hard and tried to keep from hating this grandma.

As she shuffled away, he saw his dad filling a Styrofoam clamshell to-go container with noodles and veggies. "Jesus, Dad," he said. "Really?"

His dad blushed. "The Chens were adamant," he said. "I didn't want to argue."

Bullshit. This was all complete bullshit. Chad glared at the empty steamer basket, and stalked away.

He'd meant to return to a table and eat, maybe find another glass of that plum wine, but once he started walking Chad didn't want to stop. He continued out of the private room, downstairs and into the restaurant's waiting area, past the lobster tank, and onto the sidewalk.

It was seventy-five and sunny.

Of course it fucking was.

"Hi," said the girl from the cousin cluster. The one who'd seen his move with the wineglass. She smiled without showing her teeth.

"Hi," Chad said.

"You okay?"

He shrugged.

"You were his best friend, huh?"

He coughed to clear something caught in his throat.

"I needed some fresh air myself," she said. She tucked a long strand of silky black hair behind one ear. She wore tiny gold earrings in the shape of birds. "Maybe it'll help?"

He shrugged again.

"It's kind of crazy in there," she said.

He didn't want her to be reasonable, didn't want to calm down, didn't want to feel any way but awful, yet he felt his pulse slowing as they moved toward each other.

And then they were kissing, there on the sidewalk in front of a sign saying CART SERVICE SAT/SUN 9-2. They were kissing and Chad wasn't thinking about anything besides her lips and her tongue and the mingling tastes of the food they had eaten to honor the memory of Walter Chen.

Fast Falls The Eventide

The teachers, even Mr. Farris, gave them the week off from homework. Due to *recent tragic events*—this was the euphemistic phrase Paly used to cancel a Shooter Drill, suspend assignments, and apologetically hope that seniors might still be able to enjoy their field trip to Great America. Whatever the phrase was intended to do, it most effectively conjured the month after 9/11, when the nation's funereal mood had pervaded every interaction. And of course, there was a special assembly. From the gymnasium floor the principal, flanked by the guidance counselors, assured them that it was completely normal to feel anxious and uncertain, but they should not put undue pressure on themselves.

The last time Chad had seen the guidance counselors was at 9th grade orientation, when he was sitting next to Walter as the same two women told them it was never too early to start their college selection process. They listed strategies for burnishing the application, advised summer "externships" when possible, and then said, "don't forget to enjoy yourself!" The kids in front of them, taking notes, added the bullet item "Enjoy yourself!" after "Service/learning" and "SAT prep classes." Walter and Chad rolled their eyes at each other.

Not that Chad was surprised by adult hypocrisy, anymore.

The hallway outside the high school office was lined with color photographs of each year's graduating class, all wearing sweatshirts from their chosen universities. Chad and Walter had noted the way there was always a guy in the back row positioned so the person in front of him obscured a shirt that said "Cal State." All those Stanfords and Yales and Browns and Berkeleys weren't supposed to "pressure" them, they were assured by the counselors, only to "inspire." Walter had tapped one of the photos and said that the Cal State dude looked the happiest of all of them.

Now, at the assembly, they were told of the danger of copycat "contagion," as if whatever led Walter to go meditate on the Caltrain tracks might be transmitted the way mono had spread through the cast of the fall musical.

Chad felt that this diminished Walter, who, damn him for it, had done something brave and unexpected. His act should stand alone.

But from the stage, the other counselor reminded them that two juniors had died the same way last year. She said this broke her heart: so much lost potential. As she spouted clichés—flowers plucked before blooming, the unknowable heights to which they might've soared—Chad wondered whether Walter had known about this precedent, and whether he himself had been a copycat.

The principal announced a grief support group to meet at lunchtime, that they should look for the purple table tent in the cafeteria.

Chad dug his fingernails into his palm, and made a mental note to avoid that tent.

The chorus held their dopey battery-powered candles and sang in a minor key. "Though he was with us here only briefly," said the principal, Palo Alto High School mourned the loss of Wilber Chen.

Fuck this, Chad thought, and walked out.

He didn't know where he was going, but he knew he couldn't stay there. He picked up speed as he crossed the quad, glancing at the bell tower and wondering how much longer the assembly would drag on.

Leaving campus was easier than expected. He simply kept walking; no one stopped him at the edge of school property; no alarms sounded.

The train whistled, approaching the downtown station. Four blasts. Chad put in his headphones, and turned up Jay-Z. He kept walking until he found himself in the record store, clapping angrily through racks of CDs.

Music and poetry were useless, he knew, but no more useless than anything else.

The clacking sound pleased him: it sounded like rage, like something that could break apart. It was the best he had felt since he'd found out about Walter, except for the few minutes he'd spent with the girl with bird-shaped earrings. Kissing her, he had almost forgotten to be angry.

He left the record store to find a snack. He didn't have enough money for CDs—his mom had cut off his allowance after what had happened at the mall bookstore, and when the weeks of punishment were up, his dad had not reinstated it. "We could all do with a little belt-tightening," he'd said. He sounded like a fifties sitcom but Chad hadn't called him on it because what would be the point?

"Just ask us, when you need something," his mom said, and this was the worst: the united front they'd been putting up. He missed the old way his mom would second-guess his dad sometimes, the way they would tease each other. This new routine felt false and insulting.

At the bagel store around the corner, Chad counted the change in his pocket before ordering. "Anything to drink with that?" the cashier asked.

"Just a cup for water," Chad said.

He took a free Palo Alto Express and sat down at one of the tables outside. The cashier brought out his bagel in a tiny plastic basket lined with wax paper. To a man at another table, the cashier said, "Just bring the forms back whenever you're ready."

The man at the other table was Chad's father.

"Hey, Dad," Chad said, as if he weren't surprised to find his father filling out paperwork at the Palo Alto bagel/smoothie shop instead of being in San Francisco at his advertising firm. As if Chad himself weren't supposed to be in bio lab right now. Fuck it, what were they going to do, take away the allowance they weren't giving him?

His dad looked up. "Hi, Chad," he said, as if none of this surprised him either.

"They had an assembly about Walter," Chad said. "I kind of couldn't deal with it."

His dad nodded. There were two metal tables between them, but neither of them stood up to move.

"I felt like I might punch somebody."

"I can understand that," his dad said, smirking. "But violence isn't the answer," he added. "It doesn't really solve the underlying problem."

"You sound like *Mom*," Chad said.

Three tables away, his dad shrugged lightly. "Better to address the real reasons for your anger. That's a healthier option. That's why your mom made that appointment for you with the therapist, this weekend."

"She brainwashed you good, huh?"

This should've been a punchline, the two of them snickering at his mom's save-the-world tendencies. But his dad smiled like a cult member awaiting the rapture.

Jesus. His mom had coached yet another at-risk member of society back to the light. The guy who'd taken a baseball bat to a car a few months ago now preached, violence isn't the answer. Chad saw that his dad was maybe her biggest, and longest-term, project of all.

"If you need a personal day," his dad said, "we'd understand."

This did sound like a script his mom had written: Consoling a Teenager in Mourning, a short play in three acts. Chad knew most of the lines from the way she'd talked to him about Grandma Marchese—at least when she was able to talk about it. He couldn't remember his dad ever using the phrase "personal day" before, ever.

He didn't want to be at school, but neither did he want to be at home with his thoughts and what-ifs. What if he hadn't let Mrs. Chen chase him away that day? What warning signs had Chad missed, in his focus on his own family drama? What was the point of keeping clean, of being good, if the train was going to get you anyway?

His parents' new attention made this more acute: how wrong they all were to think *Chad* was the one who needed their concern.

Chad felt his anger rising; he needed to change the subject. "What's with the forms?"

His dad's cheeks grew pink.

"Seriously, Dad."

"I'm taking a break from the firm right now."

Chad's eyes narrowed. "You got fired?"

"Actually, it's called a leave of absence."

"So you're going to work at the Posh Nosh?" He knew this was the kind of cutesy name that gave his father hives. The only thing worse than wearing a branded polo shirt and spreading flavored cream cheese schmears on these bready West Coast bagels would've been—what? Maybe an internship at MacAvoy.com. He hadn't said the bagel store's name to rankle his father, but he didn't mind knowing that it rankled him.

"If they'll have me."

Chad's curtailed allowance, the carton of banquet leftovers, all clicked into place. "Why didn't you just tell me?"

His dad shrugged and looked down at the metal table. "I didn't want you to worry about this," he said. He looked up sharply, as if he'd remembered part of the script: "How does it make you feel?"

Jesus Christ. Fuck this new solicitousness. Chad didn't want to be paid attention to; he wished, again, to go unnoticed. Goddamn Walter for screwing everything up. Chad wrapped his bagel in the wax paper lining the basket, and stood up. "I gotta get back to school," he said.

The Meal Equally Set

The marquee out front hadn't been updated since Chad's last visit. Black letters still spelled out the holiday-themed message:

GIVE PRESENCE THIS SEASON
(A GIFT THEY WON'T RETURN)

Chad walked up the concrete stairs and into the sanctuary of Marcus's church, St. John the Missionary. It was empty on a weekday afternoon; a lanky man pushed a whirring vacuum down each aisle. Chad took a seat, and flipped through the offertory envelopes and prayer requests lined up next to the hymnals. The sound of the vacuum was comforting, like ocean waves. For the first time since he'd rushed to the hospital, Chad exhaled deeply.

Another man entered the sanctuary, and moved behind the pulpit. He was wearing a shirt and khakis, not his robes, but Chad recognized him as the minister who'd given the sermon on forgiveness. *Jesus is NOT a BEAN counter* was a phrase he and Marcus had imitated since.

After arranging some books and papers, the man noticed Chad. "May I?" he asked, and when Chad nodded, he slid into the pew in front of him so that they sat side by side, but staggered. The minister half-turned to say, "Thanks for coming in."

Chad said, "I like it here."

"You've been with us before?"

He nodded. "Right before Thanksgiving. I really enjoyed your sermon, Sir."

"Good move," the man said. "Flattery is always a nice way to start. But it's Godfrey, please."

"You talked about forgiveness," Chad said. "It was on my mind."

"You hoping to be giving it, or getting?"

Chad shrugged. He hoped his mother would forgive him for sins he hadn't confessed, that Kara would forgive his awkwardness and sweaty-DVD-getaway. If either were offered, he'd be grateful. He hoped he could forgive himself for having his last word to Walter be *Whatever*. "Both, I guess."

Godfrey seemed to contemplate this. "You'll need to decide whether to grant it, and whether to accept."

"Why wouldn't I accept someone's forgiveness?"

The minister's arm rested along the pew in front of Chad, as if he were sitting on a park bench. His skin was several shades darker than Chad's. "I don't mean to say you'd turn it down," he said. "But it takes grace to receive forgiveness lightly, without feeling burdened by it."

Chad nodded. "That's exactly what I was worried about. I think my dad would think it was a burden."

"And whose forgiveness is your father looking for?"

"My mom's."

The minister bowed his head. "An old story."

"I don't really know why I came here today." Chad wiped his palms on his jeans. "I got confirmed last fall."

"Praise be to God."

"I mean, not in this church."

"This is a Baptist church," the minister said kindly.

"I suspected as much." Chad remembered his own minister saying that Confirmation completed what Baptism started. "Whose flock are you wandering away from, then?"

Chad named his own church.

Godfrey nodded again. "How's it been for you, there?"

Although the question was not specific, Chad felt that the man knew precisely what Chad's own congregation looked like, and could imagine how it felt to be the one drop of Loudermocha in a creamy sea of milk, and had intuited something even Chad couldn't quite articulate.

Godfrey's voice was so calm, without the punctuating bombast he'd used to deliver his sermon. Chad wondered what his voice would sound like reading a bedtime story. Or eulogizing Walter Chen. He inclined his head, ready to listen to whatever the minister had to say.

"I trust you've read the Book of Esther? After Mordecai took her in, young Hadassah became a Queen."

"On the other hand, though, you have Moses."

Chad grimaced. "That didn't go so well for his adoptive parents."

The minister smiled. "If you can find the strength to forgive," he said, "that will be rewarding for you. Forgive them for *everything*. For whatever they're not. And love them for who they are."

Chad felt his throat clench. Was *this* what he had come for? Permission to stop counting beans? A sense that his grandmother's lifetime of prayer had gotten her somewhere? And what the hell could he hope for Walter's soul?

He remembered his Grandma's rosary beads, the Latin she would hum to herself. Rituals and habits practiced so long they were almost unconscious. She had believed in a kingdom of Heaven, once, and he had never asked her whether the trials of her last months had shaken that belief.

"Hineni," said the minister. "In Hebrew, *Here I am.* This is what Abraham says when God summons him to sacrifice his son. It's an announcement of Abraham's presence, his readiness to do what is asked."

Here I am, Chad thought. He wasn't sure about his own readiness to do the work the minister suggested, but he was here. He would not take Walter's exit ramp. When he felt safe to speak, he said, "You're good, Sir."

"Godfrey," the minister reminded him. He offered a warm smile. "I'm going to pray for a moment; you're welcome to join me."

Nodding, Chad cast his eyes downward.

Outside the church, the sky was gray, sagging with moisture as if it had been sloppily watercolored. Chad made his way down the steps, hoping he could beat the rain home. The minister's words echoed as he walked. He wondered what it would be like to have a father with natural authority, who basically twinkled with wisdom. Ready with a verse for all occasions. Morgan Fucking Freeman, is what Marcus would've said. Although Marcus wasn't there to say it.

And then, suddenly, he was: Marcus, Andre, and Kevin Hernandez were walking down the sidewalk toward Chad.

Andre looked from Chad to the church. "You been praying, son?"

"No," Chad said. He tried to keep his poker face. "My friend died," he said. It was the first time he'd said it out loud.

"Shit," Marcus said.

Kevin pretended to do a head count. "You got friends, Palo Alto? Besides these fools?"

"Shut up," Marcus told Kevin. He nodded toward Chad. "Come on, we headed to the park."

They sat on top of the park picnic table, resting their feet on the bench. A eucalyptus in the corner was nested in its own sheared strips of bark.

Another group of guys had claimed the basketball court, and Kevin Hernandez joined their game, which was more or less fine with Chad. "My school is bull-shit," Chad told them.

Andre made a face that meant *No kidding, are you new here?*

"They had a special assembly for my friend Walter who died. They called him Wilber."

Marcus chuckled. "That's messed up."

"They seem worried that we're all going to go stand

in front of trains now. Like anyone ever did something because Walter Chen did it first."

"This the dude from the record store?" Andre said. "'Hi there, I must be going?'"

Chad nodded.

"So his mom got him away from your corrupting blackness, and look what happened. He wasn't any safer at the fancy private school." Marcus shook his head.

"My 'corrupting blackness.'"

"It's a thing," Marcus said.

Andre asked, "What do they do at a 'special assembly,' sing Kumbaya and shit?"

"Kind of," Chad admitted. "The counselors told us not to stress out over our grades."

"They do some yoga with y'all?" Andre had folded his hands into a prayerful *Namaste* pose.

Chad grinned. "No," he said. "But the school nurse taught us to meditate."

"Holy shit," said Andre. "Did she like hypnotize you?"

Marcus laughed. "When I snap my fingers, you will believe you are a chicken."

"Like I said," said Chad, relaxing for the first time since he'd gone to the hospital, "my school is bullshit."

Marcus snapped his fingers, watching Chad's face eagerly for signs of chickendom.

"I'm gonna try that with my probation officer," said Andre. "Some deep breathing exercises would do that guy a world of good. Man is wound *tight*."

For a long moment Chad felt as if Walter were sitting there with them, before the phantom of his friend got up and walked away.

"That the first time, huh?" Andre said.

"Since my Grandma last summer, yeah."

"I mean, first time someone your own age."

Andre and Marcus exchanged a look, but no one said anything. They sat for a long moment in silence, watching the basketball game. The players shouted as they jockeyed for position in the key.

"He didn't, like, leave a note or anything?" Andre said.

Chad shook his head. What Chad didn't know about Walter was a much longer list than he'd ever expected.

He took the dog out for a walk before dinner, for once outpacing Red—his stride quickened by acid fury. He hated this neighborhood, its relentless prosperity, his father's vain quest to belong here.

Scot MacAvoy 's SUV passed him, gleaming again and with no trace of the damage Chad's dad had inflicted. It was a rolling advertisement for the futility of rage. Scot's window descended as he glided up to Chad.

"Hey, C, how's it going?"

Chad shrugged.

"It gets better, man," said Scot.

"Thanks," Chad muttered. *Go to hell*, he thought, though an evening of mindless video games on Scot's couch didn't sound half bad. "You up for hanging out later?"

Scot made an apologetic face. "Not tonight, pal. Got some VCs to woo."

"Right."

"Let's do it soon, okay?"

Before Chad could answer, the window slid back up, and Scot's SUV continued down the street. Chad shook his head and let Red pull him around the block again.

He felt like he could walk all night, just a guy and his dog.

At home, his dad set the table and complimented his mom on the smells, as if he never missed a family meal. Chad gritted his teeth, refilling Red's bowl with kibble as the dog lapped at his water dish.

Everything was bullshit.

Chad showily ate food he wasn't hungry for as evidence that he was all right, and tried to fend off the unified assault of his parents' concern.

His dad was suggesting a trip to the beach, reminding Chad of how he had loved the rides and games at the Boardwalk as a kid. Chad could already imagine how this day would go, his parents indulging him with cotton candy and soda and persistently reliving those happy memories. He could picture himself crammed into a bumper car, his mom laughing hysterically as she crashed into him. Just look how well they were doing! Without Grandma! Without Walter! They were just fine! Would a family that wasn't doing absolutely fine ride a roller coaster three times in a row? Would they?

Minimum Wage

In the mornings, Ray wrapped sandwiches in wax paper for the train commuters. Lox and cream cheese, turkey and cheese, egg salad. He always put extra napkins in the bag because he knew the challenge of eating on the train without getting greasy smears on your work clothes.

He had been issued two embroidered polo shirts with the store logo; he wore a white apron. He was not surprised by the parts of this he hated.

After the early rush, there was a lull: time to restock the condiments and fill some takeout containers of flavored cream cheese. Before he opened, Ray had mixed up batches of each flavor: one with flecks of shredded lox, another with green onions, one with dill, and an abomination with cherries and strawberry jam that was the Posh Nosh's "signature blend" and the most popular flavor by a mile.

Things picked up again with the morning workout crowd, coming in for a smoothie after their yoga or Pilates classes. At least that's what Ray assumed from the clothes they were wearing. It took him some time to make each smoothie, with the regulars' tweaks and customizations: soy yogurt instead of dairy; mangos in place of apricots; extra protein powder; no bananas. Sometimes he set out a tray of complimentary bite-size pieces of bagel; at first, he had done this in an attempt to appease those waiting for him and his blender, but he soon realized that the tray's primary purpose was to give the smoothie drinkers the opportunity to publicly perform their vocal disdain for carbohydrates. His manager scolded him for wasting bagels that wouldn't be eaten, until Ray showed him the tip jar stuffed full by customers grateful for the opportunity to advertise their own virtue. For that moment the Posh Nosh was the best place on earth.

The lunchtime crowd mostly wanted sandwiches. This was a busy hour of toasting bagels, spreading them with mustard, stacking deli meat and cheese, pouring kettle chips into the sandwich baskets. He could do this without thinking, which was nice, because when Ray stopped to think, he got hung up on the injustice of his making sandwiches for tips, or worried about whether Allison would come around, or fixated on the impossibility of knowing whether Chad was really ok—but what was left to say except, for the love of God please don't go throw yourself in front of a train.

A long afternoon was spent ensuring the coffee cambros remained full for the prematurely retired techies who balanced their laptops on the tiny Posh Nosh tables. Ray assumed this was their second or third choice of hangout, as there were two boutique coffee places within a block, one featuring "artisan-roasted" brews. That was, he figured, truth in advertising, as the baristas were mostly artists and writers. But the techies drank up Ray's coffee and the Posh Nosh's Wi-Fi bandwidth, staring into their screens blank-eyed with yearning for a time machine to fourteen months ago when they were millionaires.

Ray wouldn't have minded rewinding, himself.

But unlike the laptop jockeys, he'd never even dreamed he was a millionaire, even in hypothetical stock options.

And the still-employed dot-commers—in their uniform of blue button-downs with Dockers—came to the Posh Nosh, too, for a tray of drinks to take back to the office. A flicker passed between them and the guys on their laptops, a shudder of vertiginous acknowledgment of the knife-edge between being in and out of the game.

Another lull before the afterschool crowd—Ray needed to make sure the chillers were full of soft drinks, Snapples, and bottles of water. Some of the kids wanted bagels or smoothies, but nothing too complicated, so Ray was able to keep the line moving. He was attentive to the details: backpacks slung over one shoulder, t-shirts with bands he hadn't heard of, moments of apparent intimacy. He imagined that some of these kids knew Chad, but they hadn't connected their classmate with the white counter guy in the polo shirt. A relief that his nametag only used his first name: he could debase himself at the Posh Nosh without humiliating Chad in the bargain.

Though Ray didn't *feel* debased. He was surprised to

find that he took pride in his work. His suggestions—a water dish for customers' dogs, the addition of an egg-and-cheese sandwich to the breakfast menu—were well-received. Anticipating customer needs was satisfying in a way he hadn't expected. Two weeks had passed easily. He found himself thinking of his father, who'd worked as a machinist back in Nutley; coming home from work with sore feet and the need to shower, he felt a kind of kinship.

The Posh Nosh had been more or less a one-man operation prior to Ray's coming on board. The afore-mentioned man seemed pleased to have given himself an implicit promotion by hiring Ray.

It didn't pay much, but with Allison earning a paycheck again, it was enough to cover COBRA. They might just hold onto the house long enough for him to "find his voice" and return to Goldsmith & Wong. If that was what he wanted.

It was a Wednesday in February, and Ray had just presented a smoothie to the last of the workout women—mango tango with a protein shot—and was wiping down the blender bank when he heard the door behind him. The women assembled at the front table offered warm greetings to whoever had come in.

Ray performed a quick visual inventory and hoped the new customer didn't order anything with straw-berries. He'd need to wash and slice more before the next batch of smoothies. He was still holding the towel when he turned to greet Irene MacAvoy.

"May I help you," he managed to say. His voice sounded tinny and strangled.

Her surprise was visible for a fleeting moment, smoothed over so quickly that he could've convinced himself he'd imagined it. Only a flush in her cheeks remained. "Hello, Ray," she said.

He twisted the towel in his hands, damp from the cleanup. What should he do with it? Lay it on the counter between them? Tuck it under? He would still be a guy in a polo shirt selling bagels to a woman he'd almost believed he was in love with.

"Doing research?" she asked, assuming he was at the Posh Nosh to develop an ad campaign—or doing him the kindness of appearing to assume this. Irene's smile revealed neither her teeth nor her intentions.

"Not exactly," he said.

She was beautiful, still. Her dark eyes, her hair twisted up with a silver chopstick, a charcoal dress that looked molded to her form. This was the closest they had been to each other in months. "How've you been?"

An impenetrable look. "I've been fine," she said.

She didn't ask him the same question, so he didn't have to talk about Chad's friend Walter, or his leave of absence, or the way he had begun to feel like a hotel guest in his own home. Instead he asked, "What can I get you?"

"Two dozen bagels," she said. "Just an assortment."

"Having a party?"

"There's a group of us making signs for the protest this weekend." Her nails rapped on the counter. Nails that would never again leave scratch marks on his back.

"The protest?"

"Against the war. Iraq? It's a terrible mistake."

"Allison thinks so, too."

This was not the most awkward thing Ray could

have said, but it was plenty awkward. They looked at each other for a moment.

Irene cleared her throat. "Is she, um…is she marching?"

"I think she has to work."

Another awkward silence. The distinction between having to work, and not, had sliced the air between them. Irene adjusted her earring.

"Would you like any spreads with that?"

"Two plain, one lox, thanks."

He glanced over at the table of women, then at the twenty-somethings huddled over their laptops. They had no idea, he thought, no way of understanding all that had happened between him and Irene. No one watching them now would know. He was proud of how coolly they were behaving.

Then again, who would ever have suspected that Irene MacAvoy would have slept with the Posh Nosh clerk?

He hadn't expected that she might be the one he was debasing.

"We have a special," he said. "Buy one, get one free. If you'd like a fourth spread, I mean."

"I only need three," Irene said.

"I'm just saying."

The bargain declined, she handed him a credit card to slide through the machine, thanked him, embraced a few of the smoothie women before leaving. None of them looked back at Ray.

He began to brew another pot of coffee. Stacked plastic lids next to the array of cups. Removed a few packets of Equal from the bin of Raw Sugar envelopes. Refilled the soy milk thermos, always the first to be emptied, followed by the half-and-half and then the fat-free. Tapped the stir sticks so they fell into a more symmetric arrangement. These were small things, but Ray's customers would notice, and it would please him.

Pack Up The Moon

A week passed almost without Chad noticing. On the Paly bulletin boards, fliers for the Model UN club were papered over by audition announcements for the spring musical, *Rent*. The lunchtime guitar circle of theater kids gossiped about the war that must've been waged in the teacher's lounge to select something so "edgy" and "downtown." It was the first show in years that would not require a box step! Their stage whispers and strains of their audition songs could be heard from any corner of the cafeteria.

Chad overheard his classmates making holiday weekend plans; most of them involved Tahoe or, sometimes, Whistler. Despite local weather conditions, the school passageways rang with the sound of GoreTex shoulders zipping against each other, enabling the ritual display of ski tags. It was the practice of Chad's classmates to accumulate lift tickets over the season; they applied each sticker over the last, on the same metal hook, so that by March they wore a layered collection. The thickness of your stack, and the prestige of the locations you'd skied, was yet another Paly measuring stick.

No doubt the guidance counselors would tell him not to worry about this.

Homework and class projects had gradually returned to pre-*tragic-events* levels, a distracting facsimile of normalcy. As the rain had dried up, more and more students streamed across the street for lunch at the lowslung Town & Country shopping center. Chad thought if he joined them he might never return to campus. Also, his "just in case" money wouldn't cover the cost of even one California roll.

Instead, Chad sat by himself in the less-crowded cafeteria, serenaded by the strains of bespectacled, bowl-cut Ken Wang's rendition of a searing rock ballad and the other kids' *Rent* preparations.

When he could focus, he attempted to read the book he'd brought for protective company. But sometimes he stared at a page for so long he thought he must've read it by now, and when he turned the page, he retained nothing. This did not bode well for his Brit Lit paper. Was Grendel or Beowulf the true monster? Who the hell knew?

He had rerouted his path between classes to reduce the risk of running into Kara. World History, the only class they shared, had been his favorite. Now he longed for a Shooter Drill, an excuse to crawl under his desk and stare at the floor. He had become an increasingly avid note-taker; the other day, Mr. Farris had paused to compliment him on the detail.

Chad knew he'd screwed everything up, as surely as he knew poor Ken Wang was destined to play the passive best friend, no matter how hard he tried to be the rocker hero.

After school he found himself, for the third time that week, sitting on the curb across from the Chens' pseudo-Spanish house. Once again he felt unsure of how he'd gotten there, as if he'd been sleepwalking and had just awakened to the feeling of asphalt under his palms as he curled his hands around the curb.

A dog walker strolled by across the street, a young woman in a Santa Clara University sweatshirt holding four mismatched leashes. She had become familiar to Chad during his visits to the curb across from the Chens', and they nodded at each other as she passed.

Chad watched as a small car pulled up, and a woman carried a casserole dish to the Chens' front door. When there was no response to her knock, she left the foil-wrapped dish on the wicker table on the porch. She stood watching the house for a long moment, and then she got in her car and drove away.

Chad's mother was part of this casserole brigade. She had delivered a frittata over the weekend while Chad and his dad dropped Eggo waffles into the toaster. Yesterday he'd seen another woman leave a flower arrangement. In all his years visiting the Chens, Chad could not remember any furniture on the porch, or anyone sitting there. The table must have been set out only to receive these offerings, to insulate Mrs. Chen from her well-wishers. He pictured her, unbent, at the funeral service.

The Place You're Supposed to Laugh

As the Chens' front door swung open, Chad had the urge to run. He had half-turned away from the house, curled into his backpack, when Mrs. Chen said, "Chad."

He looked up from his bag. "Yes, Ma'am."

"Come in, please."

She was so solid, so intense. He wished he'd thought to tell someone where he was going, in case he was never again to emerge from the Chen bungalow.

He followed her to the kitchen. Carrying the casserole, Mrs. Chen pointed her elbow at one of the stools for him to sit in. She found a spot for the casserole dish in the refrigerator, and then she stood on the other side of the counter.

They watched each other.

"Would you like some water?" she asked.

"Thanks," Chad said, because this would give her something to do, and him something to hold while he was reminding himself not to spin on the stool.

The house seemed the same: he looked around for signs of the way everything had changed. But there was still a magnetic calendar on the side of the fridge; still a napkin holder next to the jar of duo jiao hot sauce on the counter; still a construction paper hawk silhouette taped to the sliding glass door to the forbidden back patio; still foam corners on the piano bench to protect Walter's little sister. The six year old who was going to grow up with a half-remembered brother, like an imaginary friend she'd always wonder whether anyone else could see. "How's Julie?"

"She's strong," said Mrs. Chen. "She has enrichment today."

Chad nodded and drank from his water. "How are you doing?"

Mrs. Chen just stared at him, as if to say that they both knew that this was a stupid question unworthy of an answer, but she wanted to be sure Chad knew that she knew it was a stupid question.

"So, what's for dinner tonight?" he gestured toward the fridge full of sympathy casseroles. He remembered, after Grandma Marchese died, eating a dozen variations on chicken and broccoli.

"I hate this, this theater of sympathy," she said angrily. "This performance robs me of the one thing I love to do, cook for my family. All I want is to feed them. But it would be obscene to buy groceries or cook, when rations for an army are rotting in my refrigerator."

"You don't have to eat this food," Chad said. He thought of Godfrey, of families like his own, over-stretched.

She slammed her palm on the counter, hard. Chad imagined the way her hand must have felt: numb, at first, and then gradually beginning to throb and burn. Her face revealed nothing but her rage at the foil-wrapped casserole dishes.

He realized then that none of the flowers from the Chens' porch were on display in the house. He wondered what she did with them. Probably she put them with the compost, or chopped them into shreds or flung them into the garbage disposal for a satisfying thrashing. Or maybe there was a special private place where she'd built a personal shrine to Walter. He wasn't sure which of these he most wanted to believe.

He considered asking whether she had any plum wine on hand.

Outside the sliding glass door, two hummingbirds

squabbled over the sugar water feeder hanging from the eaves. They hovered, wings moving too fast to see, and then they took turns at the feeder.

Mrs. Chen followed his gaze. "So much work to just hold still," she said.

Chad agreed that this was true.

She opened a drawer for something, placed it on the counter before Chad. Walter's pocketknife from Boy Scouts. With this blade, they had whittled twigs into spears; torn holes in their own skin out of clumsiness; dug worms out of the earth. "It was his," she said.

"I know."

"Now it's yours."

He stared down at the knife, unable to touch it.

"You're welcome," she said.

"Thank you," he responded to the prompt. "Are you sure?"

She gave him another withering look. If he had come here to confirm that she'd been right to judge him unworthy of her son, it was working.

"Thank you," he said again.

Mrs. Chen nodded once.

He assumed he was being presented with an artifact, and sent away with his consolation prize. He watched as she filled a plastic watering can from the sink, and walked toward the sliding glass door. "You coming?"

Chad followed, watching her pour water into the hanging flower baskets that surrounded her hummingbird feeder. Leave it to Mrs. Chen to remember to water the plants.

Across the cement patio stretched a chalk pathway

for a hopscotch game. The boxes were uneven and the seven was backwards. He pictured Walter's sister Julie tossing her stone, hopping along the numbers. Here at last was proof that something had changed: Mrs. Chen would never have allowed Chad and Walter to draw on the patio. It had been poured new, back when they were in second grade or so—just a little older than Julie, he guessed. Where had the chalk even come from?

I'm surprised you let her draw that," he blurted. *Shit*, he thought as she turned toward him. He braced for another of her disappointed looks.

She looked past Chad, though, and moved toward the last flower basket. "Why surprised?"

"It's just—the cement, I remember when you put it in. You didn't want us to even *breathe* out there."

Now, Mrs. Chen looked straight at him. Her mouth twitched upward in what he would've described as a smile if it had been anyone but Mrs. Chen. She laughed.

"What?"

Her laughter overcame her, and she grabbed at his arm, pulled him to the edge of the cement slab, the corner nearest the house. She used her foot to push aside the leafy fronds of a flowering plant. Pointed down at the place where—he'd nearly forgotten—the letters were carved into the ground. Walter's initials, and his, and the date, 8-13-95.

Right. In a flash he saw the stick they'd used to dig into the wet cement, the point they'd sharpened with Walter's knife. The t-shirt Walter had worn that day, emblazoned with a velociraptor. The smack of Mrs. Chen's slap on Walter's cheek. Banning the vandals from the patio: *Don't even breathe on it.* He remembered now this edict had been not just in case, but because.

She had been furious. But now she was laughing. He bent to his knees, traced their damage with his finger. WJC, CAL, 8-13-95. Years of California sun and the annual month of rain had smoothed the edges of their letters and numbers; his fingertip followed them easily. With his other hand he swept aside the leaves of the greenery that Mrs. Chen had almost certainly planted to conceal their vandalism. "I'm sorry," he said to Mrs. Chen, without looking up from the cement.

For a moment she stood watching him, then she knelt to trace the letters herself.

Walter was gone, and what she had left was what she had punished him for. All the antibacterial soap and foam corners on the sharp edges, and still she was here on her knees.

And now Mrs. Chen was hoping and wishing and choking down dinners made in other people's kitchens with other people's recipes, that used chili powder instead of cumin, pork in the dumpling filling when you preferred shrimp, a celery stalk when you needed a hug.

Chad understood that Mrs. Chen would never not be Walter's mother.

They ran their hands over the letters, traced the numbers, until their fingers knew the way. Walter's pocketknife was heavy in the pocket of Chad's shorts. "I have to pick up Julie from enrichment," Mrs. Chen said. "Okay?"

"Okay," he said.

She stood slowly, watching as the leaves fell back over the inscription. She patted Chad's arm, robotic again, protective exoskeleton back in place. "Thank you for coming," she said. "Please don't be a stranger."

What Chad Knew

He was six pounds, nine ounces at birth. Twenty inches long; brown eyes. Blood type O+; Apgar score 9/10. Box ticked next to African American. Trenton's St. Francis Hospital had issued him a blanket with blue and pink stripes, and a tiny knit cap that matched. The blankets and caps were donated in bulk by the Grey Nuns of the Sacred Heart, who knitted them and signed the small printed cards sent home with each new mother.

In the spirit of our foundress St. Marguerite d'Youville, the Grey Nuns of the Sacred Heart strive to be signs of God's unconditional love in a more just and compassionate world.

Navigating the digressive internet with this sentence as his polestar, Chad had learned that Marguerite d'Youville was a "genteel but impoverished" eighteenth-century Montreal woman who married unwisely, to a bootlegger who found the local Native tribes a lucrative market. Montreal society frowned on this, and Marguerite and her sisters were gossiped about as "les souers grises;" *grises*, grey, was slang for "tipsy." Despite her shame, Marguerite dedicated herself to helping others, particularly the poor, elderly, and ill. It was not clear whether she had offered reparations to those natives who became addicted to her husband's merchandise.

So now, Chad knew more about Marguerite d'Youville than he did about the woman who had given birth to him. His mom had learned, later, that this woman's name was Tami. He could ask the court to find out her last name, if he wanted, but she had not named a father. She had been terribly young: sixteen, his mom thought; and she had died on the bed where Chad was born.

St. Francis Hospital was in Trenton, New Jersey, at the corner of Hamilton and Chambers. He could zoom in on the internet map. What Chad knew about Trenton was that his grandma made a show of shuddering whenever it was mentioned, and that it was the state capital. If Chad's parents hadn't moved to California, fourth grade would've been New Jersey history. Instead of celebrating Father Junipero Serra and making sugar cube models of his missions, instead of panning for gold in the schoolyard, Chad would have visited the New Jersey State House and constructed a Lenape wigwam. The Trenton motto—"Trenton Makes, the World Takes"—was a slogan his dad would've been proud of. Surely people in Trenton were still good with their hands. And also, it sounded like a city with a chip on its shoulder.

Trenton was 50.1% African American, with a 2001 median income one-tenth that of Silicon Valley. If you entered "Trenton, New Jersey" into a search engine, your top three hits were "homicide," "State Prison," and "1968 riots." On a ranked list, it was named the fourth most dangerous city in America. Possibly, this was why his grandma shuddered.

Chad had asked Grandma Marchese about the riots. It was a horror show, she said. She told him angry men pulled fire alarms to summon the fire engines, then threw bricks into the cabs because they wanted to hurt the men in uniform who'd failed them. That did sound terrible, Chad said. No, she said, annoyed with him for cutting her off. It was a horror, she said, that *Dr. King had died.* And it was terrible that they got RFK too. Grandma's "they" were not the men with bricks. But then again, she didn't claim the men with bricks as "us," either.

Chad's whole concept of *us* and *them* might have been different, if he still lived in Trenton. Or even in that first apartment the three of them shared in Hoboken. For one thing, the attacks that had felt so distant and cartoonish would've been in his backyard. Earthquakes, on the other hand, would not have been as urgent a concern. But also, there might've been more kids like him at school. Maybe, in Trenton, they would've covered Langston Hughes *first* instead of *after* he'd spent months with Whitman; he could imagine a whole class, reciting together: *I, too, sing America. I am the darker brother.* Perhaps his teacher would've been less awkward and skittish in presenting Hughes to him, as if Chad could've been insulted somehow by being offered the work of a poet who resembled himself.

If Chad had grown up in Trenton, he would have learned the Battle of Trenton in 1776 was a "small but pivotal" moment in the Revolution. General George Washington had crossed the Delaware River the previous night in order to fight the British at daybreak. By noon, the victorious army had crossed back to Pennsylvania. In Trenton, a marble Battle Monument stood at the center of a five-way intersection, less than two miles northwest of St. Francis Hospital. Chad would've learned, in fourth grade, how critical the Trenton victory was to American morale, and the Revolution's momentum.

Trenton makes, the world takes.

Chad knew his parents had driven to Trenton as soon as they got the call. *He's here*, Allison said to Ray, one hand over the mouthpiece. Because a woman they'd never met had died, they had come running. They'd peered through the glass at his plastic bassinet, and swaddled him in the nuns' knit blanket.

The Loudermilks hadn't flown to Kenya or Ethiopia to bring him home from a tribal orphanage, but they'd named him for an African country, as Marcus had pointed out. His mother said only that as soon as they saw him they knew it was his name. Chad did not know what the girl called Tami might have been thinking of naming him.

His parents were both from New Jersey; the three of them lived in a one-bedroom apartment in Hoboken. In baby book pictures, his parents held him, swung him into the air, pushed his stroller around the neighborhood. At the pizza joint, Chad loved to watch the cooks hurl their dough skyward. In Hoboken, he started teething and disdained his rice cereal. This was all well-documented in his mom's careful script. Then, nine months after Chad was born, they moved to California. Chad took his first steps in their Palo Alto living room.

He knew the sun set over the ocean, and never understood why this so perplexed his New Jersey-born parents.

In first grade he'd been asked whether his skin color washed off. Walter Chen told the guys to shut up, and since then Chad had paid less attention to the rest of his classmates.

He had learned to use chopsticks adroitly; he could write code in three computer languages (four, if you counted Java; Scot MacAvoy, and therefore Chad, did not); he scored well on standardized tests. He had built his fourth-grade model of the mission of St. Francis (sometimes, incorrectly, known as Mission Dolores, as he'd informed his classmates), stacking sugar cubes.

When Chad was born, his mom had completed her psychology degree and was doing clinical hours. She put this aside to care for him. It wasn't until he started middle school that she began working with the "at-risk" clients people referred to her. What Chad knew about her meetings was that she tried to guide her clients toward more prudent choices, to help them build the skills and confidence to steer themselves away from danger.

One thing Chad did not know was whether his mother's counsel, had it been offered to a girl named Tami in 1986 and 1987, might have meant that Chad himself would never have been born.

Enjoy Yourself
(It's Later Than You Think)

On campus, the signs of spring were evident: the black squirrels becoming more brazen, sneaking in through open dorm windows to munch on pizza crusts or speaker wires; the chalk-drawn muted post horns that always began to appear on campus sidewalks when the English department's Modern Novel survey got to Pynchon. In the two months since Christmas, Diana had taught a dozen grad students most of what they needed to know about perturbation theory; she had drafted one paper and reviewed two others; and she had made a hundred lists in hopes they would help her respond to Arthur.

She had kept herself busy enough to have plausible excuses when he'd tried to arrange a meeting between her and the woman who was willing to serve as a surrogate. That was the word Arthur had used: she'd written it down when he said it, underlined it in her notebook. Pretending to herself that it didn't mean *mother*.

On days like today, when she had started the morning by stepping on an abandoned Lego brick and was now watching Molly set out a tea party at which only stuffed animals were welcome, Diana could think of a *pro* or two for Arthur's offer to renegotiate their custody arrangement. Surely a better mother wouldn't feel bored at the tea party, wouldn't wonder whether she could excuse herself to check her email.

Molly had her own gravitational pull, but Diana experienced this as a second sun, or even a large moon. For her whole adult life, she'd told time by the way it felt on campus, lived on the academic calendar rather than the one with holidays and weekends. Here in her apartment, she felt aware of its blankness. Molly was its only source of color and life—setting aside the decaying ficus in the corner. Of course (this was a *con*), if Molly spent less time here with her, and more time with Arthur and Tommy as they'd offered, this blankness would get worse.

In the living room, Molly deliberately placed small wooden fruit and sushi on plastic plates. She pantomimed pouring into her cup, then served the two stuffed animals she'd seated at the ends of the table. Diana offered what she hoped was a patient, not-at-all-bored smile.

Her mother had laughed when Diana learned she was having a daughter. "What a joke on you," she said. "The woman who doesn't like girls."

And it was true that Diana had worried about pink, about princesses, about the possibility of cheerleading. She was concerned about the way middle school could turn smart girls into boy-crazy gigglers. When pregnant she had pictured a boy, imagined him growing inside her, for nearly twenty weeks, had searched the ultrasound display screen for a hint of maleness. Somehow, despite the challenges of conceiving Molly, she had still believed the future would correspond to the plans she had made.

But Molly was teaching her things about girls that she had not known. Mostly, that it wasn't either/or. Molly demanded sparkly pink barrettes, and then climbed a pile of rocks, or spent an hour poking sticks into mud. She chose to wear tutus, and did not cry when she skinned her knees.

They were well into the construction of a Duplo Lego village when her townhouse doorbell rang. Diana heaved herself into a standing position, limped a little on a foot that had fallen half-asleep, and peered through the peephole: surprised to see her nephew, Chad.

She swung open the door, and Chad scooped Molly into a flying embrace. "Do you mind if I hang out?"

She tried not to look surprised, or as if she could imagine anything more appealing than playing with her toddler. "Of course not," she said. "Can I get you a drink?"

He asked for a Coke, if she promised not to tell Allison. "You know what else," Diana said, "I'm not going to use a coaster." At once they were conspirators. "I don't even *have* coasters."

He grinned back, and praised Molly's Duplo construction. "I like the bell tower."

Molly beamed proudly.

Chad put together a wall that subtly reinforced Molly's listing tower, and asked her to find some more red pieces. She dove into the pile to please him.

Diana snapped together a pair of Lego cars that could cruise down the village's central boulevard. She handed the yellow one to Molly and the green to Chad.

He was so much like his mother: smart and shy, so reserved she would think him aloof if she didn't know better. He was trustworthy, which was almost supernatural in a fourteen-year-old boy. All of this was Allison. The more they talked the more Diana could see Ray's influence, too: he could tap into a silly recklessness, and he had Molly bubbling over with giggles.

It seemed impossible that Chad was the same age as the boys whose girlfriends went to Allison's free clinic. He sat cross-legged, guiding his car toward the bus stop Molly indicated.

"Do you think you'll have another?" he asked, nodding toward Molly.

"Oh, not you, too."

"Just wondering."

"Arthur and Tommy would love to," she said. "And Arthur's a very good salesman. But——." She let the thought fade into nothing.

"I always wanted a brother or sister," Chad said.

She nearly said, *Your mother would've loved that, too*, but the words clogged in her throat, and she wondered whether this was true.

Chad grinned, disarming her. "I guess I won't hold my breath." He said, "Supposedly my mom died in childbirth."

"Supposedly?"

"Well, that's what my parents told me. Were you, um, around then?" He said this tenderly, as if he knew how thoroughly his mother had logged Diana's absence from important moments.

"I was in grad school, in Cambridge," she said. "It was intense at the beginning, like hazing; I felt like being smart wasn't enough anymore. Especially since I was the only girl." She could hear how inadequate this was, her MIT anxiety an unpersuasive excuse for having stayed two hundred miles away from Chad. A four-hour Amtrak ride. She winced an apology, and said, "I missed my college roommate's wedding, too, because of prelims."

He steadied Molly's hand as she fit a large block on top of a narrow tower. "It's funny, you and mom both moving to the same town in California."

"I guess it is," she said. "To be honest, I didn't even realize she lived so close to campus. I was just, like, awesome, I got a job at Stanford. And Arthur lives in San Francisco." Too late she heard the undercurrent of this sentence, the way her sister would've heard it: how low Allison had ranked.

"I'm glad," he said. "I'm glad you and Molly are here. Especially now."

"Me too," Diana said. She wondered whether having Chad and Allison nearby might make it easier this time around, if she did agree to try again with Arthur.

Later they would take Molly for a walk, spend an hour at the corner playground. Molly would leave them to race up the climbing structure, and they would stand and watch her, both grateful for this moment. For now they sat together, architects of their Lego world. Brick by brick, they built walls, archways, and high windows.

Map of the Night Sky

The paint store clerk spoke in a lazy cowboy cadence. Chad heard his mom unconsciously slowing down her speech to match the man's accent, the words stretching out in her mouth as she placed her order. The clerk kept his left thumb looped into his front pants pocket, and nodded knowingly when Chad's mom held up a green Granny Smith apple. "Sure, we can match that for y'all," he said. "You want flat or gloss?"

"How much we going to need?" the clerk asked Chad's mom.

"Now it's *we*," Marcus muttered. "Like he's gonna change into overalls and ride over to the clinic with us."

Over at the counter, Allison was showing the clerk a sheet of graph paper.

"Okay, four gallons, then," he said. "With custom mixed it's easier if I make a little more than you need, 'cause I might not make it exactly the same next time."

"You can match an apple," Allison said, "but you can't match a can of *paint?*"

The clerk grinned. "Let me just get started," he said.

Kara was standing near a display of rollers. "Thanks for coming," Chad stared at her, a beaming idiot.

"Thanks for inviting me," she said.

The Clinic project had been Aunt Diana's strategy; they'd worked out the details on the park bench, while Molly clambered up the molded rock wall. Diana was footing the cost, on the condition that Chad did not reveal that it had been her idea but instead claimed to have asked her for help when he'd dreamed it up. "Then just call up this Kara, and say you need an extra pair of hands," she said. "And whats-is-name, Marcus, too." When Chad balked, Diana laid out the twofold importance of Marcus's presence: "If your friends are around," she said, "you both appear normal to Kara, because normal guys have friends, and you actually act more normal. It's win-win."

The Free Clinic was quiet except for the sound of his mom's Paper Tiger scoring perforated spirals through the floral wallpaper borders. Chad's mom couldn't stop smiling as she tore the borders down. This was what she needed, his aunt had said. Something new; something she was doing on her own.

Marcus was a surprisingly conscientious painter. He showed Chad and Kara how to make a big "W" on the walls with the roller, a technique learned from those shows where people got their rooms remodeled overnight. "Don't get too much paint on it," he cautioned, "it'll drip."

Kara giggled. "I know I just met you," she said, "but

I didn't expect you to be a home makeover maven."

"See, that's where stereotypes'll get you," Marcus said. "I appreciate clean lines and a splash of color as much as anybody."

Kara laughed again, and Chad worried that Marcus's charm might overpower his own. He might have miscalculated, inviting both of them to help with the Clinic painting. His aunt Diana had thought this would lower the stakes for Kara, but she didn't know Marcus. Chad almost wished that Andre were there too; he might've kept Marcus from dialing up his charisma. But Dre had an unmissable date with his probation officer.

"Would yew look at this heah brush, pardner." Marcus used a vaudeville version of the paint store clerk's accent. "Y'all got poly's shape reteyntion, and the dew-rabilit-ay of this heah nylon."

Chad saw Kara's back stiffen. "You have a problem with Texas?"

"No, Ma'am," Marcus said. "Nor with Texans."

"Kara, maybe you can help us," Chad said quickly. "We've been working on this theory." If he hit the *us* and *we* a little hard, it was only to remind Marcus they were supposed to be on the same team.

Neither Kara nor Marcus responded; they both went on painting green W-shapes on the walls.

Chad sucked in air to keep talking: "About *Star Wars*, and *Lord of the Rings*? Like, there are all kind of connections."

Kara dipped her roller in the paint tray, and applied another green-apple W.

"You know, Chewbacca is kind of like Gimli the dwarf, sort of barely articulate, with a mix of cuddly and scary? And Gandalf is Obi-Wan, right, that's obvious."

Marcus was shaking his head. Chad could imagine how Marcus would tease him later: way to go, man, *Star Wars* and Hobbits will win her heart for sure. Maybe he'd repeat what he'd said at the mall, when Chad had turned sweaty and speechless, his shirt full of stolen goods: If you want to get around the bases with that girl, Marcus had said, you oughta swing, not just keep bunting.

Without turning from the wall, Kara said, "And how do the droids fit in?"

"*The droids*," Chad and Marcus said thoughtfully, together. At this further evidence of Kara's unique specialness, Chad's heart sped.

His mom walked in holding a ragged strip of the lilac border she'd removed. She pulled a metal folding chair from the hallway and placed it in the middle of the room. "You guys are doing wonderfully."

"They're coming along," Marcus said with paternal pride.

Chad's mom asked Kara how she liked California, and Kara said that before they'd moved, they'd painted every room in her house. It was kind of sad, she said, to see her room painted a soft pink, but the real estate agent had said it would be good for people to be able to *visualize* it as a girl's room. Also she had to box up most of her books, the Trixie Beldens and Nancy Drews, not to mention taking down her Map of the Night Sky and hiding her microscope in the closet, because all those prospective buyers didn't especially want to visualize themselves having a *nerdy* daughter.

Chad remembered the aggressively inspiring décor

in Walter Chen's bedroom, and he felt grateful to Kara's parents for having allowed her to choose her own dreams—at least prior to the real estate agent's open house. He told her his cousin Molly's dad, Arthur, was a real estate agent. Arthur paid a guy to stage the houses he put on the market, to clear out the clutter and furnish the place with just enough impersonal style that almost anyone could imagine themselves living there.

But in the end, Kara said, it was okay painting and packing, and it was really fun picturing their new house, imagining all the new people they'd meet in the new place. A fresh start. You could be anyone; you didn't have to be the girl who used to wear a retainer and whose Mom gave her a spiral perm. You could start over, with a clean slate.

Chad's mom was quiet for a long time after that, and then she poured some paint into a fresh tray, and she walked into the other Exam Room. Chad hoped she wasn't thinking about calling Arthur's staging team into their own house. He could imagine some guy trashing their stuff, announcing that Chad's room telegraphed all of his peculiarities to the world.

"Microscope, huh?" Chad asked Kara.

She held his gaze, in that fantastic way she had of not giving an inch.

"Sometimes," said Marcus in an instructional tone, "you need to zoom in, when things are very small." He looked pointedly at Chad's jeans.

"Shut up," Chad said.

Kara grinned. "I have a telescope, too," she said to Marcus. "That helps me see things that are—and will always be—very, very far from my bedroom." She made her hands into a pirate's scope, and peered at Marcus through curled fingers.

"Your friend is funny," Marcus said to Chad.

Maybe Aunt Diana had been right about including Marcus. He had not expected this. They painted another ten minutes in companionable silence. He decided to swing for the fences. "Are you, um, doing anything later?"

Kara asked him what he had in mind.

Chad hadn't expected Kara to say yes: he was imagining a strikeout, waiting to feel the whiff. The jolt of making contact had his whole body thrumming. He showered and changed, and then he called Scot MacAvoy in a panic.

"This the new girl?" Scot asked. "From Texas?"

"That's the one." In the background Chad heard the peppy soundtrack of *Mario Kart*. "Good memory."

"Oh, I don't forget Inconvenient Hard-ons so easily."

"So, like, a movie?"

"You can't talk to her during a movie," Scot said. "Don't you want to talk to her?"

"I just want to sit next to her."

"No." The Mario soundtrack stopped suddenly: Scot had paused his game to ensure that Chad received his message. "Legends of Flight," he directed. "It's a flight simulator place. You'll each be in your own little pod. You can talk over the radio, you can make up a sexy code if you want. *Permission to buzz the tower* and shit."

"Are you for real with this?"

"Dead straight. What time you going, I'll meet you there."

"*No*." After battling Marcus for Kara's attention all afternoon, he had little interest in taking Scot MacAvoy along on what might conceivably be called a date.

He chose a gray polo and jeans, played some Wu-Tang to gear himself up. Chad arrived early, but Kara was already out front, reading the sign that promised *Amazing Thrills* and *Six Degrees of Freedom*, but warned that pregnant women and those with heart conditions could not experience said thrills. She had changed, too, into the fantastic striped shirt from the mall. "You come here often?"

"First time," Chad said. "My friend Scot says it's amazing."

Kara gestured to the sign on the Legends of Flight window, where the word *Amazing* was repeated several times. "Apparently."

The Paradox of Kara: there was nowhere he felt more like an idiot than standing before her, but this was where he most wanted to be.

Inside, they dressed in flight suits covered with quasi-military patches, and entered a briefing room with four other people: their squadron consisted of three guys in Stanford gear, one girl in a Phish t-shirt, and Chad and Kara.

Their so-called commanding officer explained the mission they should try to carry out, and provided rudimentary pointers on using the controls inside their simulator pods. He asked them to choose their own call signs, like in *Top Gun*. Two guys wanted to be Iceman, and did rock-paper-scissors to decide.

Chad struggled to think of a cool pilot handle that

wasn't from a movie or some terrible pun on "joystick" or "thrust." He wondered desperately what Scot would do, and spat out, "Sultan."

"Can I be Jedi?" Kara said, and Chad's heart surged. Around the briefing table, all the other men nodded approval.

Their flight pods were plastic cockpits on three-axis gimbels. As soon as they all had their headphones on, the Stanford guys began trash talking: "I'll see you in hell," "Not if I see you first," "Eat my jet exhaust." The CO's voice asked them to "Keep it clean up there, flyboys."

In the pilot's seat, Chad had a monitor showing the horizon, several virtual gauges, a wheel for steering and a throttle. Over the radio he could still hear the Stanford guys jawing. "Hey Sultan," he heard Kara's voice say, low and soft in his ears. "You ready for takeoff?"

Chad shifted in his seat.

His pod tended to roll; he struggled to maintain level flight, and quickly forgot the details of the mission because of the urgency of Not Crashing. But he laughed, and Kara laughed, and before they knew it the CO was calling them back to base. "That was surprisingly awesome," Kara said. "One might even say, *amazing.*"

"Nice maneuvers, Jedi."

She blew lightly on her fingernails: *no sweat.* "My mom's picking me up at the Starbucks. Want to get something?"

Over drinks at a table painted with a checkerboard, Chad learned that Kara had a big brother who was much older, almost done with college at UT, back in Austin.

"Were you mad, when your parents moved away from Texas?" Chad tapped one of the dark painted squares. "I mean, because you liked it so much there?"

Kara laughed, her green eyes shining. "I had zero friends in Texas. Like, complete outcast. Plus, my parents are happier now. They fought a lot back home, and it was still bad when we first got here, but this place has chilled them out."

"I guess," Chad said. He thought again about his parents, about the way the bond between them had been weakened.

"You grew up with cool people," she said. "Like your friend Marcus."

Chad shook his head. "I actually just met him, in September."

"You're telling me that Star Wars-Hobbit thing— you just came up with that?" She shook her head in fake awe. "You guys are full-on pop culture geniuses."

"You know, I don't really appreciate that tone," Chad said.

She grinned at him. "I'll grow on you," she said.

He would very much like that, he thought. "I get your point, though, about new friends. Marcus and this other dude Andre, I'm really glad I met them. Mostly."

"Rachel and Yvette dragged me into Prom Committee, and it's the kind of thing I never would've done back home, but it's actually pretty fun."

"Sounds really...great," Chad said. It sounded awful: paper streamers and holsters of Scotch tape.

"Last weekend after the meeting, we went to see *Rent* à la Paly. Oh my god, Ken Wang is *incredible* as Roger. There are like eight girls who sat in front and just screamed for him."

"Ken Wang?" Chad struggled to square this with the theater kids' cafeteria circle. Superdork Ken Wang was the lead, not the nerdy best friend? Ken Wang was the object of screaming?

"That's what I meant before, though, about the blank slate. Like if the kids back in Texas knew *I* was on Prom Committee, they would've savaged me. The newspaper, sure. But—"

"That's the thing," Chad said. "Kids here have known me forever."

"No," Kara said. "I'm not sure they know you at all."

Their mothers arrived at the Starbucks to retrieve them at the same time, and the proud glances they exchanged instantly dissolved whatever confidence Chad might have rebuilt over the evening. At once, instead of a fighter pilot with a superhot wingwoman, he was a preschooler who'd managed to turn his handprint into a credible Thanksgiving turkey. His mom thanked Kara, again, for her help with the Clinic painting, and then beamed beatifically as Chad and Kara said goodnight to each other.

"Did you have fun?" his mom asked as she pulled out of the parking lot.

Chad made an agreeable murmuring sound that he hoped made clear how little he wanted to discuss it further. For an expert in communicating with teenagers, she missed a lot of signals.

"She seems very nice," she tried again.

He repeated his noncommittal *mmmm*.

"I guess you'd rather replay it in your head than

talk to me, huh?"

Chad shrugged and stared out the window. The thing was: he couldn't stop thinking about what Kara had said. That übergeek Ken Wang was now some kind of guitar god with groupies. That you could stage yourself right out of your own bedroom, just put the microscope in the closet. Show up at a new school and sign up for Prom Committee. Even the flight place tonight had allowed them to rename themselves.

How could it be that Walter had felt so trapped? Hadn't he known how easy it could be to slip into a fresh flight suit and take on a new call sign?

Or hadn't that been what he wanted?

What it had been like for Walter, from the blue blazer to the tennis bag to the hours roaming hallways full of zombies to the moment of impact on the rails—of this, Chad knew nothing at all.

He closed his eyes against the streetlights of El Camino. The tapping of his mother's fingertips on the steering wheel sounded like rain.

Chad saw Mrs. Chen bent over the vandalized cement, laughing. His index finger traced a "W" onto his leg.

His mom leaned into his room to say goodnight, lingering in the jamb, and revealed she'd been chewing on the blank slate thing too.

She held a legal-sized mailing envelope. "This is everything I could find out," she had said. "It's not much, but inside there's a number to call if you still have questions. We can investigate together. Or you can do it yourself."

Chad stared back at her.

"I just thought you might be curious," she said. "I didn't want you to think we couldn't talk about it." She tucked her hair behind her ears.

"I know who I am," Chad told her. "It's not in that folder."

She paused for a beat before yielding a small smile. "I love you," she said.

"Me too, Mom." He slid the envelope, unopened, into the drawer of his desk, curled himself into bed, and dreamed of knifing through the stratosphere.

Puppy of Shame

In one corner of the Loudermilk living room sat a half-filled shipping box, a package under construction for Ray's new apartment. By the time Diana arrived, Allie had packed a new clock radio and bare-bones slimline phone, a spare set of sheets, and the two issues of *Sports Illustrated* that had arrived since he'd moved out. Also: three-quarters of a bottle of his preferred shampoo, an extra cartridge for his electric shaver, and two shirts that had been in the laundry hamper when he'd packed.

Diana leaned back into her chair; it was soft and welcoming, an upholstered embrace. Leave it to Allison to make sure even the furniture was like this. In the kitchen, Molly performed a small dialogue between two Play-Doh blobs. Allie's stereo played Joni Mitchell as they drank lemonade that tasted freshly made. The house smelled of cinnamon—Diana suspected unseen baking, perhaps a batch of cookies for Ray's care package.

Diana's initial take was that the package indicated things were only temporary, just like Ray's month-to-month lease. The cheapness of the items Allie had selected, the absence of extra batteries for the alarm clock, and the kindness of the package in itself—the special trip she'd made to shop for Ray—suggested she didn't mean the separation to be permanent.

But in the last hour, sipping lemonade and talking with her sister, Diana had begun to read the package as a send-off: cigarettes and extra socks for a departing soldier. The inelegance of the slimline phone, with a cord that was likely to become tangled instantly, irrevocably; a phone that was *not* wireless, *not* digital, for which she'd probably had to search—clearly one big *fuck you* by way of Southwestern Bell.

Diana had come to help Allie pack, and to check on Chad. But Chad was out, Allison said.

"Oh, right, the thing with Kara."

Her sister looked startled. "You know about Kara?"

"I didn't know she was a secret," Diana said.

Allie's face contorted, then seemed to smooth by the force of her will. "She's not. I just—I didn't know you knew."

So: Chad was gone, and her sister had never really needed her help, thus the lemonade and conversation, and soon Diana had ended up blurting out Arthur and Tommy's proposal. *Quietly* blurting, once she was sure Molly was out of earshot in the kitchen, distracted by the Play-Doh Allison seemed to have had on hand for just such an occasion—unless she had intended it for Ray's care package—but blurting just the same.

In a hoarse whisper, she revealed her hopes, her fears, several versions of the pros-and-cons lists she'd compiled.

"Of course you're scared," her sister said. "You're a mom, it's our default state."

"By the skin of my teeth," Diana said.

"That's the only way," Allison said. "This has nothing to do with what you and Arthur decide," she went on, "but you really need to get yourself some friends who are mothers. People you can compare notes with." Seeing Diana's face, she emended: "Not compete with, just sort of calibrate."

"Calibrate," Diana repeated. She traced a line in the condensation on her lemonade glass.

"When Chad was little, I did this toddler nutrition class, and every week we'd pass around a little stuffed dog. We called it the Puppy of Shame."

"Okay."

"Just as a joke, whoever felt like they'd been the 'worst' mom that week, they got to hold onto the Puppy of Shame. Maybe you forgot to pack a snack in the diaper bag; or you ignored the symptoms of an ear infection for so long that when you finally went in, the pediatrician said, *WOW, This is a bad one*; or once—." Allison held up a finger. "*Once*, you held onto your kid's hand too tight when he wanted to run, and he dislocated his elbow."

"Puppy of shame," Diana said.

"I mean the stakes are so high, but at the same time, everybody drops a stitch sometimes."

Diana waited a beat, thinking, and then gave a throaty laugh. "Mom dropped her share, I guess."

"She was human." Allison shrugged.

"I guess I've never really had that," Diana said. "That Puppy of Shame kind of circle. Things are different, with Arthur. I remember this one time, Molly was maybe six weeks—two options, nursing or crying—and Arthur came over and said, 'Okay, I've got this, you go take care of you for a couple of hours.' And honestly, I was so touched and grateful that I just sat in my car for about ten minutes, weeping at his generosity. And then I dried my tears and I realized there was nowhere I wanted to go. Like, *nowhere.*"

Allison gave her a sad smile that Diana guessed was pity.

"So I went to Peet's and had a cup of tea. Just kind of sat there in a daze. And then I went grocery shopping. I was in a trance, up one aisle and down another, just filling the cart with things I didn't really need." Diana paused, ran her fingertips over the nubby fabric of the chair. "I guess if I'd had someone to go see, maybe. To hand off the Puppy of Shame."

She noticed then that Allison's face shone with tears.

"Allie, are you okay?"

Quietly, Allison said: "I live ten minutes away."

"I know."

"I would drop everything to sit and drink a cup of tea with you."

Suddenly Diana pictured the basket her sister had brought over when Diana moved in: the binder full of takeout menus, maps from various local attractions, the gift cards for cafes and even a hair salon. She remembered rolling her eyes at this, at the profligate squandering of her sister's time it represented.

"I'm an asshole," Diana said. "I should have been

there, with you and Mom."

"It's okay," Allison said.

"It's not. I'm sorry I wasn't there, at the end. Before. And I'm sorry for every cup of tea we haven't had."

Allison reached over and squeezed her hand.

Relief unclenched Diana. She did not deserve such easy forgiveness, but Allison had offered it anyway. Her family would give her strength and support, as families were meant to do. She was a fool for not having known this. For having allowed the ten minutes between them to dilate. She smiled, sheepish, at her sister.

They made grilled cheese for Molly's lunch, and sat at the kitchen table with a centerpiece of stacked Play-Doh coils. They offered extravagant praise for this construction, which Molly accepted as she munched on her sandwich and slurped yogurt from a tube.

You could read Chad's afternoon in his face: when he returned, he had the glazed, blissful look of a boy who had spent an hour talking with a girl, mustering his courage and falling deeper into teenage love with her; and another hour kissing her, until her chin was pink and raw from the stubble on his own. He looked as if his only regret was that he hadn't figured out how to kiss and talk at the same time.

Diana was in the big chair, reading, when he staggered into the house and slumped against the door to close it. Allison was soothing Molly into a nap in the master bedroom.

She put down her magazine. Chad was so dazed with happiness it felt as if it would be rude not to return his beaming smile. He offered a blissed-out nod on his way to his room.

Despite Allison's enveloping compassion, Diana felt tense and unsettled. She found she couldn't focus on the article, and instead took Molly's sippy cup into the kitchen to wash.

She wondered what had happened to Allison's Puppy of Shame friends, why they weren't crowding around her table with wine and laughter, telling Allie she'd get over Ray, that she'd been too good for him anyway. Had Allison seemed too good for them, too? Had they felt, as Diana had, so inadequate that it was easier to keep their distance?

She wished she'd known earlier how to look harder, how to see Allison's home as welcoming instead of reproachful.

"Stay," Allison's voice came from behind her.

"What?"

"For dinner. Molly's having a good nap, you should stay."

"I don't want to put you out," Diana said.

"It's soup night," Allison said. "Easy peasy."

While Molly slept, they folded baskets full of laundry. Chad's polo shirts and jeans, Allison's khakis and sweaters. For a long time there was only the flapping sound of shaken-out clothing, and the soft thumping rhythm of folding. The smell of scented dryer sheets perfused the living room.

Diana wrapped a pair of clean socks into a ball. She remembered something her sister had said, the last time they met for coffee on campus. One of the many things Diana had heard incompletely. "You said Mom had pictures of Molly up, at the hospital," she said.

Her sister nodded.

She swallowed hard, afraid she knew the answer before she asked. "Did she put up any pictures of Chad?"

Allison sucked in her breath, and shook her head.

"Oh, Allie, I'm so sorry." She had been so completely wrong. Each time her sister had mentioned the pictures, described the way their mother had asked after Molly, Diana had heard judgment and reproof. Somehow she had not been able to hear the ache in her own sister's voice. Jesus, she hated getting things wrong; it was infuriating. "Jesus, I'm sorry."

Allison's eyes glistened. "Maybe we made it harder than it needed to be."

Her sister was brave: this was what Diana had thought, when she'd first seen the picture of the boy she and Ray adopted. She wasn't sure she would've been able to do it herself.

"Chad's marvelous," Diana said. "So smart, so kind. He's just like you."

"He's like Ray, too," Allison said.

She wrinkled her nose.

Her family was like a rosebush: a thorny tangle of beauty, fraught with the potential to draw blood. Maybe all families were like this. Diana had thought the family she'd given Molly was complex enough, but she was coming around on the potential of further entanglements.

From the bedroom, Molly sighed in her sleep: a light honeyed gasp.

By the time Chad emerged from his room, they'd set the table for dinner. Allison told him, "We'll eat after

Molly wakes up. Do you mind picking some music?"

"I was planning on going out," he said. "With Marcus, Dre, and Kara. Okay?"

"Didn't you just see Kara?" Allison said.

Chad nodded, glancing at Diana.

Allison bit her lower lip, which meant she didn't want to say what she was about to say. This had been her childhood tell, and she looked as pained and rueful now as when she'd been about to sink Diana's battleship. Still, she persevered. "I just don't want you to rush things," she said, haltingly. "I don't want you to get hurt."

Chad said, slow and low, "You don't want me to get hurt."

"No," she whispered.

"This year has well and truly sucked," Chad continued.

Diana felt her chest contract.

"And I'm not saying I want Dad to move back, or anything. I just feel like, I want to go out to dinner with the people who came *into* my life. Is that okay with you?"

Allison, nodding wordlessly, wrapped her arms around him.

He was taller than his mother; he was closer to adulthood than childhood now. But in Allison's embrace, right up until she let him go, Chad was a beautiful boy.

The Eternal Backseat

What did Chad know about 1987? President Reagan had asked Gorbachev to tear down the Berlin wall. The second of the Unabomber's home-made devices exploded in Utah; the Irish Republican Army bombed a memorial service; a plane crashed on takeoff in Detroit, and another was blown up in Korea. An American baby named Jessica had fallen down a well, transfixing the nation for anxious days until she was safely recovered. A tornado ravaged Saskatchewan, in Canada, and a typhoon devastated the Philippines. A girl named Tami gave birth to him in Trenton, and died.

The internet provided documentation: bullet lists, names and dates, without context or causality. The information was not always verifiable, and betrayed the biases of whoever had compiled and posted it. This was just a larger-scale version of the "What's going on in the world" page in his baby book.

His mother listed the popular songs of the year of his birth: REM's "It's the End of the World as We Know It (And I Feel Fine)," George Michael's "Faith," Los Lobos's version of "La Bamba." She liked REM best, and so that was the album cover she'd scanned and printed in a one-inch by one-inch square, pasted into the book next a pair of handwritten music notes and her selected list of facts. In 1987, U2 released *The Joshua Tree.*

"Fuck this," said Marcus. "Michael Jackson released *Bad*, how about that?" He punched the comforter on his bed. "How about Jody Watley, how about Public Fucking Enemy released *Yo! Bum Rush the Show*, how about Rakim?"

Chad gave him a look. "You just happen to know that *Yo! Bum Rush the Show* came out in eighty-seven."

"You're not the only motherfucker who can do research, Loudermocha." Marcus shook his head. "I doubt Tami was all about Wang Chung, all I'm saying."

I, too, sing America, thought Chad. From his backpack, he pulled the folder his mom had given him. He let it fall onto the comforter. "So let's do some research."

From the way Marcus lunged for the folder, Chad saw that maybe Marcus hadn't been prodding him to explore his roots entirely for Chad's sake. Marcus had his own ghost life, the one where his mother answered to Mrs., not Ms., Johnson—where his father stuck around, taught him to play catch or whistle or make his signature chili. In the ghost life Marcus's jump shot might've been a copy of his dad's, not Jordan's.

Engrossed, they pored over the folder's facts and

data. A hospital admission form filled out incompletely; a certificate of adoption that had been signed by lawyers on behalf of their recently deceased pro bono client. On one form, Chad's birthday was incorrect, though it was possible that this was the only place it had been recorded correctly. There was no one to ask for corroboration.

They spent longer looking than the meager contents warranted, because this was all they had. Because maybe if they looked carefully enough, they would find something new. Something that explained them to themselves. Frankly, Chad thought poetry was putting up better numbers than data on that particular score.

"You boys want a snack?" Marcus's mother asked them from the doorway.

When neither of them looked up from the papers to answer, she came closer.

"This doesn't look like schoolwork," she said.

Chad looked up at her. "It's, um, my adoption file, Ms. J."

She nodded slowly. "No wonder my son looks to be reading for comprehension for a change."

"There's not much here," Chad said.

"What are you looking for?" Oh, she was good, just like Chad's mom. Those simple-sounding questions that opened things up. Maybe it was nursing and counseling that had given them these skills, or maybe they were nurses and counselors because they were so good at coaxing people to talk about the places that hurt.

"He looking for a clue," Marcus smirked, but his mom shushed him.

"I guess I want to know more about the woman who gave birth to me," Chad said. "I don't know if I have uncles, or cousins, or a sibling even, back in Trenton." He tossed the page he'd been reading back onto the small pile. "But there's not even a last name."

"Just *Tami*," Marcus said.

"Tami," his mom repeated. And there was something powerful in hearing her name aloud. If it didn't exactly conjure her into Marcus's apartment, it made her real.

"Tami," Chad agreed.

"She was sixteen?" Ms. Johnson asked, confirming something Marcus must have told her.

Chad nodded.

She smoothed the pant leg of her scrubs. "And when she died, they called your parents, the Loudermilks, right away?"

He nodded again. "They were waiting," he said. "It took a long time to move up the list, my mom said."

"Like for a liver," Marcus said. "You were their liver."

"Shut up," Chad said.

"Maybe spleen."

Marcus's mother exhaled loudly, the way she did when she first came home from work and stepped out of her soft white shoes. She reached for Chad's hand, and held it.

"That girl," she said, then began again. "*Tami* was somebody's lost daughter, you know. She never did come home. Who knows how long she'd been lost to them."

He felt a chill go through him, wiggle up his spine. Marcus played with the strings of his sweatshirt hood. "I get what you're saying," he said. "Like Tami's family didn't come to get the baby."

She nodded and drummed her fingers on the empty manila folder. "Her medical records will be sealed, of course," she said, almost to herself. "She must not have known there was a problem with the baby."

"Problem?" Chad's voice squeaked.

"For the labor to have killed her," Marcus's mom said. "Could've been obstructed, or she could've had a clot, or—I'm sorry, Chad—she might've tried to end the pregnancy."

This had not occurred to him. He felt a strange pressure in his gut, now that it had.

"We do everything we can," she said. "So in an American hospital, in nineteen eighty-what, six?"

"Nineteen eighty-seven," Chad and Marcus said together.

"It's unusual," she said. "For a mother to die." She lifted her hands. "Not to say never, but—" With a *whoosh*, she exhaled again, and stood. "Okay, now. Snack time."

She steered them into the kitchen, fed them oranges, and put out a bowl of potato chips. As usual, Marcus doused the chips with hot sauce and ate them four at a time.

Chad rolled an orange around in his hand. He remembered the way he and Walter used to hide wedges of fruit in their mouths and grin crazily at each other. Busting into giggles until Walter's mom would scold them. Now, with his thumbnail he dug into the peel.

"I'm on tonight," Ms. Johnson told Marcus. "I'm going to lie down for a while before I head back in. You boys don't get in trouble's way, understand?"

"Ma, sometimes trouble finds us even when we don't go looking for it."

"Oh yes, I know all about that," she said. "You best be polite to trouble, though."

Trouble did have a way. When you were in the lights, in the crosshairs, you couldn't talk back. You couldn't duck and run. You couldn't smirk. And you couldn't find yourself in that position too often; statistics were not in your favor. You ought not to swagger, to intimidate. You wanted to make easy the way of those who would otherwise make it hard for you.

"I know where we need to go," Chad said. "Are we done with the talk?"

"The talk is eternal." Marcus zipped up his sweatshirt and nodded his jaw at Chad. "Let's roll, Palo Alto."

The golden mosaic on Stanford Memorial Church glowed in the evening light. They locked their bikes and asked a passing student for directions. Shifting her backpack, the girl pointed out a route.

But the Green Library desk clerk shook his head. "This facility is a resource for current Stanford students, faculty, and staff." With a raised eyebrow he took in their hoodies and high tops.

"Shit," said Marcus. "A place with gold-plated walls can't share the books? Reading is fundamental, son."

"Sorry," the clerk shrugged.

Marcus slumped, turned to leave. He wasn't going to go looking for trouble in the University library. He jammed his hands into his sweatshirt pockets.

"Wait," Chad said. "We know a professor. Can we be her guest?"

The eyebrow lifted again. "If she vouches for you," the clerk offered. "In person."

"Dude," Marcus said. "It's Friday night."

"She's working," Chad assured him.

The clerk offered to make the call. Maybe he was a gentleman, or maybe he'd decided to liven up the Friday afternoon shift with two townie hoodlums getting laughed at by a faculty member, then receiving a uniformed escort off campus. Either way, his hand had already been resting on the phone.

"Thank you very much," Chad said. He made a face at Marcus: *see, when you don't burn the place down, they can be helpful.* "Diana Marchese, in Physics?"

His aunt arrived in a few minutes, signed some forms to grant them temporary access to the library stacks and computers. "So," she asked Chad while they waited for the clerk to complete the process, "what are we looking for?"

"Trenton, Nineteen Eighty-Seven," he said.

Media & Microtext was monastically quiet. They'd assumed Diana would know what to do, but she confessed that this was not even her regular library: they kept the engineers and physicists and *their* books sequestered in a completely different building. Actually, she'd gone there first, which was why they'd had such a long opportunity to exchange awkward glances with the desk clerk, reading every flyer on the bulletin board—*a cappella* tryouts, a rally to Take Back the Night, a visiting lecture by an expert in Chinese history, a screening of a recent documentary—until finally a pair of sorority girls took pity on Diana and pointed out the library used by the rest of campus.

"What's with the ancient computers?" Marcus asked.

The reference librarian gave a snort. "Those are microfilm machines." She indicated another type of console. "That's for microfiche. But I think film will have what you're looking for."

Which was a bold prediction, considering they didn't know themselves.

"Here we go," said the librarian, lining up a spool and threading it through the machine's reader. "Times of Trenton, August Nineteen Eighty-Seven." As Chad took a seat, the librarian gestured to another machine for Marcus. "And the Trentonian as well."

"This room is only open until nine," said the librarian. "Let me know if you need any help."

They had just under two hours to look, on machines they'd never used before, in newspapers from a place they'd never been. Possibly, the desk clerk had already called campus security.

"We got this," Marcus said.

Obituaries and death notices, to start with. Nothing for a Tami on the day Chad was born, or anytime in the next week.

But someone would've had to place an obituary. Someone would've had to write one.

Just like someone would've had to pay ten cents a word to proclaim her baby's birth, like in the announcements Diana found: *Joelle and Robert Watkins welcome a baby girl.* Marcus shook his head: "Having a baby is news?"

"For my sister it was," Aunt Diana said. "It was the best thing, the most important thing, that had ever happened to her."

"Did she put it in the newspaper?" Marcus asked.

"She made cards herself," she said. "Before everybody did that. With pictures and Chad's information."

Chad said, "I thought that was just for my baby book."

Diana turned away from her microfilm screen to look at them. "She had a hundred of those suckers printed up, sent them to everyone she knew." She drummed her fingers on the back of her chair. "If she could've, she would've hired a pilot to trail a banner up and down the state."

Summer down the shore with Chad's grandma: the little planes flew over the beach all day, advertising a fish fry or a concert on the boardwalk. He could almost picture one of them saying, WELCOME HOME CHAD.

"My mom got kicked out of the house for having me, so I don't think she hired a publicist," Marcus said.

You had to look at every word; there was no search engine to lead you to what you were looking for, presuming you knew what that was. But after an hour, Chad hadn't seen anything that got close to answering his questions.

He pulled out the Trenton map he'd got from Triple A, and spread it out on the carpeted floor. He had circled the location of St. Francis Hospital. It was across the street from Trenton Central High School, less than a mile each from the state house and the prison. Welcome Home, Chad.

Marcus stood up, stretching, and came over to look

at the map. Together, they looked at the foreign boulevards, parks, and neighborhood names. It wasn't a map of anyplace Chad recognized.

"Guys," Diana said, "listen to this." She read aloud:

Family to sue over son's death
The parents of a twelve-year-old who drowned in Crosswick Creek while visiting his teacher's house have filed notice of a claim against the state.
The three boys were invited to spend the night at the home of their sixth-grade teacher as a reward for good behavior.

"Say *what*," Marcus said.

"That's what it says," Diana said. "Times have changed, I guess. I can't even pat my students on the back when they start crying in my office."

Chad made a face. "Physics makes them cry?"

"Sometimes it's physics, mostly it's not. I just let 'em talk. But no pats on the back. Leave the office door wide open."

"Sounds kind of like my mom," Chad said.

His aunt, startled, swung to look at him. Chad shrugged back.

Marcus read over Diana's shoulder. "Three boys: Kareem, Vashon, and Terrance. *Hmmph.*"

"Drowning, what a miserable way to go," Diana said. "You both know how to swim, I hope."

They nodded. Chad flashed back to Rinconada Pool, where he'd once paddled under the giant mushroom-shaped fountain, splashing as Allison watched from the water's edge. He and Walter dared each other to leap from the dive platform, and lobbed hacky sacks at each other across the lap lanes.

"Chad," Marcus whispered. "Come here." He pointed to Diana's screen.

Multiple injuries in Columbus Park shooting

Police are searching for several teenagers involved in a shooting incident Tuesday at Columbus Park. Several Chambersburg residents reported hearing gunfire that night, and seeing youths run away from the park. When police arrived, they found one victim who had been killed, as well as a young woman. The woman was taken to St. Francis Hospital, where she later died as a result of her injuries.

This was the day Chad had been born.

"Maybe," Marcus said.

"Maybe," Chad agreed.

"Who's got Thursday and Friday," Diana said, gesturing to the microfilm spools. "Shooting was Tuesday. Let's see if they found anybody."

"How hard would they try to find *us*?" Chad said.

Marcus made a mumbling sound.

"Fifteen minutes," the librarian said, leaning in the doorway.

Aunt Diana was scrolling through early 1988; none of the Columbus Park youths had yet been apprehended, and the ongoing search was mentioned more briefly, less urgently, each time it appeared. Marcus was following the story of the drowned boy, Kareem, murmuring updates when he found them.

Chad had gone back to 1971. He didn't know

for sure whether Tami's parents would've sprung for a birth announcement, and he definitely didn't know what month to look at, so he started in January and paged through. There had been a Tamika Wallace born in February, a Tamara Davis on April 2. *Monty and Renee Davis warmly welcomed a baby girl at Robert Wood Johnson Hospital. Named Tamara for her grandmother, she is the Davises' first child. She was eight pounds, ten ounces, and nineteen inches long.*

He realized he didn't know whether Tami had been born in Trenton, like Tamika and Tamara. He only knew she'd died there. Maybe she'd died because of Chad, as he had always believed, or maybe she'd been shot at Columbus Park. Maybe Chad's father was one of the youths who had fled, or maybe he was the reason she'd left home. There were too many maybes to count.

Chad had hoped to find absolutes, unconditional truths spelled out in file folders and carefully scanned newsprint. But he was made of maybes.

A conversation in the hallway at the Hotel Carcinoma, last summer: a white coat leaning close to tell Allison she ought to have some testing done, that there was a gene mutation in Grandma Marchese that had worsened her odds when the cancer returned. That the mutation ran in families. But whatever mutations were waiting to terrorize his own cells, he wouldn't see them coming. There were no drills to prepare for disaster. There were only, and always, more maybes. He could be paralyzed or liberated by them, or some of each, he guessed.

Five minutes to nine, they packed up their bags; Chad slid the new notes into his folder. The reference librarian walked them to the door. The desk clerk was still skeptical: he squinted as they passed through the metal detectors, suspicious that they might've stuffed a microfilm terminal into their backpacks.

Chad watched Marcus fight the urge to shoot his middle finger at the clerk. On behalf of himself, and Kareem, and the nameless victims of the countless shootings, stabbings, and aborted robberies they'd been steeping in for hours. Instead, they both pulled their hoods over their heads, meager protection from the violent world.

Spring

RESILIENCE had joined INNOVATION as the Valley's self-defining buzzword. Anyone would tell you: the devastated tech scene was beginning to bloom again, sending up green shoots. Seasonally appropriate regrowth, even in seasonless Northern California; it was thus proclaimed. It would be a rebuilding year.

Resilience felt apt enough to Chad, who'd been blindsided by what ought to have been the worst year of his life, when things imploded in ways unanticipated by Shooter Drills or emergency supply kits. Ears ringing from the blast, a layer of ash on his shoulders, but still standing.

Paly's Drill protocol had been refined, following recommendations from an expert consultant they'd seen walking the grounds with a clipboard and the vice-principal. Mr. Farris raised his eyebrow when he explained about the *consultant*, and the resulting *minor tweaks* to their procedure. Chad wondered whether this "school safety expert" was one more person whose Plan A had collapsed with the stock market: dotcom coder turned disaster specialist. Anyway, instead of crouching under their desks the students now huddled in one corner, after piling their desks into a barricade.

Chad had learned that the disaster you'd prepared for wasn't the one that would devastate you. But once a month he sat, silent, with his classmates, holding his breath on the linoleum.

On his way to the party at Diana's, he passed through Stanford's gauntlet of palm trees. Chad had heard, somewhere, that palm trees were not native to the area: some species had been brought from Southern California, some from Mexico, and some from the Pacific islands. Transplants, like almost everyone else he knew: but they had learned to thrive here, had come to define the place.

Molly was the only two-year-old at her own second birthday party. There was no bouncy house, no piñata in the blocky form of a beloved cartoon character, but Molly didn't seem to mind. She twirled and played with Chad, indifferent to the adults and their small talk.

Arthur said he thought the market was coming back. He'd had a few bidding wars on properties that last year he would've had to price lower. Open Houses were busier; he no longer needed to put out hors d'oeuvres and hire a band just to pull people in. Aunt Diana teased him about building custom bookcases, and he grimaced.

And Tommy talked about his new job, planting

trees along the sidewalks of San Francisco. It was called Urban Reforestation, and he was doing it one Japanese maple at a time. Somehow he and Arthur had convinced investors to support this romantic venture, and he was staffed, for now, with kids like Andre who were balancing out their permanent records.

His mom shared his absent dad's news: Ray was headed to Ecuador for three weeks, in the wake of his successful pitch to their National Tourism Board. His lease on the apartment, which had been month-to-month, was now a yearly contract. But instead of walking to the Posh Nosh, he was once again commuting by train: the Ecuador account was his ticket back to Goldsmith & Wong. There was a slim chance Allison would permit Chad to go down to Quito for a short visit. There was only a slim chance that he'd have time. For the approaching summer he had an unpaid internship at MacAvoy.com, a stack of Mr. Farris-recommended books, a real and actual girlfriend, and a paid gig babysitting Molly.

At her party, she spun to the music he'd picked, grabbed his hand and said, "Where's Marcus?"

"Sorry, Molly," he said. "He had to work."

She pouted, but he promised they'd both return tomorrow for ice cream.

"Ice cream *and Legos*," Molly negotiated.

"We so stipulate, counselor." He lifted one arm for her to twirl under.

After the dinner, after the cupcakes, after all three hours of the party playlist, he helped his mom with the dishes and debriefed on everyone's news and how *good* everyone looked, didn't everyone look *happy*, and the thing was that they did; they'd weathered the disastrous fall and winter, together they had helped each other survive calamity. And they would be there when the next one struck.

Each of them was still mourning losses—jobs, opportunities and stock options, mothers, fathers, friends—and danger lurked always in the darkness, in the trees, in the genes, around the next bend. But today, they had chosen joy.

He could see how pleased his mom was to have given this to Molly. After the party, they took Red to the park. For a sunny hour they walked together, past the duck pond and the playground, and then he led her to the Sunks.

In the grassy bowl, Chad and Walter had acted out adventures. They were Frodo and Samwise, Luke and Han; Neo and Morpheus; dueling pirate captains; explorers of an unknown world. They had each died a thousand times, by lightsaber, sword, volcano, vicious Matrix-collapsing superpunch; they had perished in agony, in exile, in glory. Generally, in slow motion. In each case the survivor swore to avenge his fallen friend, except in the rare but not unfeasible case that the two of them perished together.

Here in the park they had faced down dragons, Sith Lords, the cruelty of the sea. Death in the Sunks had never stuck; you could be impaled on a spear tipped in the poison of a rare orange frog, and still be home in time for dinner.

Each to his grief, Gwendolyn Brooks had written: *each to his loneliness, and fidgety revenge.* Chad had tried out fidgety revenge, and had found that it did not make up for his losses.

His mother's revenge for her own grief was love.

She was the starshine at the center of him, the one whose kisses had once cured scraped knees, who'd offered safety in the pool's deep end, and who ran alongside his bicycle until he pedaled fast enough to stay upright. Always, she tried so hard.

He imagined that Tami's parents mourned her. They might not have known when or precisely why to grieve, but as soon as she was lost to them, he dearly hoped she was mourned. Like the Chens, they must have been bereft, searching for some kind of understanding; he knew how sharply this ached, but still this pain was what he wished for. He hoped Tami had been well-loved.

He told his mom all of this, there in the Sunks. Together, they lay down and stared up at the twilight sky. Everything above them seared pink. All that hopeful green stuff under their backs.

Acknowledgments

Thanks to the Ashby Avenue writers' collective: wise readers and dear friends whose regular meeting over a stack of manuscripts kept this writer writing. I am profoundly grateful for Bridget Hoida, Nami Mun, Jennifer Deitz, Nick Petrulakis, Gus Rose, Anderson Berry, Laura Cerruti, Marika Brussel, MJ Deery, Marco Morrone, Megan Morrone, Christian Divine, D. Foy, Shoshana Berger, Samina Ali, Brett Gamboa, and John Beckman. Thanks especially for your patience while I wrote the three novels and countless stories that helped me learn how to write this one. Special thanks to Bridget for an apron to keep the mess off.

And thank you, Leland Cheuk, for your exemplar. For writing, editing, and living with ferocity and fearlessness, and for taking on this project. For the profound act of literary citizenship that is 7.13 Books, this reader and writer is grateful.

I have been fortunate to learn from gifted and generous teachers of writing and literature: Leonard Michaels, Bharati Mukherjee, Tom Farber, Malena Watrous, and Jim Shepard. For fostering my love of fluid mechanics, science, and engineering: Phil Marcus, Stan Berger, and Frauke Palmer. (I have shared my enthusiasm for fluid mechanics with the character Diana Marchese, and have given Diana credit for L. Mahadevan's "Cheerios effect.")

For your feedback and your friendship, thank you: Patti Carmichael Miller, Caprice Garvin, Kate Brandes, Kate Racculia, and Cate Steele Hartzell. I am glad for the nourishing community provided by the Squaw Valley Community of Writers, the Tin House Writers Workshop, the One Story workshop, and the Djerassi Resident Artists Program. Thanks to those editors who saw something in my stories and shone light on them, especially Joe Ponepinto and Kelly Davio, Christopher James, Robert Vaughan, Scott Waldyn, Robert James Russell, Jen Michalski, Rusty Barnes and Rod Slino, Andrew Day, and Rafe Posey.

Thanks to Will Allison, Hannah Tinti, and my One Story pals – the divine judy-b., Mike Dell'Aquila, Marrie Stone, and Jennifer Kircher Carr. I am indebted to Heidi Durrow and my fellow #NunBoxers Robin Farmer, Ginger McKnight-Chavers, Jessica Sick Haas, Elena Acevedo Dalcourt, Romalyn Tilghman, and Michele Beller. I raise a glass to Malena's Orphans – Mary Bernardi Edelson, Harley Mazuk, Siri Chateaubriand, Devika Mehra, and Arlene MacLeod; and my Tin Housemates Thaddeus Gunn, Bryan Hurt, Mark Chiusano, Katherine Lee, Jon Muzzall, Sharon Gelman, Teresa Burns Gunther, Renee Thompson. The praises of the guru Kathy Fish ought be sung from the highest mountaintops. Kevin McIlvoy, my vocabulary lacks words adequate to fully encompass your generosity and capacious love for the power of stories well told.

Somehow I have managed to work at two Colleges where the concept of an engineering professor writing fiction was indulged and even, in some quarters, encouraged. Thank you, Lee Upton and Alix Ohlin, for welcoming me into your fellowship.

My family taught me to love books, and enables my addiction to this day. Thank you to Jeanette and David Dossi; Sable Stroud & Joel Trinidad; Larry and Jane Stroud; Maya & Tommy Crawford; and Lynn and George Rossmann. Lynn, thank you for all the times you asked to read something, and urged me to keep working on the words and sending them out.

Above all, I am grateful for the love and friendship of Toby Rossmann, and for our clever and curious daughters Leda & Cleo.

About the Author

Jenn Stroud Rossmann writes the essay series "An Engineer Reads a Novel" for *Public Books*. Her stories have appeared in *Literary Orphans*, *Jellyfish Review*, *Tahoma Literary Review*, *failbetter*, and other magazines. Her work has been a finalist for honors including the BOA Editions Short Fiction Prize, the Disquiet Literary Prize, and Sarabande Books' Mary McCarthy Prize. She earned her BS and PhD at the University of California, Berkeley, and is a professor of mechanical engineering at Lafayette College. She throws right, bats left.

CPSIA information can be obtained
at www.ICGtesting.com
Printed in the USA
LVHW111807080119
603164LV00005B/798/P